WARRIORS

PATH
OF A WARRIOR

WARRIORS

NOVELLA COLLECTIONS

The Untold Stories
Tales from the Clans
Shadows of the Clans
Legends of the Clans

WARRIORS

PATH
OF A WARRIOR

INCLUDES
Redtail's Debt
Tawnypelt's Clan
Shadowstar's Life

ERIN
HUNTER

HARPER
An Imprint of HarperCollinsPublishers

Special thanks to Clarissa Hutton

Path of a Warrior
Redtail's Debt, Tawnypelt's Clan, Shadowstar's Life
Copyright © 2019 by Working Partners Limited
Series created by Working Partners Limited
Map art by Dave Stevenson
Interior art by Owen Richardson

Library of Congress catalog card number: 2018954175
ISBN 978-0-06-279884-8

Typography by Hilary Zarycky
19 20 21 22 23   PC/BRR   10 9 8 7 6 5 4 3 2
❖
First Edition

CONTENTS

WARRIORS

REDTAIL'S
DEBT

ALLEGIANCES

THUNDERCLAN

LEADER SUNSTAR—bright ginger tom with yellow eyes

DEPUTY TAWNYSPOTS—light gray tabby tom with amber eyes

MEDICINE CAT FEATHERWHISKER—pale silvery tom with bright amber eyes

APPRENTICE, SPOTTEDPAW (dark tortoiseshell she-cat with a distinctive dappled coat)

WARRIORS (toms and she-cats without kits)

STORMTAIL—blue-gray tom with blue eyes
APPRENTICE, BRINDLEPAW (pale gray tabby she-cat)

ADDERFANG—mottled brown tabby tom with yellow eyes

SPARROWPELT—big, dark brown tabby tom with yellow eyes
APPRENTICE, REDPAW (tortoiseshell tom with a ginger tail)

SMALLEAR—gray tom with very small ears and amber eyes

POPPYDAWN—long-haired dark red she-cat with a bushy tail and amber eyes
APPRENTICE, WILLOWPAW (pale gray she-cat with blue eyes)

THRUSHPELT—sandy-gray tom with white flash on his chest and green eyes

ROBINWING—small brown she-cat with ginger patch on her chest and amber eyes

FUZZYPELT—black tom with fur that stands on end and yellow eyes

PATCHPELT—small black-and-white tom with amber eyes

WINDFLIGHT—gray tabby tom with pale green eyes

DAPPLETAIL—tortoiseshell she-cat with a lovely dappled coat

SPECKLETAIL—pale tabby she-cat with amber eyes

LEOPARDFOOT—black she-cat with green eyes

BLUEFUR—thick-furred blue-gray she-cat with blue eyes

APPRENTICE, FROSTPAW (white she-cat with blue eyes)

SWIFTBREEZE—tabby-and-white she-cat with yellow eyes

THISTLECLAW—gray-and-white tom with amber eyes

LIONHEART—golden tabby tom with green eyes

GOLDENFLOWER—pale ginger tabby she-cat with yellow eyes

TIGERCLAW—big dark brown tabby tom with unusually long front claws

WHITESTORM—big white tom

ROSETAIL—gray tabby she-cat with a bushy reddish tail

QUEENS

(she-cats expecting or nursing kits)

WHITE-EYE—pale gray she-cat, blind in one eye

ELDERS

(former warriors and queens, now retired)

WEEDWHISKER—pale orange tom with yellow eyes

MUMBLEFOOT—brown tom, slightly clumsy, with amber eyes

LARKSONG—tortoiseshell she-cat with pale green eyes

RIVERCLAN

LEADER **HAILSTAR**—thick-pelted gray tom
APPRENTICE, BLACKPAW (black tom)

DEPUTY **CROOKEDJAW**—light brown tabby tom with green eyes and a twisted jaw
APPRENTICE, SEDGEPAW (brown tabby she-cat)

MEDICINE CAT **BRAMBLEBERRY**—white she-cat with black spotted fur and blue eyes

WARRIORS **RIPPLECLAW**—black-and-silver tabby tom

VOLECLAW—gray tom

TIMBERFUR—brown tom

ECHOMIST—pale gray she-cat

CEDARPELT—mottled brown tabby tom

OWLFUR—brown-and-white tom

OTTERSPLASH—white-and-pale-ginger she-cat

BEETLENOSE—tom with crow-black fur
APPRENTICE, REEDPAW (pale gray tabby tom)

SOFTWING—white she-cat with tabby patches
APPRENTICE, SKYPAW (pale brown tabby she-cat)

WHITEFANG—white tom with brown paws
APPRENTICE, LEOPARDPAW (unusually spotted golden tabby she-cat)

LILYSTEM—pale gray she-cat

SHIMMERPELT—black she-cat

PIKETOOTH—dark brown tabby tom

MUDFUR—mottled light brown tom
APPRENTICE, PETALPAW (tortoiseshell she-cat)

LAKESHINE—mottled gray-and-white she-cat

OAKHEART—reddish-brown tom with amber eyes

APPRENTICE, LOUDPAW (dark brown tom)

FALLOWTAIL—brown she-cat

WILLOWBREEZE—pale gray tabby she-cat with amber eyes

GRAYPOOL—dark gray she-cat with yellow eyes

SUNFISH—pale gray she-cat

ELDERS

TROUTCLAW—gray tabby tom

SHELLHEART—dappled gray tom

SHADOWCLAN

LEADER

CEDARSTAR—very dark gray tom with a white belly

DEPUTY

RAGGEDPELT—large, dark brown tabby tom

MEDICINE CAT

SAGEWHISKER—white she-cat with long whiskers

APPRENTICE, YELLOWFANG (dark gray she-cat with a broad, flattened face)

WARRIORS

DEERLEAP—gray tabby she-cat with white legs

BLIZZARDWING—mottled white tom

FOXHEART—bright ginger she-cat

WOLFSTEP—tom with a torn ear

CROWTAIL—black tabby she-cat

APPRENTICE, CLOUDPAW (white tom with blue eyes)

BRACKENFOOT—pale ginger tom with dark ginger legs

ARCHEYE—gray tabby tom with black stripes and thick stripe over eye

HOLLYFLOWER—dark-gray-and-white she-cat

MUDCLAW—gray tom with brown legs

LIZARDSTRIPE—pale brown tabby she-cat with yellow eyes

TOADSKIP—dark brown tabby tom with white splashes and white legs

FEATHERSTORM—brown tabby she-cat

SCORCHWIND—ginger tabby tom

NEWTSPECK—black-and-ginger tabby she-cat

ASHHEART—pale gray she-cat with blue eyes

AMBERLEAF—dark orange she-cat with brown legs and ears

FROGTAIL—dark gray tom

POOLCLOUD—gray-and-white she-cat

NETTLESPOT—white she-cat with ginger flecks

FINCHFLIGHT—black-and-white tom

NUTWHISKER—brown tom with amber eyes

ROWANBERRY—cream-and-brown she-cat with amber eyes

MOUSEWING—black tom with long, thick fur

ELDERS

LITTLEBIRD—small ginger tabby she-cat

LIZARDFANG—light brown tabby tom with one hooked tooth

STONETOOTH—gray tabby tom with long teeth

WINDCLAN

LEADER

HEATHERSTAR—pinkish-gray she-cat with blue eyes

DEPUTY

TALLTAIL—large black-and-white tom with amber eyes

MEDICINE CATS

HAWKHEART—stone-gray tom with flecks of darker brown fur

BARKFACE—short-tailed brown tom

WARRIORS

DAWNSTRIPE—pale gold tabby with creamy stripes

REDCLAW—dark ginger tom

WOOLLYTAIL—gray-and-white tom with bright yellow eyes

DEADFOOT—lean black tom with a twisted left paw

STAGLEAP—dark brown tom with amber eyes
APPRENTICE, SORRELPAW (gray-and-brown she-cat)

HICKORYNOSE—brown tom

APPLEDAWN—pale cream she-cat

MEADOWSLIP—gray she-cat

MISTMOUSE—light brown tabby she-cat

HAREFLIGHT—light brown tom

DOESPRING—light brown she-cat
APPRENTICE, PIGEONPAW (dark gray tom with white patches)

LARKSPLASH—tortoiseshell-and-white she-cat

SHREWCLAW—dark brown tom with yellow eyes

ASPENFALL—gray-and-white tom

PLUMCLAW—dark gray she-cat

QUEENS

PALEBIRD—black-and-white she-cat (mother to Wrenkit, Rabbitkit, Flykit, and Bristlekit)

RYESTALK—gray tabby she-cat

ELDERS

WHITEBERRY—small, pure white tom

LILYWHISKER—light brown she-cat with amber eyes and a crippled hind leg

FLAILFOOT—black tom with yellow eyes

CAT VIEW

HIGHSTONES

BARLEY'S FARM

FOURTREES

WINDCLAN CAMP

FALLS

SUNNINGROCKS

RIVERCLAN CAMP

RIVER

TREECUTPLACE

CARRIONPLACE

SHADOWCLAN
CAMP

THUNDERPATH

OWLTREE

GREAT
SYCAMORE

THUNDERCLAN
CAMP

SNAKEROCKS

SANDY
HOLLOW

TALLPINES

TWOLEGPLACE

DEVIL'S FINGERS
[disused mine]

NORTH ALLERTON ROAD

WINDOVER FARM

WINDOVER MOOR

DRUID'S HOLLOW

DRUID'S LEAP

TWOLEG VIEW

RIVER CHELL

MORGAN'S FARM CAMPSITE

MORGAN'S FARM

MORGAN'S LANE

NORTH ALLERTON
AMENITY TIP

WINDOVER ROAD

WHITE HART WOODS

CHELFORD FOREST

CHELFORD MILL

CHELFORD

KEY To The TERRAIN

DECIDUOUS WOODLAND

CONIFERS

MARSH

CLIFFS AND ROCKS

HIKING TRAILS

NORTH

CHAPTER ONE

Redpaw carefully patted some fresh moss into the corner of a nest in the ThunderClan warriors' den, then sighed. "This is so *boring*. I want to go hunting."

His sister Willowpaw dragged more moss into the den, wrinkling her nose at the taste as she dropped it beside him. "At least we're not picking ticks off the elders like Frostpaw and Brindlepaw," she mewed.

Redpaw patted the new moss into place. "But pretty soon *they'll* have their warrior ceremonies, and *we'll* be the only apprentices left, and we'll have to do all the worst jobs in camp for *moons*," he complained. "Whitestorm and Tigerclaw already became warriors. And we don't even have Spottedpaw helping us anymore."

Willowpaw peeked out the entrance to the warriors' den toward where their littermate, Spottedpaw, was laying out herbs to dry in the sun. "Medicine-cat apprentices work pretty hard, too," she purred, her blue eyes shining with amusement. "Not just you, Redpaw."

Redpaw's whiskers twitched. "I know I'm being silly," he admitted. "I just wanted to go hunting with Sparrowpelt and Tigerclaw and the others."

He *would* have gone with them, if it had been an ordinary hunting patrol. Sparrowpelt was his mentor; the tabby might be a little grumpy sometimes, but he wouldn't leave Redpaw out of a hunt. But today their hunting patrol had gone toward Sunningrocks, and ThunderClan's leader, Sunstar, had deemed the rocks near the river too dangerous for apprentices.

"We've been fighting over Sunningrocks with RiverClan for years," Sparrowpelt had explained to Redpaw, his tail twitching. "Some cats say that the rocks were *in* the river once, so RiverClan thinks of them as theirs. I don't know about that—they've been on ThunderClan land as long as any cat in the Clans now can remember. But RiverClan won't admit they're ours. We went and warned RiverClan off, not long before you became an apprentice, but Sunstar's nervous that they might be biding their time and planning an ambush."

So, Redpaw thought with another sigh, *I'm stuck freshening nests in camp instead of catching prey.*

It was all useful work, of course. Redpaw knew that, and he wanted to do whatever he could to help his Clan. But apprentice duties around camp weren't any fun, compared with hunting.

There was nothing Redpaw liked better than hunting: prowling through ThunderClan's forest territory, sniffing the air for the scent of prey, his ears pricked for even the faintest sound. After he'd spotted his prey, he loved the feeling of his muscles tensing, his heart pounding, as he carefully stalked it. And there was nothing more exhilarating than the final pounce.

Redpaw flexed his claws, imagining the squirm of a mouse beneath his paws. He felt like he might burst with pride whenever he saw his Clan eating prey he had caught. Sparrowpelt had said just the other day that Redpaw's hunting skills were coming on nicely, and the memory filled Redpaw with a warm rush of pride.

"I'm going to be the best hunter in ThunderClan," he announced.

Willowpaw flicked her pale gray tail. "Even better than Tigerclaw?" she mewed teasingly. "*No* cat is better than Tigerclaw. At least that's what he thinks."

A shadow fell across the entrance to the den, and Poppydawn, Willowpaw's mentor, thrust her broad red face through the opening.

"Sounds like there's a lot more chattering than working going on in here," she meowed briskly. "Willowpaw, put some more moss in that corner. I don't want to be sleeping on rocks."

"Yes, Poppydawn," Willowpaw mewed, dipping her head respectfully.

"And Redpaw, why don't you go get some feathers?" Poppydawn went on. "Those would make the nests nice and soft."

"There aren't any good feathers on the fresh-kill pile," Redpaw replied, a little less respectfully. Poppydawn wasn't *his* mentor.

"There will be now," Poppydawn told him. "Sparrowpelt's patrol is just getting back, and it looks like they have a couple of nice starlings."

"They're back?" Redpaw rushed past Poppydawn out of the warriors' den, Willowpaw close behind.

"Don't forget to finish that job," Poppydawn called sternly after them.

Outside the cozy warmth of the warriors' den, Redpaw shivered as the chill of leaf-fall seeped into his fur. But the sun was still shining brightly: They had some time left before the bitter cold of leaf-bare. In a patch of warm sunlight in the center of camp, the two older apprentices, Frostpaw and Brindlepaw, paused in their grooming of the elders beside them.

"Looks like it was a good hunt," Frostpaw mewed cheerfully. Beside her, Larksong arched her back in annoyance.

"Are you gossiping or getting rid of my ticks?" she asked grouchily. Frostpaw rolled her eyes and turned her attention back to the old she-cat's pelt. Redpaw suppressed a purr of amusement and looked up at the returning hunters.

Sparrowpelt was already beside the fresh-kill pile; the starlings Poppydawn had mentioned were on the ground at his paws. Despite his good catch, Sparrowpelt's face was dark with anger. Redpaw hesitated, glancing back toward the camp entrance at the rest of the hunting patrol coming in.

Speckletail was striding across the clearing toward the fresh-kill pile, a squirrel dangling from her jaws and a stormy expression in her amber eyes. Redpaw craned his neck to see past her. Tigerclaw was just pushing his broad shoulders through the gorse tunnel. He looked angry, too, but Redpaw was distracted by the prey that hung from his mouth. A fat rabbit and two juicy voles! So much prey that Redpaw wondered how the big warrior was managing to carry it all.

"Wow," Redpaw breathed to his littermate. "You're right. Tigerclaw's the best hunter in camp."

Willowpaw flipped her tail. "He's still an arrogant furball, though," she mewed softly. "*We* know that."

"Yeah . . . maybe," Redpaw agreed, his eyes following Tigerclaw as he crossed the clearing behind Speckletail. "He's changed a lot since he became a warrior, though."

When Tigerclaw had been the oldest of the apprentices, he had taken every opportunity to make it clear that *he* was the best fighter and the best hunter among the apprentices and that Redpaw, Willowpaw, and Spottedpaw, who were the youngest of the apprentices, were far, far beneath him. Redpaw hadn't forgotten that.

But ever since Tigerclaw had gotten his warrior name, he'd stopped bullying the apprentices. Instead he seemed to be intensely focused on becoming the best warrior in the Clan. *Someday he'll probably be leader,* Redpaw thought, looking admiringly at the dark brown tabby's broad shoulders and huge paws.

All three cats who had been on the patrol had dropped their prey on the fresh-kill pile now and were gathered together in the clearing, their faces dark with fury. "I wonder what happened," Willowpaw meowed softly.

Curious, Redpaw moved closer, approaching Sparrowpelt.

"Um, how was the hunt?" he asked his mentor, feeling awkward. "Did you have to sneak up on those starlings, or did you jump—"

"Not now, Redpaw," Sparrowpelt interrupted, turning away. "We have to report to Sunstar." He hurried toward the leader's den, Speckletail and Tigerclaw following close behind.

"We'd better get back to work," Willowpaw mewed, glancing nervously across the clearing at Poppydawn. "I don't want to get in trouble."

Redpaw hesitated, watching Tigerclaw disappear into Sunstar's den at the bottom of the Highrock. After a few moments, Sunstar's long-furred ginger face pushed through the lichen that covered the entrance. "Tawnyspots!" he called, and the Clan's deputy hurried to join the others in the leader's den.

Something bad must have happened, Redpaw thought, the fur rising along his spine. He glanced around. Maybe they'd seen something scary in the forest, like badgers or foxes. Or maybe Twolegs and their dogs were nearby. Redpaw shivered.

From opposite sides of the clearing, Bluefur and Thistleclaw had raised their heads to gaze thoughtfully toward Sunstar's den. Every cat thought that Sunstar would pick one of them to be his next deputy when Tawnyspots retired to the elders' den, and they each paid close attention to what happened between ThunderClan and the other Clans, as if they were preparing themselves.

While a few other faces were also turned with interest toward the Highrock, no cat was watching Redpaw.

Willowpaw was dutifully heading back toward the warriors' den, while Frostpaw and Brindlepaw were busily grooming the elders. Poppydawn was sharing a vole with Rosetail, their heads close together in conversation. *She won't notice if I don't go straight back to changing bedding,* he decided.

Trying to look like he *wasn't* eavesdropping, Redpaw strolled closer to Sunstar's den, his ears pricked up.

"This is the third time, Sunstar!" Sparrowpelt was yowling.

"You actually caught the RiverClan patrol marking Sunningrocks?" Sunstar demanded, his voice a deep growl.

"It was Owlfur, Softwing, and Ottersplash," Speckletail confirmed. "We tried to chase them off, but we didn't want to leave the prey we were carrying."

"We should have taught them a lesson they wouldn't forget," Tigerclaw hissed angrily. "It would be worth it to lose a little prey."

"We thought that Hailstar listened when we warned him away from Sunningrocks," Tawnyspots meowed. His mew sounded tired, and Redpaw shifted uncomfortably. The deputy looked sicker every day, ribs showing through his thin, dry coat. "Maybe we should talk to him again. His warriors might be acting without his approval."

"Enough is enough," Tigerclaw growled. "We need to stop just *talking* and show RiverClan that they can't get away with this."

"What are you suggesting, Tigerclaw?" Sunstar asked calmly. Redpaw could almost see his leader's level gaze as he carefully considered each cat's words.

"We need to *fight*," Tigerclaw hissed. There was a scraping sound inside the den, and Redpaw pictured Tigerclaw's paws flexing, his long, sharp front claws extending and retracting with the big tabby's anger. "We should attack RiverClan's camp. Teach them what happens when they mess with ThunderClan."

"I'm not sure fighting is the best choice," Tawnyspots argued. "RiverClan has more warriors than we do right now. Do we want to start something on their own territory, knowing we'll be outnumbered?"

"We'll bring the apprentices, then," Tigerclaw replied coolly. "They should have the experience of being in a real battle anyway."

Redpaw's whiskers stiffened in surprise. *The apprentices? Tigerclaw thinks we should fight RiverClan?*

His head spun, and for a moment he lost track of the conversation in Sunstar's den. He snapped back to attention at the sound of his mentor's angry voice.

"We can't take the apprentices into battle!" Sparrowpelt yowled. "They don't have any real fighting experience!"

"They're not ready," Speckletail agreed.

"And they never will be, if they never get to fight," Tigerclaw mewed. "They need to be properly trained, and facing a battle with another Clan is the only way to learn."

There was a long silence, and Redpaw pictured the warriors looking to Sunstar for his decision. *He might take Frostpaw and Brindlepaw, but Sunstar won't let Willowpaw and me go,* Redpaw thought. *He thinks we're too young to fight.* He swallowed hard. *Do I even* want *to fight?*

When he dreamed of being a full warrior, Redpaw never imagined a battle. He wanted to hunt and patrol for his Clan. He knew he'd have to fight someday. *But not yet.*

"We will go to RiverClan," Sunstar meowed at last. "And we'll take all four of the warrior apprentices." Redpaw stiffened in shock.

"But Sunstar—" Sparrowpelt began to object.

"We're not going to start a war," Sunstar interrupted firmly. "We'll go onto their territory with a full force of warriors. We'll make a show of strength, and remind Hailstar that he'd better stay away from Sunningrocks. That's it."

"We've done that before," Tigerclaw objected. "And it only kept RiverClan away for a little while."

"This time we'll be asking Hailstar for a promise," Sunstar pointed out. "Surely he understands that we can't continue fighting over Sunningrocks forever. If he gives us his word, we can trust him to see that his cats keep it."

"I don't think we should take Redpaw and Willowpaw," Sparrowpelt mewed again. "They're nowhere near full-grown, and they could get hurt."

"Frostpaw and Brindlepaw are almost warriors," Speckletail agreed. "But Redpaw and Willowpaw haven't had much battle training yet. They're practically just out of the nursery."

The fur rose on Redpaw's shoulders. He might not have learned how to fight yet, but he wasn't a kit!

"Tigerclaw has a point about the apprentices' training," Sunstar meowed. "But Sparrowpelt and Speckletail are right, too. If the apprentices are going to come onto RiverClan's territory, we need a plan to keep them safe."

"We could try dividing our forces," Tawnyspots suggested. "Most of our warriors can approach RiverClan across the river, but another group can come over the bridge from Fourtrees. If there's a battle, they can attack from behind, when the RiverClan cats are already distracted."

"And we could keep the apprentices well to the back of that group," Sunstar mewed thoughtfully. "Along with you, Tigerclaw."

"I'm the best fighter ThunderClan has!" Tigerclaw yowled, outraged.

"And I'm hoping to frighten RiverClan off without actually starting a fight," Sunstar replied calmly. "You're the one who suggested bringing the apprentices, and I think you should be responsible for making sure they come home safely."

"I'm not their mentor," Tigerclaw growled, sounding sulky.

"Surely the Clan's best fighter is the one we need protecting our apprentices," Sunstar meowed.

There was another long pause, and then Tigerclaw muttered, "Yes, Sunstar." Redpaw could imagine him dipping his head, his amber eyes stormy with silent frustration.

"We should announce the plan to the Clan," Sunstar mewed briskly, and Redpaw leaped back from the Highrock before Sunstar could come out of his den and see him eavesdropping.

I'm going to be in a battle! he thought, his heart pounding with excitement.

Then a cold chill ran across his spine, and he felt his tail droop. Redpaw swallowed hard.

I'm going to be in a battle.

CHAPTER TWO

"See this?" White-eye asked, angling her face so that Redpaw was looking directly into her cloudy, sightless eye, so different from the sharp yellow one beside it. An old scar knotted its lid. "A badger's claw caught my face when I was just a kit. One wrong move in a battle can mark you forever. Be careful today, Redpaw."

Redpaw's stomach turned over. "Do you really think we're going to fight?" he asked, his mew sounding shaky to his own ears.

The pale-gray she-cat twitched her whiskers thoughtfully. "I don't see how we can avoid it," she replied. "Sunstar told Hailstar that the RiverClan cats had better stay away from Sunningrocks. Now that they're coming back again, I think ThunderClan will have to fight." She sighed. "I just wish I could help. I hate being useless."

"Well, having kits is really, um, important, too," Redpaw mewed awkwardly, glancing at the she-cat's rounded sides.

"Thanks, Redpaw." White-eye dipped her head, her mew a little lighter. "Just don't rush into the fight today, okay? Let the warriors handle it."

"Are you trying to scare my apprentice?" An amused meow came from behind them, and Redpaw jumped, then licked his chest fur in embarrassment. *I'm* not *scared.*

White-eye turned her muzzle up toward Sparrowpelt's and purred. "I only want you both to be careful," she mewed. "My kits will need their father."

Sparrowpelt rubbed his cheek against hers, closing his eyes, and Redpaw averted his gaze.

"I'll just . . . be over there . . . ," he said uncomfortably. Redpaw turned his back and hurried away, not stopping until he was almost to the fresh-kill pile.

He took a deep breath. Now that he was away from Sparrowpelt and White-eye, his embarrassment went away and his pelt prickled nervously as he thought about what White-eye had said. *One wrong move in a battle can mark you forever.*

Nearby, Stormtail was giving Brindlepaw some last-minute advice. "Now remember," the tom instructed, "if they get you on your back, slash your hind paws up at your opponent's belly just like I showed you. Don't be afraid to use your claws."

Redpaw swallowed hard, panic spiking through him. *I haven't even learned that move yet!*

Sunstar strode to the center of the clearing and yowled for attention. "It's time for us to confront RiverClan," he announced. "Bluefur will be leading the apprentices and their mentors, as well as Tigerclaw, to approach the RiverClan camp across the Twoleg bridge. Lionheart and Goldenflower will be staying behind to defend our camp." The large golden tom and his smaller ginger sister exchanged disappointed glances but bowed their heads in agreement.

"Every other warrior, take the herbs that our medicine cats have for you; then we will go. Remember, right now we're just giving them a warning. No cat is to attack unless I give the order or RiverClan attacks first."

Featherwhisker and Spottedpaw moved between the warriors, giving out herbs. Spottedpaw came to Redpaw and dropped a small packet at his paws. "For strength," she explained, and Redpaw dipped his head to lap them up, grimacing at their sharp taste.

Once each warrior and apprentice had finished their herbs, Sunstar paced to the camp's entrance. "Follow me!" he yowled.

The warriors streamed out of camp behind their leader. Their tails were held high and their eyes were bright and eager. Redpaw watched them go, his stomach sour with nervousness. *What's wrong with me? I want to be a warrior. It's all I've ever wanted. Why am I afraid to fight?*

"What's got your tail in a twist?" Tigerclaw had stopped beside him and was looking at Redpaw curiously.

"White-eye was talking to me about how she lost her eye," Redpaw explained reluctantly. "She said that one wrong move can mark you forever, and she told me to hang back and let the warriors fight."

Tigerclaw's tail flicked dismissively. "White-eye's just jealous because she's chosen to have kits instead of fighting for her Clan," he meowed coolly. "Don't let her discourage you. *She* can't fight right now, but *your* best warrior days are just beginning."

They are? Redpaw's pelt tingled. He liked the idea of becoming a strong warrior more than he did the idea of needing to be protected.

Tigerclaw was so *confident*. If he thought Redpaw was well on his way to being a strong warrior, he was probably right. Warmth spread through Redpaw's chest.

"The best warriors don't try to avoid a fight," Tigerclaw went on. He slid out his sharp claws and raked the ground with one paw, leaving long deep lines in the dirt. "If River-Clan tries to argue with us, I'll attack. We can't hesitate if we want them to respect us."

Redpaw knew that what Tigerclaw was saying was reckless: They should be waiting for Sunstar's commands. But he couldn't help the warm curl of admiration that ran through him. *He's so brave.*

Redpaw watched as his father, Adderfang, disappeared through the gorse tunnel, the last of the warriors following Sunstar.

"Apprentices and mentors! Tigerclaw! With me!" Bluefur called. Her apprentice, Frostpaw, was standing beside her, wide-eyed.

Sparrowpelt touched noses with White-eye one more time, then turned away. "Come on, Redpaw," he meowed as he strode toward Bluefur.

Redpaw's eyes met his sister Spottedpaw's again. She was standing outside the medicine cat's den with Featherwhisker, her tail lashing excitedly. "Good luck, Redpaw!" she yowled. "Good luck, Willowpaw!" Waving his own tail to her in

farewell, Redpaw took a deep breath and followed Sparrowpelt out of camp.

Bluefur took the lead, Sparrowpelt and Poppydawn side by
side behind her. Stormtail followed with his apprentice, Brindlepaw, beside him, her sister Frostpaw eagerly chattering to
them both. "Do you think we'll see any of the RiverClan cats
actually *swimming*?" Redpaw overheard her asking.

Willowpaw fell into step beside Redpaw as they paced
through the forest, and Tigerclaw brought up the rear of the
patrol. Recently fallen leaves crunched beneath their paws,
and sunlight came between the trees' branches, making bright
patches on the forest floor. Redpaw shivered suddenly, only
partly because of the leaf-fall chill in the air.

Willowpaw shot him a sharp glance. "Are you scared?" she
whispered.

"A little bit," Redpaw admitted, keeping his voice low so
that Tigerclaw wouldn't hear.

"Don't worry," Willowpaw told him. "Remember, we're
just delivering a warning to RiverClan. And if something
does happen, we're not alone. We've got the whole Clan; we've
got Sparrowpelt and Poppydawn looking out for us. . . ." She
pushed closer, her fur brushing his, and whispered even more
quietly, "And Tigerclaw thinks he's the best warrior in the
whole forest. He won't let us get hurt. It wouldn't be good for
his reputation."

While the rest of the warriors headed straight for the
RiverClan camp, Bluefur led her patrol up past the Owl
Tree and close to Fourtrees before turning and following the

river toward the Twoleg bridge.

"This is a waste of time," Tigerclaw muttered. "We should be attacking the camp, not wandering around at the edge of RiverClan's territory."

"Sunstar wants us to come from this direction," Bluefur mewed sharply. "And we're not planning to fight unless we have to." The blue-gray she-cat looked preoccupied, her eyes searching the open plains of RiverClan's territory as if there was something she was expecting, or hoping, to see. Tigerclaw narrowed his amber eyes at her balefully, but said nothing.

As Redpaw followed Frostpaw onto the bridge, he wrinkled his nose at the sharp, unnatural Twoleg scent. It smelled strange.

They were only a few paces across when a cry sounded in the distance. Stormtail's head shot up. "That's Smallear," he meowed. "They're fighting."

Another agonized yowl made all the cats flinch. "Dappletail," Bluefur observed tensely. "It sounds like she's in trouble."

"Come on!" Tigerclaw yowled. He began to run, easily shouldering past the apprentices. Redpaw tensed, running after him, the surface of the Twoleg bridge hard beneath his paws.

Tigerclaw was side by side with Bluefur at the front of the patrol when a sudden harsh screech came from above. A huge brown shape blocked out the sun, swooping down at them. Panicked, Redpaw dodged backward, but Bluefur and Tigerclaw were on their hind legs, their claws extended, swiping at the brown thing above them, which Redpaw could now see was feathered—a bird!

"Protect the apprentices!" Stormtail yowled, and the other warriors began aiming sharp-clawed blows at the bird, too.

The bird screeched again and rose out of their reach. Its yellow eyes glared at them beadily, and its tawny wings were spread wide. *A hawk!* Redpaw realized. Sparrowpelt had told him how dangerous the huge birds could be. "They'll carry a kit off to eat if they can," he remembered his mentor saying. "Or even a lone full-grown cat, but they're no match for a whole patrol." They'd attack smaller cats, Redpaw remembered, ones they could lift in their claws. He gulped, flinching. He and Willowpaw were the smallest cats here.

"Bunch together," Poppydawn instructed, and Sparrowpelt and Stormtail hurried back toward the apprentices, herding them into a smaller, tighter group.

Redpaw couldn't take his eyes off the hawk circling above them. Its long, sharp talons and the cruel curve of its beak looked horribly dangerous. He realized just how exposed they were on the bridge, with nothing between them and the vicious bird, no trees or bushes to shelter beneath.

"Run!" Bluefur yowled. She pointed her tail toward a small grove of birch trees near the far end of the bridge. "Get under those trees!"

Warm pelts brushed against Redpaw's as the rest of the patrol began to run. Redpaw wanted to run with them, but he felt as if his paws were stuck to the Twoleg bridge. He crouched low, panting. *I have to run.*

He couldn't run.

He looked up just as the hawk swooped lower, its huge

wings fully extended. Redpaw backed away quickly, his paws scrabbling against the hard surface of the bridge. The space between him and the rest of the patrol widened.

I'm going the wrong way!

Everything was slowing down, everything except for Redpaw's heart, which was beating faster and faster. He gasped for air, his paws feeling too slow and heavy to lift.

"Redpaw!" Willowpaw wailed from the other end of the bridge. The others had noticed at last that he hadn't run with them. He'd been left behind.

If I run now, maybe I can still get away.

But the hawk was circling above him now, coming lower and lower. Redpaw could see the bright gleam of its beady eyes. He cringed back, flattening his body against the bridge.

"Run, Redpaw!" Sparrowpelt yowled. He and Tigerclaw were racing back toward Redpaw, their long strides eating up the distance between them, but the hawk was closer. It dived toward him, its talons extended. Redpaw couldn't breathe.

A hawk will go for a lone cat.

And, with nothing to hide him from the diving hawk, Redpaw had never felt so alone.

CHAPTER THREE

The hawk screeched, its shadow falling over Redpaw. It was so huge above him, so much larger than he was, that it could probably swallow him whole, he thought, his heart pounding hard. He squeezed his eyes tightly closed.

Redpaw whimpered, his ears pressed flat against his head.

The bird's next screech was almost drowned out by a powerful snarl. Redpaw's eyes snapped open just in time to see Tigerclaw slam into the hawk in midair, knocking it with a thud into the side of the bridge beside Redpaw.

The hawk slashed at Tigerclaw with its beak, giving an angry squawk. Tigerclaw dodged backward easily, using his big paws to pin the huge bird's wings to the bridge. He began ripping away feathers, blood beading in red droplets across the bird's brown wings. The hawk thrashed, almost throwing him off, but Tigerclaw held on.

"Redpaw!"

At the sound of Sparrowpelt's voice, Redpaw tore his gaze away from the fight. His mentor was only a tail-length away, panting from his run. "Come on," his mentor hissed urgently. "Now, while Tigerclaw's got it distracted."

"But . . ." *Shouldn't we help him?* Redpaw looked back at the battling cat and hawk just as Tigerclaw jerked to one side and bit into the hawk's neck hard, his sharp white teeth bright against the hawk's dark feathers. He tore at the bird's throat and more feathers scattered across the bridge. It didn't look like Tigerclaw needed their help at all.

"Come on, quickly!" Sparrowpelt growled. Finally, Redpaw ran. Together they dashed toward the rest of the patrol on the opposite side of the bridge.

Redpaw couldn't quite keep pace with his mentor. As fast as he was running, he was still falling behind.

"Don't leave me," he whimpered, his mouth dry with terror. With a horrified glance at the sky, Sparrowpelt doubled back. Snatching Redpaw up by the back of the neck—like a *kit*—he hauled him toward the far end of the bridge.

"Hey!" Redpaw sputtered as they got closer to the others, his legs churning helplessly. "Put me down! I'm fine!" When they finally reached the end of the bridge, Sparrowpelt dropped him, immediately beginning to nose gingerly along Redpaw's sides.

"Are you hurt anywhere?" he asked. "Did it scratch you?"

Before he could answer, Willowpaw threw herself on Redpaw and buried her head in his shoulder. "Oh, Redpaw," she mewed shakily. "I was so *scared*. When I saw you weren't with us, I . . ." She gasped and pressed her head harder against him.

Redpaw backed a little away from them both, embarrassed. "I'm *fine*," he insisted. "I promise."

"Good," Bluefur mewed briskly. "Stay under this tree, all

of you. Hawks usually hunt alone, but we should be cautious. There could be another one up there."

On the bridge, the fallen hawk flapped its wings desperately, throwing Tigerclaw off. He landed on his feet, snarling, and leaped toward it again, but the bird fluttered its damaged wings and, with an awkward lurch, launched itself off the other side of the bridge.

"Wow!" Frostpaw said, her eyes wide. "It's running away! Flying, I mean."

The bird plummeted for a moment, then rose again, flapping its way slowly into the sky. It looked battered and unsteady. A few more feathers drifted down onto the bridge. Now that Tigerclaw had bested it, it didn't seem quite so fierce.

As it flew off over the trees, Tigerclaw strutted back toward his Clanmates, his tail held high over his back. Redpaw shook off his sister and ran to meet him.

"Tigerclaw," he gasped, coming to a halt before the warrior, suddenly feeling shy. "You saved me!"

Tigerclaw licked his own front paw smugly. "It's all right, Redpaw," he meowed. "You're safe now."

"Thank you," Redpaw told him. Just saying thanks didn't seem like enough, really: He could still feel the horrible dread that had filled him as he'd waited for those wickedly sharp talons to sink into his sides. "If—if there's anything I can ever do for you, T-Tigerclaw, just name it," he stammered. "I owe you *everything*."

"You did very well, Tigerclaw," Bluefur mewed as the rest of the patrol came up behind Redpaw. "We're all grateful to you."

There was a murmur of agreement from the other cats, all of whom were looking at Tigerclaw with respect. Redpaw squirmed, feeling hot with shame. No cat would have had to be grateful to Tigerclaw, if only Redpaw had followed the order to run, if he hadn't stupidly put himself in danger.

"We need to keep going, though," Stormtail pointed out. "The other warriors may need us."

Bluefur and Sparrowpelt exchanged a worried look. Suddenly Redpaw noticed that he could no longer hear the yowls and sounds of fighting from the RiverClan camp.

"I can't hear them anymore." Brindlepaw echoed Redpaw's thoughts. "Is the fight over?"

"I don't know," Bluefur mewed. "We'd better go and see. I think that Redpaw and Willowpaw should stay here, though."

"I'm *fine!*" Redpaw insisted again. His knees were still trembling, but he didn't want to be left behind. "And it's not fair to make Willowpaw stay back," he added. Willowpaw cast him a grateful look.

Bluefur ignored him, instead looking at Sparrowpelt. "Will you stay with them?" she asked.

"Of course," Sparrowpelt replied, and Bluefur dipped her head gratefully.

"Stay under the tree in case the hawk comes back," she warned as she left, the rest of the patrol following her. They were hurrying, the three warriors in front and Frostpaw and Brindlepaw behind, both apprentices gazing at Tigerclaw admiringly.

Redpaw watched until they disappeared over a hill, and

then he flopped down near the birch tree's roots. "This is all my fault," he groaned.

"You're not responsible for the hawk," Sparrowpelt replied. He was looking toward the RiverClan camp, his ears pricked for any sound.

Willowpaw lay down next to Redpaw and pressed her side against his. "I was so frightened when I saw you were still on the bridge," she confessed, her voice unsteady. "What if that hawk had carried you off?"

Redpaw shuddered at the thought and pushed his nose against his sister's shoulder, inhaling her comforting familiar scent. "It didn't, though," he mewed, to himself as much as to her. "I'm still here. Tigerclaw saved me."

Willowpaw blinked slowly at him, her gaze warm. "I'll never call Tigerclaw a show-off or an arrogant furball again," she promised. "He saved your life, and he can be as proud as he wants to be."

Redpaw's heartbeat had only just calmed down when Sparrowpelt suddenly stiffened. "Here they come," he meowed, lashing his tail.

"It hasn't been very long," Willowpaw muttered, getting to her feet, and Redpaw shook off his shakiness and rose, too. "Is everything okay, do you think?"

Sparrowpelt didn't answer, but stepped forward to greet the other warriors. He and Bluefur touched noses briefly, and Bluefur sighed. "We were too late."

"The fight was over?" Sparrowpelt asked.

Poppydawn's tail drooped. "The rest of ThunderClan had to retreat," she mewed. "There were just too many RiverClan cats."

Because we didn't get there in time. Redpaw's mouth went dry.

"We weren't there to fight, because of me," he blurted guiltily. "I'm sorry!"

Sparrowpelt sighed. "We'll talk about this when we get back to camp, Redpaw."

"The important thing is that you're all right," Poppydawn meowed firmly. "Let's get back and see if we can help Feather-whisker and Spottedpaw with any injuries from the fight."

Redpaw trailed behind the other cats as they headed back toward the ThunderClan camp, his head bowed. *This is all my fault.* The thought kept repeating in his head. *My fault.* If only he hadn't frozen in his panic! If he had run with the other cats, maybe they would have arrived at the RiverClan camp in time to be of use in the battle.

Tigerclaw dropped back to walk beside him. "Hey," he meowed, bumping his side against Redpaw's reassuringly. "Stop worrying."

Redpaw's whiskers twitched miserably. "I'm not sure I can."

"It'll be fine," Tigerclaw assured him. "We might have lost *this* battle because of you, but we'll have other chances to beat RiverClan."

Redpaw stumbled. *Because of me?* Tigerclaw was confirming all his worst fears.

"I'll back you up when we talk to Sunstar," Tigerclaw went on. "He'll see that you just didn't know any better. It's not like you ruined everything on purpose."

Redpaw's heart sank. "D-do we have to tell Sunstar what I did?" he asked, his mew quavering.

Tigerclaw's ears twitched in surprise. "Of course we do," he replied. "Sunstar's our leader and he needs to know why his plan failed. But I'll stick up for you, no matter what the others say. After all, every warrior in the Clan did some dumb things as a 'paw." He shot Redpaw a glance out of the corner of his amber eyes. "I mean, those things don't usually have such awful effects, but that was just bad luck, really."

Redpaw felt sick. What was Sunstar going to say, what would he do, when he realized that Redpaw had lost Thunder-Clan the battle? Still, at least Tigerclaw was on his side. He breathed out a small sigh of relief.

"Thanks, Tigerclaw," he mewed meekly. "I really owe you one."

Tigerclaw's tail curled high above his back. "You owe me more than one," he purred cheerfully. "You owe me your life!"

CHAPTER FOUR
❧

"*Redpaw, do you promise to uphold* the warrior code and protect and defend your Clan, even at the cost of your own life?" Sunstar's eyes, warm and steady, gazed into Redpaw's.

"I do," Redpaw promised. He realized that he was trembling. Willowpaw—no, Willow*pelt*, since a few heartbeats ago—stood shoulder to shoulder with him, a steady support.

"Then, by the powers of StarClan, I give you your warrior name. Redpaw, from now on you will be known as Redtail. StarClan honors your bravery and your loyalty. We welcome you as a full member of ThunderClan."

With a purr, Sunstar rested his muzzle briefly on Redtail's head. "Serve your Clan well," he mewed. "You'll be a fine warrior."

Joy ran through Redtail as he bent his head and licked his leader's shoulder. *A fine warrior.* Six moons ago, back when he was that scared 'paw who'd been responsible for losing the battle with RiverClan, he'd hardly dared to imagine he might someday hear those words.

The cats around them cried out, "Willowpelt! Redtail! Willowpelt! Redtail!" As their Clanmates chanted their new

names, Redtail could hear their father Adderfang's voice rising, loudest of all.

As Redtail broke away from Sunstar, he saw Sparrowpelt,
usually so stern, looking at him proudly. Beside him, White-
eye purred. Their kits, Runningkit and Mousekit, tumbled
around her paws.

Near them, Spottedpaw was quivering with excitement.
She wouldn't get her own name for a while—she had a lot to
learn before she would be ready to become a full medicine
cat—but she seemed as proud and happy for her littermates as
if everyone were calling her new name, too.

At the back of the crowd of cats, Redtail caught sight of
Tigerclaw. The big cat wasn't cheering or purring like the rest,
just watching, his expression unreadable.

Does he think I'm not ready to be a warrior? Redtail thought anxiously. He hadn't forgotten how Tigerclaw had saved him
from the hawk moons before, or that he himself had ruined
the battle with RiverClan.

No cat in ThunderClan had seemed to hold it against him:
Sunstar hadn't even scolded him, just praised Tigerclaw for
driving off the hawk. But Redtail blamed himself, and he
knew that Tigerclaw remembered, too.

"I can't believe we're finally warriors!" Willowpelt said
excitedly. "I've been waiting for this moment *forever!*" Beside
her, their mother, Swiftbreeze, nuzzled her cheek.

"My kits are so grown-up," she mewed.

Redtail pulled his gaze away from Tigerclaw's and looked
at his sister affectionately. "Yeah. You're going to be a terrific

warrior," he said, and Swiftbreeze purred in agreement.

Willowpelt puffed out her chest a little, her head high. "Do you think so? I know you will, too," she added.

I hope so. Redtail's eyes caught Tigerclaw's again. After Redtail had made that terrible mistake back in leaf-fall, he had tried hard to make up for it. He'd worked through leaf-bare without a word of complaint, bringing back prey even when the snows had reached above shoulder height and the forest seemed empty of life.

It had been a long, hard leaf-bare. Bluefur and Thrushpelt's young kits had been killed by a fox, to the whole Clan's horror, and Tawnyspots, the faithful and well-liked deputy, had died a slow, painful death from the illness he had suffered for so long. Bluefur was deputy now, more solemn and efficient than ever. Since she'd lost her kits, she seemed to think of nothing but the good of ThunderClan.

Now that newleaf was finally arriving, pale sunshine lingered longer every day, and tiny plants sprouted in the damp soil of the forest. It had been a *long* time since Redtail had cost the Clan that battle. Surely Tigerclaw didn't think of him as that timid 'paw anymore?

Determined to find out what was behind the other warrior's thoughtful gaze, Redtail stiffened his shoulders and headed toward him. *I'm one of the best hunters in ThunderClan already,* he thought. If Tigerclaw challenged him, he would tell that to the older warrior. *Every cat makes mistakes sometime. I can't feel bad about it forever.*

When he reached Tigerclaw, he wasn't sure what to say. *I'm not an apprentice anymore* seemed too obvious.

"Redtail," Tigerclaw purred in greeting, "I was going to go hunting. I could use a strong warrior to go with me. Can you think of one?"

Does he mean . . . ? A jolt of happiness shot through Redtail. He'd been worrying for nothing. Tigerclaw had called him a strong warrior. "I'd love to!" he meowed cheerfully.

He glanced quickly back at Sparrowpelt, who was purring with laughter as he tumbled Runningkit over with one paw. Then he realized: He didn't have to ask his mentor for permission to leave camp anymore. He didn't have to ask *any* cat. He was a warrior. Holding his head high, he followed Tigerclaw through the gorse tunnel out of camp.

They headed toward the border with Fourtrees, passing the sandy hollow where Redtail had spent so much time learning battle moves from Sparrowpelt and practicing with the other apprentices. Already that seemed like a long time ago.

As they walked beneath the trees, Redtail scented the air, his ears pricked for any sounds. The newleaf forest was rich with the scents of prey and of moist soil and fresh growing plants, so different from the cold, lifeless scents of leaf-bare.

A faint rustling came from the bracken beneath an alder tree, and Redtail tensed, dropping into a hunting crouch.

He scented the air, his mouth watering. *A vole.* He could hear the little distinct rustles of it moving through the bracken. He crept closer, moving silently, his tail held low and stiff. He could feel Tigerclaw watching him.

The soft sounds of movement in the bracken ceased as the

little animal froze: The vole must have sensed them at last. But Redtail could still hear the pounding of its tiny heart, knew exactly where it was hiding. Breaking into a run, he crashed through the bracken and pounced before the prey could try to escape. He bit down on the back of the vole's neck, and the warm body stilled beneath his paws.

"Nicely done," Tigerclaw meowed approvingly as Redtail backed out of the bracken, the vole dangling from his jaws.

"Thanks," Redtail replied, pleased at Tigerclaw's praise. He dropped the vole beneath a bush and scraped earth over it to conceal it until he could pick it up on their way back to camp.

Near the Fourtrees border, Redtail heard the quick thumping leaps of a running rabbit. Both cats stopped, their ears pricked.

"It's coming this way," Tigerclaw observed, and Redtail nodded. His pelt prickled with excitement at the thought of a juicy rabbit, big enough to feed three or four of his Clanmates. The rabbit was running fast and straight, and it was easy to guess where it would cross onto ThunderClan territory. Without needing to speak, they positioned themselves, one to each side of where the rabbit was heading.

The heavy loping bounds were coming closer and closer. It sounded like a big one. His mouth watering, Redtail tensed, ready to spring.

In a blur of brown fur, the rabbit shot out of the undergrowth, running full tilt, closer to Tigerclaw than to Redtail. Redtail let himself relax a bit, knowing the bigger warrior could take it down alone.

Just as Tigerclaw leaped, another blur of fur—a *cat*—burst
out of the undergrowth and leaped, too. Redtail watched in
horror as Tigerclaw and the smaller cat collided in midair and
fell to the ground with a heavy thud, tangled together and
spitting with rage and shock. The rabbit dodged away into
the undergrowth and was lost before Redtail even thought of
pouncing.

"Get off me!" Tigerclaw snarled, and the other cat sprang
to her paws, looking indignant.

"That was my rabbit!" she yowled. "You made me lose
my rabbit!" She was barely as big as a rabbit herself, Redtail
saw, and clearly an apprentice. Despite her size, she glared at
Tigerclaw fiercely, her brown-and-gray fur bristling with fury.

"*Our* rabbit," Tigerclaw corrected, sliding out his claws. "I'd
like to know what you think you're doing, hunting *Thunder-
Clan* prey on *ThunderClan* territory."

"It is not!" the apprentice hissed scornfully. "Is it, Stagleap?"
She looked over her shoulder, her eyes wide with confusion.
"Stagleap . . . ?" For the first time, she seemed to realize that
she was alone. But a moment later, she'd puffed up her fur and
was glaring at them both again. Despite himself, Redtail felt a
rising admiration for her bravery.

"You're a WindClan apprentice, aren't you?" Redtail asked,
recognizing her from the last full-moon meeting. "Sorrelpaw,
right? What are you doing here?"

"I'm hunting," she told him, her tail curling behind her.
"And no matter what you two say, WindClan cats have just

as much right to hunt at Fourtrees as you do. ThunderClan doesn't own *everything*." She sniffed. "No wonder you're always fighting with RiverClan over those Sunningrocks. What a bunch of bullies."

The fur rose on Tigerclaw's shoulders. "The border between Fourtrees and ThunderClan territory is five tail-lengths behind you. Don't WindClan mentors teach their apprentices how to recognize borders?"

For the first time, Sorrelpaw looked shaken. She looked back toward Fourtrees, her tail waving uncertainly. "Um—"

Tigerclaw went on. "Clearly, WindClan doesn't teach apprentices to respect their elders, either. We should fix that." His cold amber gaze swung to Redtail. "Show Sorrelpaw what happens to cats who insult ThunderClan."

"What?" Redtail blinked. "She's just an apprentice, Tiger-claw. Her mentor isn't even with her."

Tigerclaw stalked closer to him, dropping his voice to a murmur. "If she wasn't trying to start trouble, she would have stayed on her own territory."

"I don't think this is a good idea," Redtail mewed, backing away. Clearly, Tigerclaw didn't care that Sorrelpaw was only an apprentice. "We're still in conflict with RiverClan over Sunningrocks; do you really want to start trouble with Wind-Clan, too?"

"I am a *warrior*." Tigerclaw hissed. "I'm not going to let any cat disrespect my Clan or our borders. What about you, Redtail? I thought you'd grown to be a brave ThunderClan warrior." He looked slyly at Redtail out of the corner of his eye. "Are you still a mouse-hearted 'paw?"

"No!" Redtail's back stiffened. He knew Tigerclaw was talk-ing about how he'd frozen at the bridge all those moons ago. Tigerclaw had saved him then; maybe the older warrior really did know best. He owed Tigerclaw his life. He would follow his lead. Swallowing hard, he turned to look at Sorrelpaw.

The apprentice looked smaller than ever to him. *I won't hurt her too badly.*

Maybe she would be able to sense his intentions and wouldn't be too scared.

He approached slowly, growling and baring his teeth. He half hoped Sorrelpaw *would* seize the chance to turn tail and run, but instead the little apprentice arched her back and hissed at him, sliding out her claws.

Redtail glanced back at Tigerclaw, who was watching him with narrowed eyes, and sprang. Easily tumbling Sorrelpaw over, he slammed her against the ground. The apprentice gasped, the breath knocked out of her, but a moment later she was fighting hard. Her claws raked across Redtail's belly, stinging sharply. Hot with rage at the pain, he pinned her, holding her down, and sank his teeth into her shoulder.

Warm blood burst in his mouth, and Sorrelpaw shrieked in agony.

"Tear her apart, Redtail," Tigerclaw hissed. There was something nastily pleased about his voice.

Shocked, Redtail released Sorrelpaw and staggered back-ward. *Tear her apart?* He felt suddenly queasy, his mouth full of the taste of blood.

"Hey!" The voice came from the border. Redtail looked up. A stocky brown tom—much larger than most of underfed, fast-running WindClan—was pushing his broad shoulders through the undergrowth, staring at the scene before him with round, shocked amber eyes. "Get away from her!"

"Stagleap, I—I—" Redtail stammered, imagining how the scene must look through the other cat's eyes. The apprentice, trembling, her fur wet with blood. Redtail and Tigerclaw looming over her ominously, so much larger and older. Full-grown warriors attacking a lone apprentice. He felt hot with shame.

The WindClan tom ran to his apprentice's side and gently nosed her wounds. "Sorrelpaw, can you get up?" He helped the wincing apprentice to her paws and let her lean against his side, then turned to the ThunderClan warriors, his expression turning from concern to anger. "Which of you did this?"

Redtail swallowed hard and stared at the ground. *What have I done?*

"Does it matter?" Tigerclaw hissed, puffing out his chest. "The real question is, why did you let her go racing onto ThunderClan land after our prey? Is WindClan so pathetic they can't catch rabbits on their own territory?"

"Pathetic?" Stagleap echoed, bristling. "The two of you beating up an apprentice—*that's* pathetic." Nudging Sorrelpaw gently to stand on her own, he paced toward Tigerclaw, stopping less than a whisker's length from the other cat. "Why don't you pick on a cat your own size?" he growled.

Tigerclaw looked almost pleased, his tail curling above his

back as he unsheathed his claws.

"It was me," Redtail broke in hurriedly, before they could start fighting. He couldn't let Tigerclaw take all the blame. "I attacked Sorrelpaw because she was hunting on our territory." He hung his head. "I didn't mean to be so rough. And I'm sorry we didn't wait for you before—"

"We've got nothing to apologize for," Tigerclaw interrupted, his eyes cold. "The apprentice trespassed on our territory and needed to be taught a lesson."

The end of Stagleap's tail twitched and he hunkered down, ready to spring. "I think maybe it's you two who need to be taught a lesson," he muttered. He moved forward until they were nearly nose to nose. The two toms looked evenly matched, Redtail saw, both huge and muscular. But Stagleap was older and an experienced warrior; he might be more than a match for Tigerclaw.

"Go ahead and try," Tigerclaw taunted. He looked excited, almost eager.

I'll have to fight, too, Redtail realized, his stomach sinking. *I can't abandon Tigerclaw. But Stagleap is so huge!*

The big toms glared at each other for a long moment, muscles tensed and teeth bared. Then, just behind Stagleap, Sorrelpaw wobbled on her paws, giving a small whimper. Fresh blood from her wound was running down her side, Redtail noticed with a pang of guilt.

Stagleap broke eye contact with Tigerclaw to look down at his apprentice, his glare softening. "You'll be okay, Sorrelpaw," he told her. Shifting his eyes back to Tigerclaw and Redtail, he said, "I'd love to tear your fur off, but it'll have to wait for another day. I'm taking Sorrelpaw back to WindClan."

Tigerclaw hissed, but Redtail said quickly, "Okay, of course."

Stagleap looked sternly at him. "I'm sure Sunstar doesn't know anything about this," he meowed. "He's an honorable leader. Out of respect for him, I'm going to report this so Heatherstar can give him a chance to make it right. But if Sunstar doesn't get his warriors under control, you can be sure that WindClan will be back to settle this."

"Spitting threats while you run away does sound like Wind-Clan," Tigerclaw retorted smoothly. "But if you do come back, I'll be waiting."

"Me too," Redtail added, and winced at his own words. *I have to support Tigerclaw, don't I?*

With a sigh, Stagleap turned his back on them and coaxed Sorrelpaw into motion, heading back toward Fourtrees. The little apprentice was limping and leaning heavily against Stagleap, clearly in pain.

"You did well, Redtail," Tigerclaw murmured as they watched them go. "We can't let WindClan cats think they can get away with crossing our borders."

I suppose that's true, Redtail thought. But his mouth felt dry and sour, and the shallow scratches on his belly stung. There was a guilty, queasy feeling in his stomach. *If I did the right thing, why do I feel so wrong?*

CHAPTER FIVE

As he padded back into camp beside Tigerclaw, Redtail ached all over. He longed for the cool darkness of the warriors' den, where he could lie down in his nest and try to forget what had happened.

At the sight of them, Runningkit and Mousekit abandoned the ball of moss they were batting back and forth across the clearing and ran toward them.

"Redtail! Redtail!" Runningkit yowled. "Didn't you get any prey?"

We forgot the vole, Redtail realized.

Mousekit followed, her eyes wide. "Did you get hurt?" she asked, looking at the scratches on Redtail's side. "Was it badgers? Were you very brave?"

No, I wasn't brave. I was cruel. Redtail ignored them, stalking past the kits toward the warriors' den. He couldn't tell them what had happened, what he'd done.

"We don't have time to talk now, kits," Tigerclaw meowed importantly. "We have to report to Sunstar. Redtail, wait."

Halfway to the warriors' den, Redtail stopped and turned around to look at Tigerclaw. "What?"

Tigerclaw came forward and circled around Redtail, blocking his path. "Where do you think you're going? You have to come with me so we can tell Sunstar what happened."

"What *did* happen?" Mousekit asked curiously, but both toms ignored her.

"Mousekit! Runningkit! Stop bothering them and come here!" White-eye called, and the kits ran off. Redtail felt a surge of gratitude to White-eye. He didn't want the kits to hear any of this.

What would Sunstar think? Redtail had been considering the fight with Sorrelpaw on the walk back to camp. And he thought Stagleap was right—Sunstar wouldn't be too impressed that Redtail had beaten up an apprentice. "I guess I should get this over with," he said grimly.

Tigerclaw nudged him toward Sunstar's den. "Just follow my lead."

As they approached the Highrock, Sunstar pushed his way through the lichen covering the entrance to his den. "What's the matter?" he asked, seeing the expressions on Redtail's and Tigerclaw's faces.

"We've got trouble," Tigerclaw warned before Redtail could respond, and Sunstar's eyes widened in alarm.

"Come inside and tell me what you mean."

Tigerclaw and Redtail followed Sunstar into his den. *How can I explain why I attacked Sorrelpaw?* Redtail wondered guiltily.

But he didn't have to speak at all. Once inside, Tigerclaw began talking immediately. "We were hunting in the woods near Fourtrees, stalking a juicy rabbit," he explained. "Just as we were about to catch it, a WindClan apprentice, Sorrelpaw, came over the border from Fourtrees. She scared off our prey on purpose, just out of spite, then blamed us for hunting on our own territory."

Sunstar cocked his head to one side. "Just an apprentice making a mistake over border markers, surely? It happens. I hope you gave her a scolding and sent her back to WindClan."

Tigerclaw looked solemn. "I thought so, too, but when I pointed out the boundaries, she hissed at me and said it was time WindClan taught us a lesson. She said ThunderClan was just a bunch of bullies who thought everything belonged to us."

Redtail stared at Tigerclaw in surprise. *Sorrelpaw did say that, but that's not exactly how it happened.* Tigerclaw was making the whole fight sound like Sorrelpaw had been starting trouble on purpose and Tigerclaw had been calm and kind. "Uh . . ." Tigerclaw shot him a warning look, and Redtail closed his mouth again. Maybe Tigerclaw had seen something Redtail hadn't in the apprentice's behavior.

"We waited for Sorrelpaw's mentor," Tigerclaw went on. "We assumed that she was out of control and that he'd want to know what trouble she'd been starting. It was Stagleap, that big WindClan warrior."

Sunstar nodded; he knew who Stagleap was.

"When we told Stagleap what Sorrelpaw had done, he just laughed and asked what we were planning to do about it. And they scratched Redtail. Redtail, show Sunstar."

Redtail turned slightly, to show Sunstar the shallow

scratches on his side. Sunstar examined them seriously. He flicked his ear nervously. *Tigerclaw is twisting things. Sunstar wouldn't be so impressed by these wounds if he saw what I did to Sorrelpaw.*

"Stagleap said there was nothing we could do," Tigerclaw finished. "He said, 'It isn't like Sunstar will attack. He won't want to make WindClan angry.'"

Sunstar's eyes widened, and he bristled. "He said that, did he?"

"He did," Tigerclaw answered. "That's when Redtail drove them away."

Redtail winced. He'd overpowered an apprentice and hurt her, but he hadn't driven anyone away. He remembered the disgusted look on Stagleap's face, and a wave of shame washed over him.

"But as they left, Stagleap said he'd be back." Tigerclaw lowered his tail, looking worried. "Sunstar, WindClan is ignoring our border and disrespecting our leader. We need to prove to them that we can defend ourselves." Tigerclaw turned to Redtail. "Right?"

Redtail's head was spinning. Was Tigerclaw *trying* to start a battle with WindClan? Why was the big tom always so eager to fight? He'd done the same thing with RiverClan when the hawk had attacked. But then Redtail had an upsetting thought. *He didn't tell things the way they happened with WindClan. But why would he lie? Did he do the same thing with RiverClan?*

Tigerclaw nudged Redtail, waiting for his agreement. *I owe Tigerclaw my life,* Redtail remembered. He owed Tigerclaw everything. He couldn't call him a liar. But Redtail couldn't bring himself to back up Tigerclaw's story, either.

The silence seemed to stretch on for moons.

Finally Sunstar sighed. "There's a Gathering tonight," he mewed. "I'll talk to WindClan then and see what Heatherstar has to say. She's a reasonable cat. Maybe we can work this out without bloodshed."

"Yes, Sunstar." Tigerclaw nodded, dipping his head respectfully. But there was a strange, sullen light in his eyes.

Redtail was beginning to think that a peaceful solution was the last thing Tigerclaw wanted.

The cold light of the full moon shone down onto Fourtrees, throwing shadows from the four tall oaks across the cats gathered below. Redtail ruffled his pelt, his gaze sweeping over the other Clans, searching for Sorrelpaw. She wasn't there, he realized. Had he hurt her too badly for her to come? Or had she simply been left behind to help guard the WindClan camp?

"Our first Gathering as warriors," Willowpelt breathed beside him, looking awestruck.

"Yeah," Redtail muttered. If he hadn't hurt Sorrelpaw, he would have been just as thrilled as Willowpelt. Looking at the WindClan cats, he saw Stagleap deep in conversation with Talltail, WindClan's black-and-white deputy, and crouched a little, unwilling to catch the WindClan warrior's eye.

A loud yowl from the Great Rock in the center of the clearing called the gathered cats together. From the top of the rock, Sunstar looked down on the warriors below. On either side of him stood Cedarstar, the ShadowClan leader, and Crookedstar, who had recently become RiverClan's leader after Hailstar lost his ninth life. Heatherstar, the leader of WindClan, stood on the other side of Crookedstar. Redtail looked at the sleek, pale gray she-cat apprehensively.

What had Stagleap told her? And what was Sunstar going to say? Was he going to repeat the lies that Tigerclaw had told him? Near Redtail, Tigerclaw gazed up at the Clan leaders, his face calm but the tip of his tail twitching as if he was waiting for something.

What does Tigerclaw want to happen?

Cedarstar cleared his throat. "Newleaf has brought new prey to ShadowClan's territory. . . ."

Redtail's mind wandered as first ShadowClan's and then RiverClan's leader shared the news from their Clans. Heatherstar spoke, too, and Redtail listened to her attentively, but she didn't mention the conflict at the border. As Sunstar stepped forward next, Redtail snapped to attention, his heart pounding.

"After a hard leaf-bare, prey is running well in Thunder-Clan," Sunstar said. "We had a bout of whitecough go through camp, but Featherwhisker and Spottedpaw were able to treat it, and the last of the ill cats left the medicine den a few days ago."

He looked out onto the cats below him, and his eyes caught Redtail's. Redtail tensed, dread filling his belly: What would happen when Heatherstar told Sunstar the truth, and Sunstar realized that he and Tigerclaw had lied?

"We have two new warriors in ThunderClan," Sunstar announced instead. "Redtail and Willowpelt." The cats around them murmured their congratulations, and Willowpelt purred with pride. Redtail wanted to feel the same way, but he was too nervous.

Once the chatter had died down, Sunstar spoke again. "Unfortunately, something happened today at the boundary between Fourtrees and ThunderClan. A WindClan apprentice crossed the boundary, scaring away prey, and picked a fight with two ThunderClan warriors." He looked sharply at Heatherstar. "I'd like your assurances that this isn't going to happen again."

Heatherstar looked thoughtful. "I heard about the fight, although the story I heard was a bit different," she meowed. She paused, and Redtail's chest suddenly felt tight with fear. *Will she tell Sunstar what really happened?* But after a moment, the WindClan leader went on. "Mistakes will happen from time to time, especially with apprentices. Warriors should be patient with them." *Is she looking at me?* Redtail wondered. He couldn't tell. "But of course, the borders must be honored," Heatherstar went on. "I know Sunstar will agree to put this behind us so we can avoid further conflict."

In the crowd below, Tigerclaw laid back his ears. "Is she calling Sunstar weak?" he murmured to Thistleclaw beside him, in a meow that was just a bit too loud.

Sunstar clearly heard him, and the fur on his shoulders rose. "If WindClan will get its cats in line and have them show some respect, there won't be a reason to fight," he hissed.

Surprised rumblings rose from the crowd.

"Is Sunstar *threatening* WindClan?" a small white River-Clan tom asked, his eyes wide.

"It's time we showed the other Clans they can't cross ThunderClan's boundaries without consequences," Thistle-claw replied, and Tigerclaw nodded.

All across the clearing, fur was rising, and hisses and grum-bling broke through the usual friendly chatter of the Gather-ing. Redtail's chest felt hollow. Was this full-moon Gathering going to end in a battle? Surely it couldn't. The Gathering was always a time of peace.

Up on the Great Rock, Cedarstar flicked his dark gray tail. "Do we really need to air all these petty grievances at a Gath-ering? Some of us have business back in our own camps."

"I agree." Crookedstar, probably relieved to avoid get-ting caught up in a fight after several moons of peace with ThunderClan, leaped from the Great Rock. "RiverClan cats, follow me!"

As the RiverClan cats began to stream out of camp, Redtail quickly made his way across the clearing toward Stagleap. The big tom might not want to talk to Redtail. He might want to tear his pelt off—*and I'd deserve it*, Redtail thought miserably—but Redtail had to find out if Sorrelpaw was okay.

"Was Sorrelpaw too hurt to come to the Gathering?" he asked as soon as he was close to Stagleap.

Stagleap turned, looking startled. "She's sore, but she'll be all right," he replied. "No thanks to you."

"I didn't want to hurt her," Redtail mewed apologetically. "I was just doing my duty."

"Your duty?" Stagleap repeated. He stared at Redtail for a long moment before he spoke again. "You haven't been a warrior very long, have you, Redtail? Warriors are supposed to teach apprentices, not hurt them. Even other Clans' apprentices. Your duty was to scold her and send her home, or to wait for me to come and show her where she'd gone wrong."

"Tigerclaw was right that we had to defend our boundary," Redtail insisted, bristling, but he still felt hollow with guilt.

"What threat was Sorrelpaw to ThunderClan?" Stagleap hissed. "I know Tigerclaw's style. I knew before you told me that it must have been you who fought Sorrelpaw, because Tigerclaw would have torn her apart."

Tear her apart. Redtail's stomach twisted, remembering Tigerclaw's instructions. "No," he murmured. "Tigerclaw's . . . just a brave warrior. A good warrior."

Stagleap narrowed his eyes. "He's brave, sure. But there's more to being a good warrior than fighting."

Redtail felt uncertain and off balance. "I'm worried that what happened is going to cause a battle between our Clans," he mewed. "Sunstar and Heatherstar seem really angry."

Getting to his feet, Stagleap stretched, arching his back. "You've got more sense than your Clanmate, then. Much as I'd like to rip his fur off, I don't want a battle either."

"But what can we do?" Redtail felt helpless.

"Heatherstar's a wise leader. She isn't going to jump into a battle without a good reason," Stagleap explained. "And I've always heard the same about Sunstar. When we get back to our camps, let's talk to them. We're the ones who were there; maybe we can make them see that we don't have to fight over this."

"Okay." A wave of relief rushed over Redtail. Stagleap seemed so sensible, his gaze open and steady. *Not like Tigerclaw,* a little voice inside him said, but Redtail shook it off. Surely Tigerclaw would help him talk to Sunstar before a battle could begin. He'd gotten overenthusiastic about defending their borders, but no warrior wanted an unnecessary fight.

"ThunderClan cats, follow me!" Sunstar's yowl cut across the clearing, and Redtail jumped.

"I'd better go," he mewed. "Um. Thanks. I hope Sorrelpaw feels better."

The big WindClan tom nodded. "Good-bye, Redtail."

Redtail hurried along at the back of the group of Thunder-Clan cats returning to camp. Ahead, he could see Sunstar in the lead, Bluefur beside him. As he watched, Tigerclaw and Thistleclaw fell into step beside them.

What is Tigerclaw saying to them? Redtail wondered. He hoped Tigerclaw wouldn't encourage their leader toward a battle. As much as it pained Redtail to admit it, Stagleap had been right about what Tigerclaw had meant to do to Sorrelpaw. So was the WindClan cat also right that Tigerclaw was always eager to fight?

I owe him everything.

But does that mean I have to follow him, no matter what?

He would wait for a calm moment and talk to Sunstar, Redtail decided. Somehow he would make their leader see reason.

But as they entered camp, Sunstar leaped with one easy bound to the top of the Highrock. "All cats old enough to catch their own prey, gather beneath the Highrock," he called. Bluefur stood below him, her face solemn.

White-eye stuck her head out of the nursery. "What's happening?" she asked. The elders were emerging from their den, too, and the warriors who had been left at camp during the Gathering were hurrying toward the Highrock, their ears pricked with interest.

"Heatherstar has refused to discipline her Clan for crossing our boundaries and stealing our prey," Sunstar meowed grimly. Hisses and angry yowls came from the crowd below.

"WindClan cats are too hungry to be trusted," Sparrowpelt called. "They don't have enough prey on their own territory. They're always going to try to steal from other Clans."

"That's true," Dappletail agreed, her amber eyes bright. "But I always thought Heatherstar had too much pride to let them break the warrior code."

"It's time to remind WindClan that ThunderClan can defend its territory," Sunstar continued. "Tomorrow we send a patrol to attack WindClan."

Redtail couldn't believe it. "It was one apprentice crossing the border, not an invasion!" he burst out.

Willowpelt nudged his side. "I don't think they're going to

listen to a brand-new warrior," she whispered.

"It stopped being about one apprentice when Heatherstar said we wouldn't dare to break the peace over it," Tigerclaw yowled. He was standing near the Highrock, looking up at Sunstar. "The apprentice is only the first—if we don't defend ourselves, more WindClan cats will be crossing our borders and stealing our prey."

"Tigerclaw's right," Sunstar agreed, his expression hard. "If we won't fight for our territory, we'll lose it. We need to show them we're serious. Tigerclaw has suggested that a patrol enter WindClan's camp and do as much damage as they can. We don't need to hurt them, but if we show that we can easily get to their camp, they'll think twice about crossing our borders again." As he jumped down from the Highrock, he nodded to Tigerclaw approvingly.

He's not going to change his mind now, no matter what I say, Redtail realized dismally.

"I will lead the patrol, and Tigerclaw, Redtail, Thistleclaw, Thrushpelt, and Patchpelt will come with me. We'll head out first thing in the morning," Bluefur added.

Redtail's belly felt as if it were gripped by sharp claws. *I have to be part of this?*

The Clan was dispersing, heading back to their dens or to the fresh-kill pile.

Another pelt brushed his, and Redtail smelled Tigerclaw's familiar scent.

"Are you excited?" the big warrior asked cheerfully. "Maybe

you can finish teaching that little apprentice a lesson."

"This isn't the right thing to do!" Redtail cried. He felt like wailing.

"Of course it is," Tigerclaw purred. He sounded pleased with himself, and he looked it, too, his eyes bright and his tail curling high above his back. "The most important thing for a warrior is to fight to defend our Clan and our territory." His amber eyes stared deep into Redtail's. "And I want you right by my side, Redtail. I'll teach you what a warrior should be."

CHAPTER SIX

❧

"Come on, Redtail! You have to get up!" Willowpelt's voice broke through Redtail's uneasy sleep, and he raised his head, blinking blearily in the pale dawn light. As the youngest warriors, his and Willowpelt's nests were at the edge of the warriors' den, far from the warm, comfortable spots at the center, and a cool breeze was blowing through his fur.

The den was crowded with cats stretching and climbing out of their cozy nests, shivering in the early morning air.

"I wish I was going," Frostfur mewed to Brindleface, her paws resting on the edge of her sister's nest. "I'd teach Wind-Clan to keep their claws off our prey."

Redtail's heart sank. How could he go to fight WindClan today, when just yesterday he and Stagleap had agreed to try to talk their leaders into peace? If he attacked, and Stagleap had counseled Heatherstar to make peace, how could Stagleap feel anything but betrayed? Stagleap would never trust any ThunderClan cat again, and with good reason.

He followed the other young warriors into the clearing, his paws heavy and slow. As the three she-cats joined the other cats already gathered there, Redtail hesitated. *Maybe I still have time to talk to Sunstar. If I tell him Tigerclaw and I lied . . .*

What then? That would be a far worse betrayal than any-thing he could do to Stagleap. Redtail had a duty to Tigerclaw. Tigerclaw had saved his life when he was just an apprentice, and Tigerclaw had the right to expect loyalty from Redtail in return. And Redtail owed his loyalty to ThunderClan, not to any WindClan cat.

Tigerclaw was near the Highrock, sharing a piece of prey with Thistleclaw. At the sight of Redtail, he stood up, stretched, and sauntered over. "We're leaving as soon as every cat is ready," he instructed. "Get yourself a mouse or some-thing. You'll need your strength."

"Okay," Redtail mewed, moving obediently toward the fresh-kill pile. Tigerclaw followed.

"Sunstar wants us to concentrate on making a mess of their camp," he added as Redtail crouched to pick up a sparrow. "But if you see that apprentice Sorrelpaw again, or her so-called mentor, don't hesitate to claw their fur off. We need to show all the Clans what happens to cats who cross Thunder-Clan's borders."

Redtail dropped the sparrow. "Sorrelpaw didn't cross our border on purpose," he burst out. "Please, Tigerclaw, let's talk to Sunstar. If we tell him what really happened, maybe he'll change his mind about this."

Tigerclaw's eyes narrowed. "What *really* happened?" He came closer; Redtail could smell the mouse on his breath. "We *told* Sunstar what really happened."

"No, we didn't," Redtail retorted. "You told Sunstar that

we waited for Stagleap to show up after we caught Sorrelpaw on our territory. And that they insulted ThunderClan and attacked us before we drove them off. That's not what happened *at all*."

"Maybe we saw what happened differently, Redtail," Tigerclaw growled with a dismissive flick of his tail. "And I know you're young and you've just become a warrior. You don't really understand yet."

"That's not the point," Redtail insisted. "I know what the truth is." But uncertainty squirmed uncomfortably in his belly. Maybe Tigerclaw was right. Everyone knew he was one of the best warriors in ThunderClan. Maybe Redtail just didn't understand.

Tigerclaw looked amused. "What you have to remember is that WindClan is our enemy," he said. "Anything that makes them weaker makes us stronger."

Is that true? Redtail wondered. He'd always thought of the other Clans in the forest as ThunderClan's allies.

"Remember," Tigerclaw mewed softly, nodding at the sparrow at Redtail's feet. "There is only so much prey in the forest. If WindClan hunts on our territory, ThunderClan cats will go hungry."

Redtail stared down at the sparrow unhappily. "I guess you're right," he murmured. A new thought struck him, and he looked up again eagerly. "But *is* this going to make Thunder-Clan stronger? There are a lot of cats in WindClan, and we're going straight into their camp with just a patrol."

Tigerclaw gave a pleased *mrrow*. "There might be a lot of

cats in WindClan, but most of them will be out of their camp on a fine day like today, hunting and patrolling. Other than a guard or two, we'll be facing elders, queens, and kits. They won't fight us, and we won't even have to hurt them. We'll just damage their camp and teach them a lesson." With another flick of his tail, he added, "Not that I'd mind facing Stagleap again. But Sunstar wants us to do this quickly and cleanly, without much of a fight."

"Oh," Redtail murmured. "I see now." That wasn't so bad, he supposed. After all, WindClan *was* their enemy, sort of. And if no cat was really going to be hurt, perhaps it didn't matter that Sunstar didn't know the whole story.

"We won't bother trying to sneak up on them," Bluefur declared as they left ThunderClan's camp and headed through the forest toward Fourtrees. "The whole point of this is to show the other Clans that ThunderClan isn't afraid to defend what's ours."

The six cats crossed through their own territory and between the tall oaks of Fourtrees without pausing, Bluefur taking the lead. Tigerclaw and Thistleclaw followed close behind her, shoulder to shoulder. It was a clear day and the early morning sun warmed Redtail's pelt. It was a good day for hunting, or just for basking in the newleaf warmth, and Redtail could almost pretend their plans were that innocent.

Redtail dropped back to walk with Thrushpelt and Patchpelt. "Have you ever been to WindClan's camp?" he asked them.

Thrushpelt shook his head, but Patchpelt nodded. "I went onto WindClan territory a few moons ago with Featherwhisker when he needed to talk to Barkface about medicine-cat business, and the patrol escorted us into their camp." Patchpelt wrinkled his nose a little. "It was *weird*. Except for the kits and the elders, they sleep right out in the open. They don't have proper dens like we do."

"Wow," Redtail breathed. *How much damage can we even do, if WindClan doesn't have nests to destroy?* The thought eased some of the anxious feeling of *wrongness* inside him.

On the other side of Fourtrees, Bluefur paused at the bottom of a slope covered with bushes. "At the top of this is WindClan's territory," she told them, looking mostly at Redtail. "When we reach the top, I'll lead you all to the camp—it's hard to see if you don't already know where it is. If we're quick enough, any WindClan warriors out patrolling won't be able to make it back before we're gone."

The slope grew steeper and rockier as they climbed, until Redtail was leaping from boulder to boulder, clinging to the rocks, his claws out for any traction they could give him.

"You all right?" Patchpelt asked, sounding slightly breathless beside him. "This is a tough climb for smaller cats like us." It was kind of him to lump himself and Redtail together, Redtail thought—he wasn't even as big as the small black-and-white tom yet. "But this is the only way to get to WindClan territory without crossing the river, which is even harder."

"I'm okay," Redtail told him, trying not to wheeze. "But I'm surprised WindClan bothered to come down here to hunt."

Patchpelt slipped on a mossy stone, then caught himself. "They need prey," he mewed. "And it's easier for them. Long-legged rabbit-chasers, they're practically rabbits themselves." He and Redtail shared a *mrrow* of laughter.

At the top of the slope, Redtail stared wide-eyed across an open grassy plain broken by occasional groups of thin trees and scraggly gorse bushes. Outcroppings of bare rock dotted the grasslands, and the wind swept across the plain, bending the grasses and trees. It seemed chilly and bleak to Redtail, and he shivered.

The edge of the plateau smelled strongly of WindClan's earthy scent. The cats exchanged glances, and Bluefur led the way across the border markings.

"The camp's over there," Patchpelt told Redtail, pointing with his tail. "In that dip in the moorland." Redtail peered toward the hollow but saw nothing but a tangle of gorse. Blue-fur began to run across the open, scrubby land, and the other cats followed her. Redtail took deep breaths of the cool air, his paws pounding across the grasslands. It felt strange to have no trees above to shelter him, only the wide blue sky, but he tried to ignore that, instead focusing on the stretch of his muscles as he ran.

The patrol charged through the gorse, thorns scratching at their pelts. Redtail hissed as one caught painfully in his fur, but he didn't slow his pace. Bursting through the last of the bushes, they found themselves in the WindClan camp, a clearing protected by the gorse bushes all around but open to the sky. There was a tall boulder in the center of the camp, and the cats lying below it in the sunshine looked up, startled.

A light brown she-cat—*Doespring,* Redtail thought—leaped to her feet, hissing in outrage. "What are you doing here?" she yowled. "Get out or we'll rip you to shreds!" The lithe gray-and-white tom beside her, who Redtail remembered was called Aspenfall, growled at them, showing his teeth.

Despite Doespring's threat, Redtail could see that ThunderClan had been right: There were few cats in the camp, and, except for Doespring and Aspenfall, who must have been left to guard the camp, almost none of them were warriors. Two thin old cats peered out from a den carved out of the gorse wall. *That must be the elders' den.* One yowled loudly in alarm.

A hissing gray tabby she-cat blocked the entrance to another, her fur spiked and her claws out. "Stay back," she snarled.

"We're not going to hurt your kits, Ryestalk," Thrushpelt said reassuringly, inching closer to her.

Her tail bushed out even further. "Get away from the nursery!"

Before Thrushpelt could say anything else, Tigerclaw slashed his claws across Ryestalk's shoulder, making her wail with pain and surprise. "Take your kits and get out of the nursery," he hissed. "Or it'll be your fault when they get hurt."

Eyes wide with fear, Ryestalk hustled her two kits out of the nursery and as far from the invading cats as possible. The kits peered up at the ThunderClan cats, confused.

"Who's that, Ryestalk?" one of them, a small brown tom,

squeaked, his nose wrinkled. "They smell funny."

"Hush, Mudkit," she murmured. "Stay behind me." Crowding the kits into a gorse bush behind her, she lowered her ears, snarling at the ThunderClan cats. Redtail stared guiltily at the blood running down the queen's shoulder and soaking into her fur. *No one was supposed to get hurt!*

Thrushpelt had already begun tearing apart the WindClan nursery, and Redtail reluctantly moved forward to help him, yanking out soft nests and tearing at the gorse walls. As he dragged a nest of moss and sheep's wool out into the clearing, Redtail looked up to see Thistleclaw and Patchpelt doing the same thing in the elders' den, as Bluefur held off the elders, who were fiercely trying to defend their nest despite seeming frail. Tigerclaw had drawn Doespring and Aspenfall into a fight, distracting them from helping Ryestalk or the elders. As Redtail watched, Tigerclaw crouched and slashed at Doespring's belly, his claws ripping through her fur, and the she-cat lurched backward with a pained screech. Redtail winced in sympathy.

Barkface, WindClan's young medicine cat, stood squarely in front of his den, snarling protectively. As Redtail watched, Patchpelt took a hesitant step toward him.

"Not the medicine cat's den," Bluefur called sharply, dodging a blow from one of the elders. Relief rushed through Redtail. If they destroyed the medicine cat's den, WindClan cats might die. This fight wasn't worth that. *We aren't going to do anything terrible here,* he thought. *We're just teaching them a lesson.*

No matter how many times he told himself that, it still didn't feel true.

Tigerclaw hissed in exasperation, pinning Aspenfall to the ground. "You're too soft, Bluefur," he taunted the she-cat.

"I'm still ThunderClan's deputy," she answered. "And I say leave the medicine cat's den alone."

Tigerclaw seemed ready to argue, but a sudden yowl of rage drew all their attention to the camp's entrance. WindClan warriors were streaming into their camp, Stagleap in the lead.

Perhaps they'd heard the shrieks and hisses of fighting cats. Redtail didn't know. Stagleap cast him one disappointed look, and Redtail looked away, suddenly conscious of the shredded debris of the nursery all around his paws. *It's not my fault,* he wanted to yowl, but was that true? He knew what had really happened. He could have talked to Sunstar. He could have tried harder to talk Tigerclaw out of this. Guilt blocked his throat: There was nothing he could say now.

Stagleap threw himself at Tigerclaw, and, in a heartbeat they became a furiously fighting mass of fur, their dark brown pelts difficult to tell apart as they tussled. The other Wind-Clan cats were attacking: Talltail, WindClan's deputy, leaped for Bluefur's throat.

A cat barreled into Redtail's side while he was distracted, knocking him to the ground. Sharp pain spread through his shoulder. Plumclaw was holding him down, her claws ripping at his pelt.

Redtail struggled beneath the small gray she-cat, panting.

He couldn't get to his feet. He had to protect his underbelly.

Then he remembered a move Sparrowpelt had taught him. He stopped struggling for a moment, rolling fully onto his back. As Plumclaw shifted her weight to keep from falling, he kicked up with his hind legs, knocking her away so that he could scramble back onto his paws.

Thrushpelt was swiping fiercely at Hickorynose, who howled in pain, and Plumclaw turned to slash at Thrushpelt with her claws. Redtail looked up at the mass of fighting cats all around him just as Talltail slashed Bluefur across the throat.

Bluefur stumbled. Blood was running down her chest and dripping onto the ground.

"Bluefur!" Redtail yowled and sprang toward her, shouldering Plumclaw out of his way. Talltail was bracing himself for another attack.

"No!" Redtail hissed fiercely. "We're going." Talltail hesitated, and Redtail braced himself against Bluefur's side. "Bluefur, you have to call a retreat," he added urgently.

Bluefur was leaning heavily against Redtail's side. "Bluefur?" he asked. The deputy seemed dazed, her eyes fluttering shut, and Redtail could barely support her weight.

She can't do it, Redtail realized. Bluefur was barely conscious. He looked around at the clawing, struggling cats. There were too many WindClan cats now. ThunderClan was outnumbered. As he watched, Patchpelt fell beneath two WindClan warriors.

Bluefur moaned.

If we stay here, she'll die, Redtail realized. *And we've already lost this battle. Other ThunderClan cats might die, too.*

"ThunderClan, retreat!" he yowled, as loudly as he could.

Tigerclaw knocked Stagleap away from him. There was a long scratch across the ThunderClan warrior's face, but his amber eyes were alight with a fierce joy. "What do you mean, *retreat?*" he snarled.

But the other ThunderClan warriors had, like Redtail, clearly realized the battle had been lost. Thrushpelt came up to Bluefur's other side, and between them, he and Redtail supported Bluefur toward the tunnel through the gorse. The other ThunderClan warriors raced after them.

"Run away, ThunderClan!" Mocking yowls and threats rose behind them.

The race back toward Fourtrees was like a nightmare, Redtail gasping for breath as he struggled beneath Bluefur's half-conscious weight.

As their paws hit the grass of Fourtrees, Redtail and Thrushpelt paused for a moment to catch their breath.

"Cowards!" Tigerclaw hissed. Redtail turned to face him. The big brown tabby's face was contorted with rage.

"We had to retreat," Redtail panted. His shoulder ached and his paw pads were burning. Every heartbeat they stopped here to argue, Bluefur might be dying. "Look at her."

Tigerclaw's gaze slid over Bluefur. "We should have finished the fight *for* her. No *true* warrior would run away from a battle. You've brought shame on the whole Clan, Redtail."

Have I? Bluefur's breath rattled harshly in her chest, and

Redtail realized he was quite sure that he hadn't. "I did the right thing," he insisted, his eyes steady on Tigerclaw's. "True warriors protect their Clanmates. This was never a battle worth fighting."

Tigerclaw hissed again but said nothing. Thistleclaw and Patchpelt took Redtail and Thrushpelt's places supporting Bluefur, giving the other cats a chance to catch their breath, and they hurried on toward ThunderClan territory.

Redtail was at the back of the group, tired and sore, as they reached the entrance to ThunderClan's camp. As the others disappeared into the ravine, Bluefur supported between them, Tigerclaw turned to face Redtail.

"Nice move," he hissed, his amber eyes dark with anger.

"What do you mean?" Redtail asked.

"Trying to make it look like you're worried about Bluefur," Tigerclaw scoffed. "You're just a coward. You always have been—ever since you were a 'paw and I had to save you on that bridge. So much for loyalty. So much for the life you owe me."

Redtail didn't drop his head in guilt or gratitude; he glared straight back into Tigerclaw's eyes. He felt like he was seeing Tigerclaw for the first time. Where was the brave warrior who had saved him from the hawk? This cat had bullied an apprentice, had *lied* to their leader, had done everything he could to start a battle no cat needed. And Redtail had let him. He wasn't going to make that mistake again.

"I *am* worried about Bluefur," he hissed back in a fierce, low whisper. "Your stupid grudge almost got her killed. And I don't owe you anything anymore."

He pushed past Tigerclaw and headed into ThunderClan's camp. He *was* loyal, but now he knew what being loyal meant.

It wasn't Tigerclaw he owed his loyalty to. It was Thunder-Clan.

CHAPTER SEVEN
❧

"*You're the one who called a* retreat," Tigerclaw snarled, glaring at Redtail. "What kind of deputy gives up territory?"

Redtail glared back at the older warrior. Newleaf after newleaf had passed since the failed attack on the WindClan camp. Sunstar had lost his last life and gone on to StarClan long ago. Bluefur had become ThunderClan's leader and, although both Thistleclaw and Tigerclaw had expected to be chosen, she'd named Redtail her deputy instead.

Elders had died, and kits had been born, warriors had moved to the elders' den, and apprentices had completed their training and become full warriors. And yet, as Redtail stood in the leader's den, listening to Tigerclaw and Bluestar, the argument sounded exactly the same as it had back when he was a 'paw. *Tigerclaw hasn't changed a whisker.*

But things were worse now than they had been for a long time. Only a few days ago, they had lost a battle with RiverClan for Sunningrocks, the only battle they'd lost on ThunderClan territory since Bluestar had first become leader many moons before.

"The kind of deputy who protects the *cats* in his Clan,"

Redtail growled back at him, his tail slashing through the air. How *dare* Tigerclaw question him about this? There was no way that they could have won that fight! "RiverClan had us outnumbered. We had to get Mousefur to the medicine cat's den. She'd be dead now if it we hadn't retreated, and so would other ThunderClan warriors."

"We have to teach them a lesson," Tigerclaw snarled, his long front claws flexing angrily against the floor of the leader's den as he turned to Bluestar. "If we don't protect our territory, RiverClan will think they can cross our borders whenever they want. Redtail made a mistake."

"Redtail did the right thing," Bluestar mewed firmly. "Sometimes you have to lose a battle to keep your Clan safe." Tigerclaw didn't reply, his amber gaze sullen. "But you can be sure," Bluestar continued, "we *will* reclaim Sunningrocks."

Redtail shifted uneasily, the earth of Bluestar's den suddenly feeling chilly beneath his paws. *If we fight RiverClan now, our warriors will die.*

"But not yet," he put in. "We don't have enough warriors to win this battle. ThunderClan needs every warrior it has if we are to survive."

Tigerclaw hissed softly. "Just what I'd expect *you* to say," he muttered, almost too quietly for Redtail to hear. "You'll always back down from a fight."

"What did you say?" Redtail asked, feeling the fur along his spine rise angrily. It had been a long time since Tigerclaw could intimidate him, and he wasn't going to tolerate any half-veiled hostility from the other cat. Whatever Tigerclaw thought of him, he was still ThunderClan's deputy.

"We'll keep the peace inside our own Clan," Bluestar mewed warningly.

Tigerclaw dipped his head submissively. "I said nothing," he replied smoothly. "You've given wise counsel as usual, Redtail."

Redtail tensed. He didn't trust that submissive tone. *What is Tigerclaw up to now?*

Redtail glanced up at the clear early evening sky. There was still enough time for one last hunting patrol before Thunder-Clan gathered for the night. Prey had been running well lately, and his Clanmates should fill their bellies while they could.

"Lionheart," he called. "Take Whitestorm and Graypaw out for a hunt."

The big golden tom gave a yowl of agreement. "I scented a mouse nest down near the Twolegplace," he mewed amiably. "We'll bring back something juicy for the fresh-kill pile."

Redtail watched them go, the shaggy gray apprentice bouncing eagerly along at his mentor's side. Redtail's own apprentice, Dustpaw, was busily cleaning the elders' den with Sandpaw and Ravenpaw, pulling dried moss and musty leaves out of the den and piling them neatly to one side. The elders watched nearby, lounging in the last of the day's sunshine.

"Don't forget to make *my* nest especially soft," One-eye—formerly known as White-eye, before she had finally lost her blind eye and moved to the elders' den—called, her joking mew overly loud because of her own poor hearing. Sandpaw flicked her tail at the elder in amused acknowledgment.

Both of Redtail's littermates were in the clearing. Spottedleaf was pulling a thorn from Darkstripe's tail. The black-and-gray tom winced, but her movements were quick and sure. Willowpelt was sharing a vole with Mousefur, the two she-cats chatting quietly. Other warriors shared tongues, or dozed, while Frostfur's and Goldenflower's kits chased through the camp, tumbling over one another, their mothers watching them protectively from the mouth of the nursery.

ThunderClan's camp was peaceful tonight, and Redtail, his mind already busy with thoughts of the next morning's border patrol, turned toward the Highrock to make his day's report to Bluestar.

As he approached the leader's den, Redtail's steps slowed. He could hear Tigerclaw's voice. Why was the other cat meeting with Bluestar without him?

"We have to strike now," the massive tom was hissing. "We *have* to reclaim Sunningrocks and make it clear that ThunderClan won't tolerate any cat trespassing on our territory."

Bluestar's meow was thoughtful. "I understand why you want to attack RiverClan. But I think Redtail is right," she mewed. "Without more warriors, there's no way we can beat RiverClan in open battle."

Tigerclaw's voice turned coaxing, and Redtail's pelt prickled uncomfortably. Was Tigerclaw going behind his back now? "We can't just do nothing, though," he insisted. "Every Clan will turn on us if they think we're weak. Let me at least mark Sunningrocks now, to show RiverClan we're not giving our territory up."

Bluestar hesitated, and Redtail listened hard, his ears pricking forward. Did she believe that was all Tigerclaw was planning? Redtail hadn't forgotten how eager Tigerclaw was to fight. But Bluestar trusted Tigerclaw much more than Redtail did.

"All right," their leader meowed at last. "Take a small patrol and mark Sunningrocks at dawn. See if they've left fresh scent markers there, and if they have, destroy them. You're right that we need to claim our land again. But that's all I want you to do, Tigerclaw. Don't go looking for a fight."

Redtail groaned to himself, picturing the smug glow in the other tom's amber eyes. What Tigerclaw had said *sounded* reasonable, but Redtail didn't trust that he was really planning only to mark ThunderClan's borders.

Before Redtail could turn away, Tigerclaw pushed his way out past the lichen that hung over the entrance to Bluestar's den. He stopped when he saw Redtail, and Redtail felt hot beneath his fur, embarrassed at being caught eavesdropping.

"I take it you heard all of that?" Tigerclaw asked, his voice bland. Redtail nodded, a wary jerk of his head. "Don't bother trying to stop me," the larger tom went on. "Bluestar agrees with me. I'm taking a group of warriors tomorrow at dawn— warriors who aren't afraid to stand up for ThunderClan." He stalked past Redtail, so close that their pelts brushed.

"Tigerclaw, wait," Redtail called after him. Tigerclaw

turned back, his expression wary. "I'm not going to try to stop you. I want to go with you."

Tigerclaw's eyes widened slightly. "Do you?" he asked.

"Yes." Redtail padded toward him. "You're right that we need to mark our territory. I don't want to lose Sunningrocks to RiverClan either."

Tigerclaw looked at Redtail thoughtfully, his tail curling high above his back. "You might just end up being a true warrior after all," he mewed finally.

"I am a warrior," Redtail replied. "And all I want is to protect our Clan."

And if you're planning something more than you've said—if you're not being totally honest, Tigerclaw—I'll be there to stop you.

CHAPTER EIGHT

"Please let me come with you," Dustpaw begged, trailing after Redtail across camp. The sky was just beginning to get light, and the camp was quiet, most of the cats sleeping. Runningwind was standing guard at the camp's entrance and acknowledged Redtail with a tired flick of his ears.

"No," Redtail told Dustpaw, choosing a mouse from the fresh-kill pile. "Have something to eat, check to see if the elders need anything, and then I want you to train with Whitestorm and Sandpaw this morning while I'm gone. You can brush up on your fighting techniques."

"I'd rather go with you," Dustpaw wheedled. "And I've never been to Sunningrocks. I'm sure I'd learn a lot."

Redtail looked at his apprentice sternly. "I said no and I meant it. You've never been there because Sunningrocks is too dangerous for apprentices right now."

Dustpaw sighed. *"Ravenpaw's going."*

"Is he?" Surprised, Redtail looked across the clearing to where the skinny black tom sat patiently outside the warriors' den, waiting for Tigerclaw to emerge. His pelt prickled with discomfort. Tigerclaw's apprentice looked so *young*, even

82

younger and smaller than Dustpaw. "Well, Ravenpaw's not my apprentice; *you* are. And I'm not taking my apprentice to Sunningrocks."

Dustpaw's tail drooped, but he dipped his head respectfully. "Yes, Redtail."

Redtail nudged him to make him look up again and mewed gently, "I'll be checking with Whitestorm when I get back, and if you've been training hard, I'll take you out hunting."

By the time Redtail left his apprentice, Dustpaw seemed resigned, happy with Redtail's promise. Redtail headed toward the camp entrance, where Tigerclaw and Ravenpaw waited for him.

"You're planning for Ravenpaw to come with us?" Redtail asked as he reached them. "We don't take apprentices into dangerous parts of the territory."

Tigerclaw blinked at him. "We're just going to mark the border, Redtail," he replied. "There's nothing to worry about." There was the slightest trace of mockery in his tone.

Redtail hesitated. He was ThunderClan's deputy; he could order Tigerclaw to leave Ravenpaw behind. *Is it worth arguing with Tigerclaw?*

Tigerclaw took a step closer. "I won't let him get hurt," he mewed softly. "I'll look after him. *You* know that."

I do know that. Redtail had a sharp flash of memory: Willowpelt saying, back when they were 'paws, *He wouldn't let us get hurt. It wouldn't be good for his reputation..* And then Tigerclaw had saved him from the hawk. Despite everything that had happened since, he owed Tigerclaw his life. "All right," he agreed.

"But we're just marking our territory, remember."

He led the other two cats through the gorse tunnel and out of the ravine. In the forest, he and Tigerclaw padded side by side toward Sunningrocks, Ravenpaw a few paces behind. The sky was growing lighter and lighter, and a cool dawn mist hung in the air, dampening their fur.

Behind them, Ravenpaw gave a small, squeaking growl. Redtail looked back to see the apprentice rear up on his hind legs, his forepaws slashing at an imaginary enemy.

"Very nice, Ravenpaw," Tigerclaw praised the apprentice, his purr rich with amusement.

"I can't *wait* to fight RiverClan," Ravenpaw meowed happily, his tail slashing with excitement. "The best way to learn to be a warrior is to be in a real battle!"

Redtail twitched his ears uneasily. This was Tigerclaw's influence, he knew it. It was so much like what Tigerclaw had said to him, back when he was a 'paw. And it *was* important to be a strong warrior, to defend the Clan, but was a battle all Tigerclaw ever wanted? Was he teaching his apprentice to think the same way?

"We won't be fighting RiverClan today," he reminded the apprentice calmly. "Keeping our Clan safe is more important than beating the other Clans."

Ravenpaw sighed but didn't answer, and they padded on. Redtail glanced sideways at Tigerclaw. *Maybe I should talk to Bluestar about how Tigerclaw's teaching his apprentice,* he thought. In any case, today he would keep a close eye on Ravenpaw. *I don't want Tigerclaw encouraging him to do anything reckless.*

The sun was rising well above the horizon as they reached Sunningrocks, warming their pelts and bringing with it fresh breezes and scents of prey. The smooth granite boulders of Sunningrocks were still night-cool under Redtail's paws, but he knew that they would be warm enough to bask on by midmorning. A mouthwatering scent of mouse rose from the spaces between and below the stones. Redtail could also smell the strong musty scent of RiverClan.

"Spread out and mark the whole territory," he told the others. "Especially by the river."

Tigerclaw and Ravenpaw moved off across the rocks, and Redtail began to mark over the scent boundaries RiverClan had left at the edge of Sunningrocks. There was no sound but the whisper of leaves in the forest behind them and the rush of the river at the far edge of the rocks.

Maybe we won't run into any trouble, Redtail thought, beginning to relax. Tigerclaw and Ravenpaw came back across the rocks toward him.

"It's well marked," Tigerclaw observed. "But perhaps—"

He was interrupted by an angry hiss. Five cats appeared over the far edge of the rocks, their fur bristling. Leading them was a large, broad-shouldered reddish-brown tom, who advanced on Redtail, his eyes narrowing.

"Oakheart," Redtail breathed. He felt the fur on his own back rise as he paced forward to meet the RiverClan deputy.

"What are you doing here?" Oakheart hissed. "This is our territory now."

Redtail slid out his claws. "Sunningrocks is ours," he

mewed simply. "It's past time for this to be settled." His heart
was hammering, but he kept his voice calm. "Tell Crookedstar
that ThunderClan isn't backing down. This has gone on long
enough."

He saw two of the RiverClan cats behind Oakheart
exchange glances, but Oakheart's gaze was steady. "RiverClan
will not give up this hunting ground."

"Neither will ThunderClan," Redtail answered, meeting
Oakheart's eyes. "Tell Crookedstar."

The RiverClan deputy nodded. Redtail rose out of his
crouch, his haunches relaxing. Oakheart would carry the
message to his leader. More blood would be shed over Sunningrocks, but not today.

With a sudden, fierce yowl, Tigerclaw lashed a paw out at
the smaller black-and-gray warrior nearest him. Surprised,
she fell backward and blinked up at him. Blood rose from her
scratched chest. Redtail gasped.

I should have known, he thought. *Tigerclaw would never let this end
peacefully.* The RiverClan cats were frozen in shock, but that
wouldn't last. At least he could get Ravenpaw out of this. He
glanced back at the skinny black apprentice, who was gaping
in surprise.

"Ravenpaw, run!"

CHAPTER NINE

Ravenpaw glared up at Redtail, his small ears stiff with indignation. "A true warrior *never* runs away," he spat. "Tigerclaw was right about you!"

Despite the danger they were in, Redtail felt a pang of irritation. *Tigerclaw's been bad-mouthing me to his apprentice? What kind of Clan loyalty is that?*

There was no more time, though. Oakheart was moving forward with a snarl, shouldering Tigerclaw away from the smaller she-cat. His face was dark with fury.

Redtail's heart beat faster. It was just him, Tigerclaw, and an undersized apprentice against five full-grown RiverClan warriors. He and Tigerclaw were both skilled in battle, but this was a bad situation.

Maybe he could scare them off. "Tell Crookedstar that the next RiverClan warrior we catch on ThunderClan territory will die." He narrowed his eyes at the bigger tom. "We want this finished."

Oakheart's eyes widened a little in surprise, but then he took a step forward, his ears pressed back angrily. "No matter what you threaten, RiverClan has to eat. We won't give up these hunting grounds. Even if we have to tear ThunderClan apart to keep them."

The other RiverClan cats began to pace forward behind Oakheart, their tails twitching steadily back and forth. Redtail watched them warily, his muscles tensing.

With a snarl, Tigerclaw lashed out at Oakheart, knocking the RiverClan deputy to the ground. "Flea-bitten water rat!" he snarled. "Keep to your own territory."

Oakheart lay in the mud for a moment and then scrambled to his feet, his fur stiff with outrage. Tigerclaw stepped back, and Oakheart's angry eyes slid past him and fixed on the ThunderClan cat who was closest . . .

Ravenpaw.

Redtail felt suddenly cold. There was no way the apprentice could fight the RiverClan deputy.

Before Oakheart could move, Redtail flung himself between the two cats, slashing at Oakheart's chest. Oakheart reared up onto his hind legs, clawing at him. A sharp pain shot through Redtail's shoulder, but he dodged the next blow from Oakheart and sank his teeth into the tom's side.

As if Redtail's attack on Oakheart had been a signal, all around them the other cats had charged into battle. One, a dark brown tom, batted Ravenpaw roughly out of his way, claws extended, as he ran toward Tigerclaw, and the apprentice cried out in pain.

"Ravenpaw!" Redtail was half pinned under Oakheart. He kicked at the larger cat's belly with his hind paws, but he couldn't move. Out of the corner of his eye, he saw Tigerclaw trying to run toward his apprentice, but three RiverClan warriors blocked his path.

Desperately, Redtail kicked and kicked again, knocking Oakheart back a little so he could twist to look back at the apprentice. "Ravenpaw, run!" he yowled. "You'll get hurt!" *I have to protect him.* Ravenpaw was too young and too small for this battle.

Ravenpaw stared back at him. "Warriors don't run," he snarled. His voice sounded a little shakier than it had before, but he seemed to brace himself and stepped forward, toward the fight.

But you're not a warrior. Ravenpaw was going to get himself killed. The thought gave Redtail enough panicky strength to surge up and knock Oakheart backward and away from him. "Go back to camp and get help," he yowled, turning to the apprentice. "That's an order!"

Oakheart leaped onto Redtail and tumbled him onto his side, pinning him to the ground. Sharp claws were digging into Redtail's belly, but he could hear Tigerclaw's voice.

"Don't you go anywhere, Ravenpaw!" the big tom snarled. "We're already outnumbered; we need you in this fight. Are you a warrior or a mouse-hearted kit?"

Redtail couldn't see anything except the RiverClan tom above him, but he heard Ravenpaw's hiss as the apprentice threw himself into the battle. *What is Tigerclaw doing?* Fresh rage rose up in him at the thought of Tigerclaw and Ravenpaw defying his orders—was he their deputy or not?—and the indignation gave him the energy to twist free of Oakheart's paws.

Oakheart glared past him for a moment. "If that apprentice comes any closer, I'll kill him," he growled.

Protective rage flooded through Redtail. With one quick movement, he was on his feet and leaping for Oakheart's throat. He tore at the RiverClan deputy, blood filling his mouth. Oakheart lurched backward, but Redtail hung on as the other cat's struggles lessened and finally stilled.

Redtail blinked away the blood that had sprayed across his face. He watched as Oakheart staggered and fell, and finally as the light went out of the RiverClan deputy's eyes.

CHAPTER TEN

❧

Redtail staggered backward, staring at Oakheart's body at his paws. The fight was going on around him—Ravenpaw locked in battle with the small gray-and-black cat, Tigerclaw holding his own against two warriors—but the sounds of battle seemed muted and far away.

He can't be dead. I can't have killed him.

But Oakheart *was* dead.

A wail of sorrow came from the RiverClan cats as they realized what had happened, and two came to pull Oakheart's body away, their eyes wide with horror.

But the others were still fighting. Redtail tore his gaze from Oakheart's body. Tigerclaw was grappling with a large gray RiverClan tom. He snarled and slashed at the other tom's face, but his paws skidded on the muddy earth. Tigerclaw fell, slamming his head against one of the boulders.

For a moment, Tigerclaw seemed stunned, blinking confused amber eyes up at his opponent, and the other cat surged forward, his teeth bared.

He'll kill him, Redtail realized. *I can't let there be any more death today.* Feeling a sudden rush of strength, he lurched forward, biting down at the root of the gray tom's tail. With a strength and fury he'd never felt before, he flung the RiverClan cat away from Tigerclaw. The cat staggered and lurched, falling into the bushes.

Breathing hard, he turned back to see Tigerclaw staring at him in amazement.

"Redtail! You tossed that cat like a pile of leaves." The massive brown tom climbed to his paws, shaking his head a little as if to shake off the blow he'd taken. "And you killed Oakheart! I didn't think you had it in you."

Tigerclaw's voice was admiring, but Redtail just felt sick. *There was a time when Tigerclaw's praise would have meant everything to me.*

Now, though, Oakheart was dead, and for what? It wouldn't settle the conflict over Sunningrocks.

Fury burned inside him as he looked into Tigerclaw's eyes. *He is to blame for all this.* It hadn't had to come to a fight, not today. If Tigerclaw hadn't attacked the RiverClan cat, Oakheart would still be alive. Young Ravenpaw wouldn't be injured.

Redtail wouldn't be a killer.

He had never killed another cat. Not until today.

"Tigerclaw?" Ravenpaw's mew was tentative. The skinny apprentice inched closer, looking back and forth between them. Blood still dripped from his shoulder, running down his side. There were still two RiverClan warriors left—the small black-and-gray she-cat Tigerclaw had first attacked, and the larger gray tom Redtail had flung away from Tigerclaw.

They were pressed low to the ground, their ears back, snarling as they eyed the ThunderClan cats.

"Ravenpaw, go!" Redtail growled. If nothing else, at least maybe he could save the apprentice from any more of this.

Tigerclaw looked at Redtail thoughtfully, and then, perhaps seeing the fury and desperation in his eyes, yowled, "Go back to camp, Ravenpaw! Redtail and I can finish this!"

"But the fight's not done," Ravenpaw meowed. "And I owe Redtail . . . he saved me . . . Oakheart said . . ."

"You don't owe me anything," Redtail snapped.

"Go while you still can," Tigerclaw agreed. "Run back to camp now!"

Finally! Thank StarClan, Redtail thought.

Ravenpaw backed away a few paces, then turned and ran.

As he disappeared down the path, there was a blur of motion in the corner of Redtail's eye. He turned to see the black-and-gray she-cat spring at Tigerclaw's throat. The tussle was brief, before Tigerclaw flung her to the ground. He snarled, swiping a paw at her as she lay winded on the ground, but Redtail snapped. "Tigerclaw, stop!" To his surprise, the big tom listened, pulling up short, his claws near her throat.

"No more blood," Redtail said quietly. "Not now."

The two remaining RiverClan cats exchanged a short glance, then yowled a retreat. Redtail watched as they disappeared past Sunningrocks, and he heard the smallest splash as they slid into the water.

A tightness inside him relaxed. It was over, for now. He couldn't bear to think about Oakheart's death, not yet. The sun was high in the sky, its reflection off the river almost blinding.

A heavy blow landed hard on his back, driving Redtail into a crouch. Sharp pain ripped at his throat, and he felt something hot and wet run across his throat, streaming down his chest. *Blood.* He tried to rise again, but he couldn't move. Had the RiverClan cats come back?

His vision blurred, but as the weight moved from his back, he peered up to see Tigerclaw staring down at him, his face expressionless.

Tigerclaw . . . Had Tigerclaw attacked him? Redtail's mind felt fuzzy; he couldn't think properly. He tried to speak, but his mouth felt cracked and dry. "Why?" he whispered, almost soundlessly.

Tigerclaw's tail curled high above his back, and his eyes gleamed triumphantly. "You were in my way, Redtail. It's nothing personal, but ThunderClan needs a real deputy. I'm just doing what I should have let that hawk do back when you were a 'paw."

Redtail could feel warmth all around him—was it his blood, soaking into the earth?—but he was still cold. "But . . . you saved my life," he meowed slowly.

"And you should have been loyal from then on," Tigerclaw murmured, his amber gaze fixed on Redtail's face. "But you weren't. So, better for me, better for the Clan, if you're not here."

Despite the brightness of the sun, everything was going dark. Standing above Redtail, Tigerclaw was just a shadow against the graying of the sky. Redtail couldn't see his face anymore, but he remembered his satisfied expression. The big tom shifted, and Redtail thought he must be licking blood from his paw.

He's going to kill every cat who gets in his way, Redtail thought. Despair filled him, as even the sky went black.

At the last, he thought suddenly of Dustpaw. His apprentice would be back at camp, waiting for Redtail to take him hunting. *I'm sorry I couldn't keep my promise. . . .*

Redtail opened his eyes. The pain was gone. As he blinked, the blurry ginger shape above him sharpened into a broad, friendly face with one torn ear.

"Sunstar?" he said weakly, recognizing the ThunderClan leader. "But . . ." Sunstar had been dead for a long time. Redtail swallowed. "Am I . . . dead?"

"I'm afraid so," Sunstar said sympathetically. "You were very brave, if that's any comfort. I've come to take you to StarClan."

Confused, Redtail got to his paws. Nothing hurt now, and as he glanced down at himself, he saw that the long streaks of blood and dirt from the fight were gone. He looked up at Sunstar in confusion, and the ginger tom twitched his whiskers encouragingly and began to walk ahead of him. Instead of paw prints, faint stars glimmered behind him as he strolled toward the forest. Redtail followed.

They walked through a shimmering mist for what seemed like a long time, and then Redtail realized they were walking between trees, soft grassy ground under their paws. The sun shone onto his back, warming his pelt, and the air was rich with the scent of prey.

As they passed a pond, Redtail looked down at his own reflection. Spottedleaf had told him once that the cats of StarClan lived forever as they had been at their happiest times. He didn't look too different—he wasn't young again—but his eyes were bright. *I've been very happy in ThunderClan,* he thought. *Every cat I loved was there. I liked being deputy, especially watching over the apprentices. . . .*

A jolt shot through him. *ThunderClan!* How could he have forgotten the danger his Clan was in? Tigerclaw was such a bloodthirsty cat—who knew which warrior he would target next? All of Redtail's Clanmates were in danger.

"Sunstar!" he said hoarsely. "You have to send me back! I have to warn the others about Tigerclaw!"

Sunstar looked at him, his eyes warm with affection. "I can't send you back," he said quietly. "But ThunderClan will be saved. Come with me."

Side by side, Sunstar walked with him to the edge of a larger pond. "Look," he told Redtail.

Redtail gazed down. Flickering forms took shape within the water. "It's ThunderClan's camp," he realized. Raven-paw was there, Spottedleaf smoothing a spiderweb over his shoulder. And there was Tigerclaw, speaking as the other cats listened respectfully. Redtail felt a low simmer of anger within him. What lies was Tigerclaw spinning now?

But the water shimmered, and it was as if he were moving

through the crowd of cats. He glimpsed his sister Willowpelt, One-eye, Dustpaw . . . There was a stranger there, a small fiery orange cat, gazing at Tigerclaw with wide eyes. "Who *is* that?" Redtail asked. "He's not a ThunderClan cat."

"He will be," Sunstar told him. "He's about to be part of the Clan, and Bluestar will name him Firepaw."

Redtail peered more closely. Was there a spark of something special in the young cat's eyes? He looked like any apprentice. But Redtail's sister had brought them a prophecy. . . .

Spottedleaf had told him and Bluestar that the solution to all their Clan's problems lay in reach, if they could only realize what StarClan meant.

Was this the meaning of the prophecy? Warmth spread through Redtail. Firepaw, not Tigerclaw, would be the future of ThunderClan. ThunderClan would be saved.

My Clan will go on without me. . . .

"Fire alone will save your Clan," he murmured, and felt a warmth spread through his pelt.

WARRIORS

TAWNYPELT'S
CLAN

ALLEGIANGES

THUNDERCLAN

LEADER   **BRAMBLESTAR**—dark brown tabby tom with amber eyes

DEPUTY   **SQUIRRELFLIGHT**—dark ginger she-cat with green eyes and one white paw

MEDIGINE GATS   **LEAFPOOL**—light brown tabby she-cat with amber eyes, white paws and chest

JAYFEATHER—gray tabby tom with blind blue eyes

ALDERHEART—dark ginger tom with amber eyes

WARRIORS   (toms and she-cats without kits)

BRACKENFUR—golden-brown tabby tom

CLOUDTAIL—long-haired white tom with blue eyes

BRIGHTHEART—white she-cat with ginger patches

THORNCLAW—golden-brown tabby tom

WHITEWING—white she-cat with green eyes

BIRCHFALL—light brown tabby tom

BERRYNOSE—cream-colored tom with a stump for a tail

MOUSEWHISKER—gray-and-white tom
APPRENTICE, PLUMPAW (black-and-ginger she-cat)

POPPYFROST—pale tortoiseshell-and-white she-cat

LIONBLAZE—golden tabby tom with amber eyes

ROSEPETAL—dark cream she-cat
APPRENTICE, STEMPAW (white-and-orange tom)

LILYHEART—small, dark tabby she-cat with white patches and blue eyes

BUMBLESTRIPE—very pale gray tom with black stripes
APPRENTICE, SHELLPAW (tortoiseshell tom)

CHERRYFALL—ginger she-cat

MOLEWHISKER—brown-and-cream tom

AMBERMOON—pale ginger she-cat
APPRENTICE, EAGLEPAW (ginger she-cat)

DEWNOSE—gray-and-white tom

STORMCLOUD—gray tabby tom

HOLLYTUFT—black she-cat

FERNSONG—yellow tabby tom

SORRELSTRIPE—dark brown she-cat

LEAFSHADE—tortoiseshell she-cat
APPRENTICE, SPOTPAW (spotted tabby she-cat)

LARKSONG—black tom

HONEYFUR—white she-cat with yellow splotches

SPARKPELT—orange tabby she-cat

TWIGBRANCH—gray she-cat with green eyes
APPRENTICE, FLYPAW (striped gray tabby she-cat)

FINLEAP—brown tom

APPRENTICE, SNAPPAW (golden tabby tom)

CINDERHEART—gray tabby she-cat

BLOSSOMFALL—tortoiseshell-and-white she-cat with petal-shaped white patches

QUEENS (she-cats expecting or nursing kits)

DAISY—cream long-furred cat from the horseplace

IVYPOOL—silver-and-white tabby she-cat with dark blue eyes (mother to Bristlekit, a pale gray she-kit; Thriftkit, a dark gray she-kit; and Flipkit, a tabby tom)

ELDERS (former warriors and queens, now retired)

GRAYSTRIPE—long-haired gray tom

MILLIE—striped silver tabby she-cat with blue eyes

SHADOWCLAN

LEADER **TIGERSTAR**—dark brown tabby tom

DEPUTY **TAWNYPELT**—tortoiseshell she-cat with green eyes

APPRENTICE, CONEPAW (white-and-gray tom)

MEDICINE CAT **PUDDLESHINE**—brown tom with white splotches

WARRIORS **JUNIPERCLAW**—black tom

WHORLPELT—gray-and-white tom

STRIKESTONE—brown tabby tom

APPRENTICE, BLAZEPAW (white-and-ginger tom)

STONEWING—white tom
APPRENTICE, ANTPAW (tom with a brown-and-black splotched pelt)

GRASSHEART—pale brown tabby she-cat
APPRENTICE, GULLPAW (white she-cat)

SCORCHFUR—dark gray tom with slashed ears

FLOWERSTEM—silver she-cat

SNAKETOOTH—honey-colored tabby she-cat

SLATEFUR—sleek gray tom
APPRENTICE, FRONDPAW (gray tabby she-cat)

CLOVERFOOT—gray tabby she-cat

SPARROWTAIL—large brown tabby tom
APPRENTICE, CINNAMONPAW (brown tabby she-cat with white paws)

SNOWBIRD—pure white she-cat with green eyes

QUEENS

DOVEWING—pale gray she-cat with green eyes (mother to Pouncekit, a gray she-kit; Lightkit, a brown tabby she-kit; and Shadowkit, a gray tabby tom)

BERRYHEART—black-and-white she-cat (mother to Hollowkit, a black tom; Sunkit, a brown-and-white tabby she-kit; and Spirekit, a black-and-white tom)

YARROWLEAF—ginger she-cat with yellow eyes (mother to Hopkit, a calico she-kit; and Flaxkit, a brown tabby tom)

ELDERS   OAKFUR—small brown tom

RATSCAR—scarred, skinny dark brown tom

SKYCLAN

LEADER   LEAFSTAR—brown-and-cream tabby she-cat with amber eyes

DEPUTY   HAWKWING—dark gray tom with yellow eyes

MEDICINE CATS   FRECKLEWISH—mottled light brown tabby she-cat with spotted legs

FIDGETFLAKE—black-and-white tom

MEDIATOR   TREE—yellow tom with amber eyes

WARRIORS   SPARROWPELT—dark brown tabby tom
APPRENTICE, NECTARPAW (brown she-cat)

MACGYVER—black-and-white tom

DEWSPRING—sturdy gray tom

PLUMWILLOW—dark gray she-cat
APPRENTICE, SUNNYPAW (ginger she-cat)

SAGENOSE—pale gray tom
APPRENTICE, GRAVELPAW (tan tom)
harrybrook—gray tom
APPRENTICE, FRINGEPAW (white she-cat with brown splotches)

BLOSSOMHEART—ginger-and-white she-cat
APPRENTICE, PIGEONPAW (gray-and-white she-cat)

SANDYNOSE—stocky light brown tom with ginger legs
APPRENTICE, QUAILPAW (white tom with crow-black ears)

RABBITLEAP—brown tom

    APPRENTICE, PALEPAW (black-and-white she-cat)

BELLALEAF—pale orange she-cat with green eyes

REEDCLAW—small pale tabby she-cat

VIOLETSHINE—black-and-white she-cat with yellow eyes

MINTFUR—gray tabby she-cat with blue eyes

NETTLESPLASH—pale brown tom

TINYCLOUD—small white she-cat

ELDERS   **FALLOWFERN**—pale brown she-cat who has lost her hearing

WINDCLAN

LEADER   **HARESTAR**—brown-and-white tom

DEPUTY   **CROWFEATHER**—dark gray tom

MEDICINE CAT   **KESTRELFLIGHT**—mottled gray tom with white splotches like kestrel feathers

WARRIORS   **NIGHTCLOUD**—black she-cat

BRINDLEWING—mottled brown she-cat

GORSETAIL—very pale gray-and-white she-cat with blue eyes

LEAFTAIL—dark tabby tom with amber eyes

EMBERFOOT—gray tom with two dark paws

SMOKEHAZE—gray she-cat

BREEZEPELT—black tom with amber eyes

CROUCHFOOT—ginger tom

LARKWING—pale brown tabby she-cat

SEDGEWHISKER—light brown tabby she-cat

SLIGHTFOOT—black tom with white flash on his chest

OATCLAW—pale brown tabby tom

FEATHERPELT—gray tabby she-cat

HOOTWHISKER—dark gray tom

HEATHERTAIL—light brown tabby she-cat with blue eyes

FERNSTRIPE—gray tabby she-cat

ELDERS WHISKERNOSE—light brown tom

WHITETAIL—small white she-cat

RIVERCLAN

LEADER MISTYSTAR—gray she-cat with blue eyes

DEPUTY REEDWHISKER—black tom

MEDICINE CATS MOTHWING—dappled golden she-cat

WILLOWSHINE—gray tabby she-cat

WARRIORS MINTFUR—light gray tabby tom
APPRENTICE, SOFTPAW (gray she-cat)

DUSKFUR—brown tabby she-cat
APPRENTICE, DAPPLEPAW (gray-and-white tom)

MINNOWTAIL—dark gray-and-white she-cat
APPRENTICE, BREEZEPAW (brown-and-white she-cat)

MALLOWNOSE—light brown tabby tom

BEETLEWHISKER—brown-and-white tabby tom

APPRENTICE, HAREPAW (white tom)

CURLFEATHER—pale brown she-cat

PODLIGHT—gray-and-white tom

HERONWING—dark gray-and-black tom

SHIMMERPELT—silver she-cat

APPRENTICE, NIGHTPAW (dark gray she-cat with blue eyes)

LIZARDTAIL—light brown tom

HAVENPELT—black-and-white she-cat

SNEEZECLOUD—gray-and-white tom

BRACKENPELT—tortoiseshell she-cat

APPRENTICE, GORSEPAW (white tom with gray ears)

JAYCLAW—gray tom

OWLNOSE—brown tabby tom

ICEWING—white she-cat with blue eyes

ELDERS

MOSSPELT—tortoiseshell-and-white she-cat

TWOLEG NEST

GREENLEAF
TWOLEGPLACE

TWOLEG PATH

TWOLEG PATH

CLEARING

SHADOWCLAN
CAMP

SKYCLAN
CAMP

SMALL
THUNDERPATH

HALFBRIDGE

GREENLEAF
TWOLEGPLACE

HALFBRIDGE

CAT VIEW

ISLAND

STREAM

RIVERCLAN
CAMP

HORSEPLACE

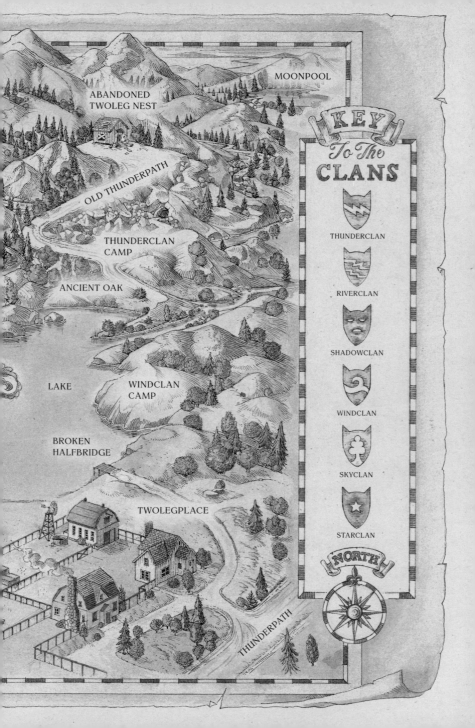

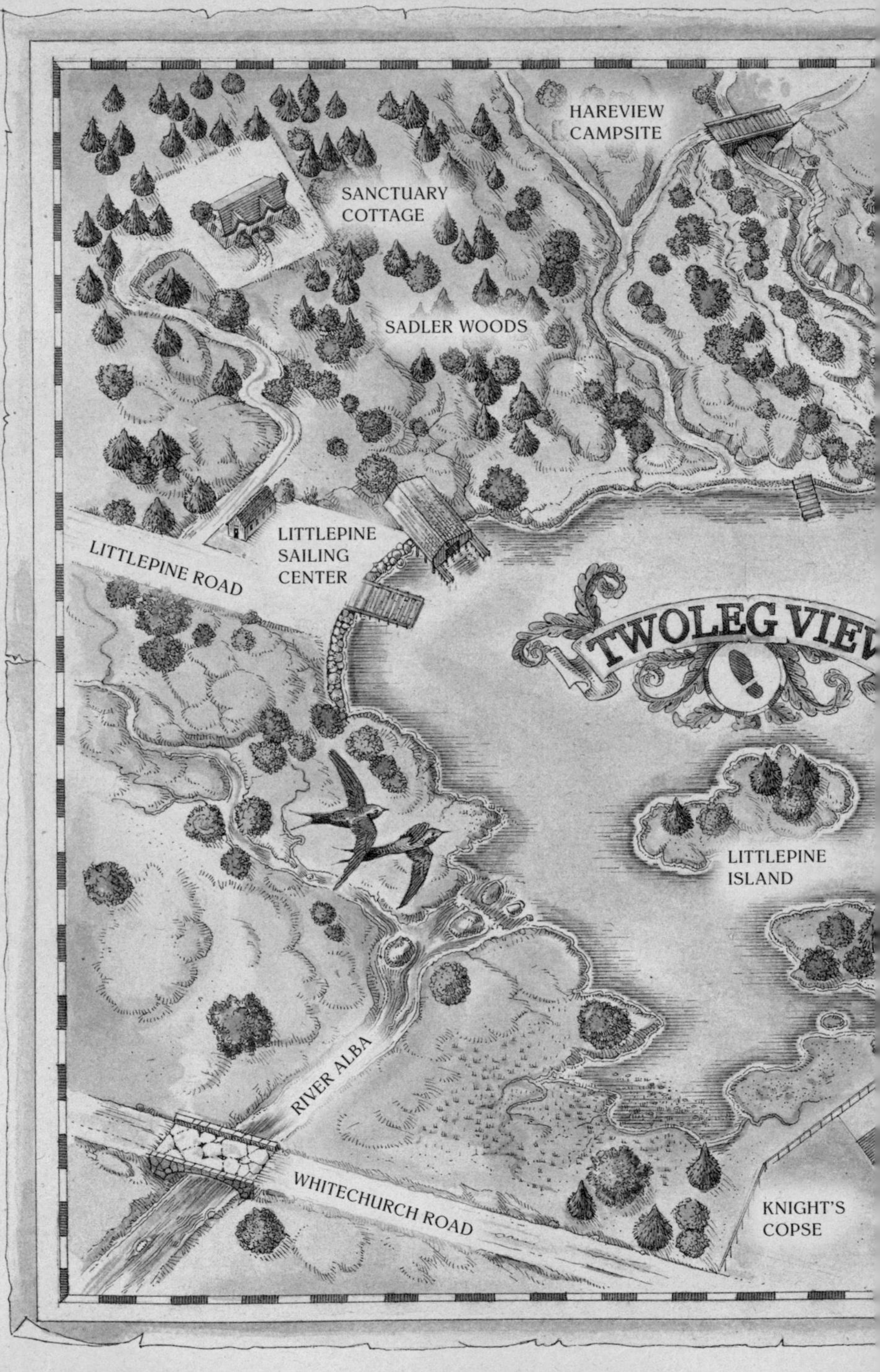
HAREVIEW CAMPSITE
SANCTUARY COTTAGE
SADLER WOODS
LITTLEPINE SAILING CENTER
LITTLEPINE ROAD
TWOLEG VIEW
LITTLEPINE ISLAND
RIVER ALBA
WHITECHURCH ROAD
KNIGHT'S COPSE

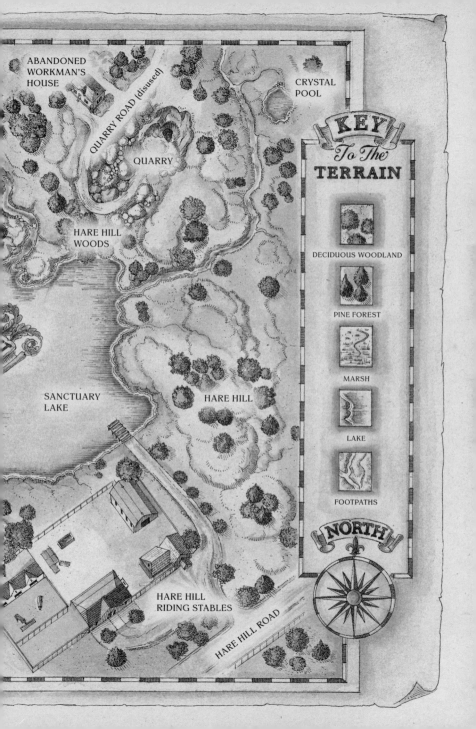

CHAPTER ONE

❧

A fresh breeze carried the smell of rabbit, and Tawnypelt's mouth watered. She tasted the air thoughtfully, following the tantalizing scent.

There. *She couldn't see it, but she knew it was there from the scent and from tiny sounds: the slight crackle of bracken, the rabbit's hurried breathing, the pounding of its heart. The prey was huddled in a clump of bracken near the base of a big pine tree. The sweet scent of pine resin, so dear to Tawnypelt, filled her nostrils.*

It's good to be home, *she thought.* It feels like I've been gone for moons!

She crouched, fixing her eyes on the rabbit's hiding place, and began to slink closer, her paw steps silent. She knew the forest floor like the back of her paws; she knew where to step to keep her approach silent. She was quite close to the rabbit when a loud crack sounded from the bracken: Her prey must have scented her. It bolted out of the undergrowth, but she could easily predict where it would go. She pounced. One strong bite to its neck, and the rabbit fell, limp beneath her.

Tawnypelt picked up her prey, satisfied. This would make a fine meal for her Clanmates.

The sun was climbing into the sky as she slid through the thorn tunnel and past the boulder into camp, the rabbit dangling from her jaws.

"*Tawnypelt!*" *Dawnpelt was washing herself outside the warriors' den. Tawnypelt's heart warmed at the sight of her.* Oh, Dawnpelt, where have you been? *It felt like ages since she had seen her kit.* "Nice catch!"

"*Oh, good, I'm starving,*" *Pinenose said cheerfully, getting to her feet. Her sides were rounded and she moved heavily.* Her kits, Tawnypelt thought. Has she really not had them yet? It's been a long time. It feels like . . .

The thought hit her suddenly: Something's wrong. *Tawnypelt dropped the rabbit in the fresh-kill pile and stared, puzzled, at her Clanmates and at the peaceful camp.* Dawnpelt shouldn't be here. And Pinenose . . . *Tawnypelt remembered those kits being born. There'd been four, hadn't there? They'd taken a long time coming, and Pinenose had borne the pain bravely.*

But now that pain was still in the future. This wasn't right. This wasn't real.

Tawnypelt shivered as if she'd fallen into the lake in winter. This felt so familiar, so right, but this wasn't ShadowClan . . . not anymore. Dawnpelt and Pinenose were dead. So many of her Clanmates were dead.

"*It was a good hunt, then?*" *The voice came from behind her.*

"*Rowanstar!*" *Joy flooded through her as she turned to face her mate. He blinked his amber eyes affectionately and she stepped closer, brushing her cheek against his, breathing in his familiar scent. It felt as if it had been longer than one morning since she had seen him.*

Much longer. Wait, *she realized again.* Something's wrong.

She flinched, and Rowanstar's tail twitched in concern. "What's the matter?"

"This isn't ShadowClan." *The words tumbled out of Tawnypelt's mouth. She grew surer as she went on, remembering.* "I mean, it is, but it's not real

ShadowClan, not as it is now. This is before the sickness, and before Dark-tail came. . . ." Her voice trailed off as Rowanstar stared at her, puzzled.

"You must have had a complicated dream last night," he purred at last. "I told you that vole didn't look right."

"Are you sure?" Tawnypelt turned slowly, staring around the camp. She desperately wanted to believe him. Crowfrost, ShadowClan's deputy, had joined Dawnpelt outside the warriors' den. Pinenose was sharing the fat rabbit Tawnypelt had caught with Kinkfur, the crotchety elder. She could hear kits squealing happily in the nursery.

Please let this be real!

A sense of peace lay over the whole of ShadowClan's camp. As she watched her Clanmates, Tawnypelt relaxed for the first time in a long time. She let her side press against Rowanstar's, shoulder to shoulder with him. "This is real?" she asked hopefully.

Rowanstar's tail brushed across her back, reassuring. "This is the only real ShadowClan."

Tawnypelt purred. "I'm so—"

"Pouncekit! Pouncekit, wait for me!" A yowl rang across the camp. Tawnypelt opened her eyes and stared at the brambles of the warriors' den, her heart sinking. A dream. *I was right. It wasn't real.* Rowanstar was dead. So many of her Clanmates and kin were dead.

"That's not how you play, Shadowkit!" Lightkit's yowl grated across Tawnypelt's nerves, shaking away the last of her dream. The light in the den was the pale pinkish glow of early dawn, but she knew she wasn't going to fall back asleep. Climbing from her nest, she headed out of the warriors' den. As she stepped outside, the cold of early leaf-bare sliced through her fur, and she shivered.

"Get *off* me, Lightkit!" Pouncekit screeched.

"Oh, that's *enough!*" Juniperclaw, his black fur tousled from sleep, brushed past Tawnypelt and stormed to the center of the clearing. "You kits need to settle down right now," he growled furiously. "You're waking up the whole camp!"

The three kits froze, staring up at him with identical wide amber eyes, so like Rowanstar's that Tawnypelt's heart gave a strange little throb. *No, not Rowanstar. Rowanclaw.* Rowanclaw had given up his status as ShadowClan's leader and become Rowanclaw again before he died. Her dream had left her confused.

"Sorry, Juniperclaw," Dovewing mewed easily from the entrance to the nursery. "But they're only kits."

Juniperclaw's thin black tail whipped back and forth angrily as he stared at Dovewing. "Maybe that's how kits act in *ThunderClan*," he snarled. "But here we expect them to have some consideration for their Clanmates."

Dovewing looked taken aback, but before she could say anything, Tawnypelt's son, Tigerheart—*no, Tigerstar, he's leader now; what is wrong with me today?*—stepped out of the leader's den. "Kits, you need to be quieter," he said sternly. "And Juniperclaw, you've got no right to talk to Dovewing that way. She's as much a ShadowClan cat as you are."

Juniperclaw dipped his head in acknowledgment, but his green eyes were stormy with resentment. "Whatever you say, Tigerstar," he muttered.

As Juniperclaw headed back toward the warriors' den, Tawnypelt tried to give him a sympathetic look, but the tom avoided her gaze. *We're all kin,* she thought sadly, *but it doesn't feel like it these days.* Juniperclaw was one of Dawnpelt's kits. *Maybe things would be different if Dawnpelt were still alive.* Fairly or not, it felt like Juniperclaw still blamed Rowanclaw, and even Tawnypelt herself, for not doing a better job of holding ShadowClan together when the evil rogue Darktail had moved into their territory. He'd eventually convinced enough ShadowClan warriors to join his "Kin" that ShadowClan was nearly destroyed. For a brief period before Tigerstar became leader and revived the Clan, ShadowClan had ceased to exist altogether, folding into SkyClan.

"Hey, Tawnypelt, want to play with us?" Pouncekit, the gray she-kit, was peering up at her. "What are you doing, anyway?"

"Just thinking," Tawnypelt said gently. The kits were still young enough that their eyes looked huge and round, surrounded by layers of fluff. It felt like it hadn't been long since Tigerstar and Dawnpelt were that small.

"We're sorry if we woke you up," Pouncekit's brother, Shadowkit, said, and both she-kits nodded earnestly.

"It's fine," Tawnypelt told them, feeling a surge of affection. They really were sweet kits.

"Come on," Lightkit said cheerfully to her littermates. "We'll be so quiet now, as quiet as when we used to hide from the Twolegs."

Tawnypelt blinked in surprise as the three kits ran off. *Kits that age shouldn't even know about Twolegs,* she thought, and then corrected herself. Of course these three did. They'd been born in a faraway place, surrounded by Twolegs and strange Clanless cats, after Tigerheart and Dovewing had run away together.

She loved them, of course. They were her kin, and they were good kits.

But they were so strange. *Not like real ShadowClan cats at all,* she thought, and immediately felt guilty. It shouldn't matter that they had been born among strangers, and it shouldn't matter that their mother was a ThunderClan cat. They were ShadowClan now, weren't they?

Sort of.

"Sorry about that." Tigerstar and Dovewing had come to stand alongside her. Tigerstar brushed his cheek against hers, and she touched noses with Dovewing.

"Would you like to share a vole?" Dovewing asked politely.

Tawnypelt's dream was still fresh in her mind: the intense focus of the hunt, the exhilaration of the final leap, the satisfaction of feeding her Clan. "I think I'll go hunting, actually," she said. "Build up the fresh-kill pile a little."

Tigerstar's ears twitched. "I sent a patrol out with Strikestone last night," he said. "They brought back so much prey, I don't think we need any cat to hunt again before sundown."

Tawnypelt's ears flattened with annoyance. Tigerstar had named *her* his deputy. She'd never asked for the position. But since he'd chosen her, Tigerstar should let her *be* deputy. Organizing hunting patrols was the deputy's job.

She took a slow breath and pricked up her ears again.

Tigerstar is a new leader. And I owe him my support. He'll grow into the role, just like Rowanstar did. But he has to find his own way.

"I'd like you to stay in camp and help strengthen the warriors' den," Tigerstar went on.

Tawnypelt sighed. "I think I'd be more use hunting," she meowed, making sure to keep her voice pleasant. Her paws were itching to get out of camp, to be alone in the pine forest for a while. How desperately she had missed the forest while ShadowClan had been living with SkyClan!

Tigerstar exchanged a glance with Dovewing. "The more cats we have restoring the dens, the sooner ShadowClan's camp will be back to the way it was," he said firmly.

Tawnypelt looked around. Two of the new apprentices Tigerstar had brought with him from the strange Twolegplace where his kits had been born—Blazepaw and Antpaw—were sharing tongues outside the warriors' den. Juniperclaw and Scorchfur were picking over the prey in the fresh-kill pile. Slatefur was sharpening his claws on a tree at the edge of camp.

And there were others, all over camp—cats who had been born outside ShadowClan, cats who had betrayed their Clan and their leader for Darktail, cats who had abandoned their dying Clan out of fear and had only just returned to the lake.

"Okay," Tawnypelt agreed, but deep inside, despite herself, she was thinking: *ShadowClan will never be the way it was.*

Tawnypelt sneezed. Dust was settling on her fur and getting into her eyes, making them itch. The sun was high overhead. They'd been at this for a long time, and their task was nowhere close to finished.

Scorchfur shoved a wad of moss into a hole in the side of the den, then hissed with annoyance as it immediately fell out again.

"When you put the moss in, hold it there and wait for Stonewing to weave twigs through it to fix it into place," Tawnypelt recommended.

Ignoring her, Scorchfur picked up the moss with his teeth and jammed it back into the hole. Irritation pricked up Tawnypelt's spine.

"Stonewing, bring those twigs over here," she snapped.

The white tom glanced at her, then away, shifting uneasily from one paw to another. "I'm working on this side," he said.

Digging her claws into the sandy floor of the den, Tawnypelt tried to keep herself from ripping the two toms' pelts off. "I told you—" she began.

"How's it going in here?" Tigerstar stuck his head through the den's entrance. Peering at the walls, he crouched and came all the way in. "You'll make quicker progress if you work in pairs," he suggested. "Stonewing, bring those twigs over here. Scorchfur can hold the moss in place and you can weave the twigs through it. It'll make for a warmer den."

Scorchfur and Stonewing looked at each other. "Okay," Stonewing said, and bent to pick up the twigs at his paws.

Hot rage shot through Tawnypelt, so sudden and violent that it frightened her. "I'm taking a break," she announced, and hurried out of the den. She didn't stop until she reached the fresh-kill pile, breathing hard.

It's fine, she tried to tell herself. *They don't have to listen to me. What matters is that ShadowClan has its territory back, and we're in our own camp again.*

When Rowanstar had decided to give up his role as ShadowClan's leader, she'd wanted very badly to hold her Clan together. But after the battles with Darktail and his Kin, there had been so few ShadowClan warriors left that Rowanstar had felt they'd *had* to join SkyClan to survive. He'd stopped being a leader, become Rowanclaw again. And then he'd died, trying to save a Clanmate's kits. Tawnypelt's grief had been so overwhelming that Tigerstar's return, and the return of several Clanmates they'd given up for lost, had seemed like a gift.

But reviving a Clan was hard. Rowanclaw was still dead. Some of the ShadowClan cats still resented him for decisions he'd made when Darktail had invaded their territory. And they resented Tawnypelt for standing by him, for loving him.

Some of those same cats betrayed him by joining Darktail, she thought bitterly. *Do I even want them as my Clanmates?*

Sighing, Tawnypelt picked up a mouse and sat down outside the nursery to eat. *I need to be patient.*

"Sweet little kits," she could hear Dovewing purr from inside the nursery. "If I get mine down to sleep, will you watch them while I grab some prey?"

"Sure," Berryheart sounded distracted. "Does Hollowkit look like he's getting a cold?"

"He's fine; don't worry," Dovewing said.

Irritation rose up in Tawnypelt again. *Doesn't she care if a ShadowClan kit is ill?*

Dovewing hadn't lifted a paw to help with the camp rebuilding. Yes, her kits were still in the nursery, but they were almost apprentice age; they didn't need her with them constantly. Dovewing could help if she wanted to.

But why should she? Dovewing's a ThunderClan cat, even if she's living in ShadowClan now.

Tawnypelt had been born in ThunderClan, too, but once she had chosen ShadowClan as an apprentice, she had been a ShadowClan cat through and through. More fierce and loyal, with more to prove, than cats who had always been part of the Clan. She doubted that Dovewing felt the same.

Tawnypelt had tried to like her son's mate, but sometimes she thought that Dovewing's presence was just another sign that ShadowClan had fallen apart. *What would Rowanclaw have said about Tigerstar taking a ThunderClan cat as his mate?*

"Are you all right?" Tigerstar's voice startled her. He had followed her out of the warriors' den and was padding cautiously toward her.

"I'm fine." Tawnypelt took a bite of mouse.

"You've seemed irritated since I've come back," Tigerstar said, sitting down beside her. He hesitated, then went on. "I know some of the Clan wanted you to take over as leader. If you were angry that I became leader instead, I would understand."

Tawnypelt sighed, the frustration draining out of her. Tigerstar was trying so *hard*. "That's not it," she said. "I'm glad you're leader. You have a better chance of making Shadow-Clan whole again than I would have. But I feel . . ." She paused, remembering with a sting how the younger warriors had ignored her suggestions earlier. *That never would have happened in the old ShadowClan.* She took a deep breath and finished, "I'm just not sure how I fit into our Clan now."

Tigerstar stared at her in surprise. "You're very important to our Clan," he insisted. "You're my deputy."

"Not if no one listens to me," Tawnypelt told him.

The fur began to bristle along Tigerstar's back. "If any cat thinks they don't have to listen to you, I'll make them listen," he said fiercely.

"Getting angry isn't going to make them accept me," Tawnypelt said. "A lot of ShadowClan cats were furious at Rowanclaw, and some of them had reason to be. Maybe I'm too much of a reminder of a time ShadowClan needs to forget."

Tigerstar flicked his tail dismissively. "Don't be ridiculous," he said. "If I—"

"Help! Help me!" Tawnypelt's pelt prickled as Dovewing's desperate yowl cut through Tigerstar's words. It came from the nursery behind them.

Tigerstar leaped to his feet and dashed for the den's entrance, Tawnypelt a few paces behind.

"It's Shadowkit! Help!" Dovewing cried. Tawnypelt put on a burst of speed and caught up with Tigerstar; they pushed their way through the nursery's entrance together.

On the floor of the nursery, Shadowkit was shaking, his

small limbs flailing as if he was caught in a nightmare. His littermates and Yarrowleaf, Berryheart, and their kits were pressed against the walls of the nursery, staring at him in horror.

Dovewing, crouched beside Shadowkit, looked up, her green eyes desperate. "I can't get him to wake up."

CHAPTER TWO

❧

In the medicine cat's den, Tawnypelt gazed down at Shadowkit. He looked so small, all by himself in the nest. Once the kit's fit had passed and he'd regained a groggy consciousness, they'd brought him here for Puddleshine, the ShadowClan medicine cat, to examine him. Dovewing and Tigerstar had sat by his nest all through the night.

It was morning now, and they'd asked Tawnypelt to watch over him while Dovewing checked on their other kits and Tigerstar spoke to the rest of the Clan. Puddleshine, who'd spent all night trying to find the cause of Shadowkit's sudden illness, was curled tightly in his own nest, catching a short nap while Shadowkit slept.

Bending over Shadowkit's nest, Tawnypelt pressed her cheek against the small gray tabby's. His milky kit scent was mixed with the rich pine scent of all ShadowClan cats, which Tawnypelt inhaled with relief. These kits had been born in a faraway Twolegplace,, but they were ShadowClan now, and they always would be. *I'm still getting to know you, but I do love you, little one,* Tawnypelt thought helplessly. *I will protect you,* she added silently.

Shadowkit's eyelids fluttered. "It's falling," he whimpered. "We have to stop it; it's falling."

"What's falling, little kit?" Tawnypelt kept her voice soft.

Shadowkit's eyes opened wider, and his amber gaze was sleepy but full of anxiety. "There's something I have to do," he murmured. "I'm not sure what . . . but if I don't, cats will get hurt. Cats will *die*." His mew was desperate.

What does a kit your age know about death? Tawnypelt wondered, nuzzling him gently. "Don't be silly," she told him. "It's just a bad dream."

"I'm not sure . . . ," Shadowkit mumbled. He seemed half-asleep again, his eyelids drooping, and she licked the top of his head.

"It's all right," she said soothingly. "Just rest."

But when Shadowkit had fallen back asleep, Tawnypelt hurried out of the medicine cat's den. Even if it had only been a dream, Tigerstar and Dovewing should know how agitated their kit had been.

Dovewing was waiting just outside. "What's wrong?" she asked immediately. "Did something happen?"

"It's okay," Tawnypelt hurried to reassure her. "Shadowkit woke up for a moment, but what he said was just nonsense— something about falling, and something he had to do. He fell back asleep, but I wanted to tell you he was upset."

Dovewing's eyes widened. "Tell me exactly what he said."

Tawnypelt told her, Dovewing looking more alarmed at every word. "I'm sure it was just a bad dream," Tawnypelt said at last, but Dovewing shook her head.

"I think it was a vision," she declared. "Tigerstar told you about the visions Shadowkit had on our journey back to the lake."

"He said you all *thought* he was having visions," Tawnypelt meowed cautiously. Tigerstar hadn't told her much, just that they thought Shadowkit saw things most kits didn't. And what Shadowkit had just experienced looked like a nightmare, not like the vision of any medicine cat Tawnypelt had ever heard of.

Dovewing shook her head. "Trust me. It was more than that."

She looked like she was about to say more, when a sharp, distressed cry—the wail of a kit in pain—came from the medicine cat's den.

They raced in to find Shadowkit writhing in his nest, his whole small body shaking violently, his eyes rolled back so that only the whites showed through their half-closed lids.

"Puddleshine!" Tawnypelt yowled. The medicine cat was still sleeping. He'd probably perfected the art of catching whatever sleep he could, whenever he could. With no time to spare, she and Dovewing tried to hold Shadowkit still with their front paws. The kit's thrashing body felt disturbingly rigid under Tawnypelt's paws.

"It's falling!" the kit screeched. "It's falling!"

Though she kept her eyes on Shadowkit, Tawnypelt could hear Puddleshine jump up from his nest and rush over.

He pulled up beside Tawnypelt just as Shadowkit abruptly stilled.

"Shadowkit," the medicine cat mewed, his voice soft. "Can you hear me?"

The kit didn't answer. His sides were moving up and down rapidly as he panted. The whites of his eyes were no longer showing, but his gaze was glassy.

Tawnypelt looked at Dovewing. Her mouth was open, but she looked relieved—Tawnypelt guessed she'd seen this happen before.

Puddleshine looked up at Tawnypelt, his expression matter-of-fact. "Would you get some wet moss, please?"

Tawnypelt hesitated for a heartbeat, not wanting to leave the suddenly frail-seeming kit, but then ran. She raced past the guard at the camp entrance to the pond near camp, and made her way back to the medicine cat's den as quickly as she could. When she returned, Tigerstar had joined the group in the medicine cat's den, and was pressed as closely as possible against Dovewing. Both parents stared at their kit, but Tigerstar's gaze looked more troubled than his mate's.

Shadowkit still seemed dazed, but his breathing had slowed to normal. Puddleshine took the moss between his teeth and gently wiped the kit's face. Shadowkit blinked and his eyes focused a little more.

"Can you hear me, Shadowkit?" Puddleshine asked again.

"Yes," the kit said slowly, blinking a drop of water out of his eyes. "We have to help them," he said, his voice quiet but full of fear. "They need us. It's going to destroy them!"

"Who?" The medicine cat kept his voice soft and soothing. "What did you see?"

Shadowkit looked confused. "Other cats. There were . . . I don't know. It was . . ." He shook his head, distressed. "I can't *remember*!"

"It's all right, Shadowkit," Tigerstar mewed, touching his nose to the kit's cheek.

"It's not all right. . . . I was seeing all these things, and they were really *important*! And now . . . now I just can't remember—it's all mixed up!" the kit wailed. "I'll never be able to help if I can't remember!"

"Right now, your job is to rest," Puddleshine instructed the kit firmly, glancing at Tigerstar and Dovewing. "It seems like maybe you had a vision that overwhelmed you and made you lose control of your body. You can't help any cat unless you take care of yourself."

"Did it hurt when you had this vision?" Dovewing asked, her green eyes large with worry.

Shadowkit hesitated. "Not hurt, exactly . . . ," he murmured. "It just felt . . . bigger and bigger and louder. Like something was pressing on the inside of my head. And then my body was moving, but all by itself, without me wanting it to, and I couldn't think at all."

Tawnypelt shivered. That sounded *awful*. "You were saying that we had to stop something that was falling." *What if this is a true vision? Puddleshine thinks so. . . . Are ShadowClan cats in danger?*

Shadowkit stared intensely into space, concentrating, for a

long moment. Then he gave a squeak of frustration. "I can't remember *anything*!"

"Maybe it'll come back to you," Puddleshine soothed. "Give your mind a chance to rest."

Shadowkit shifted unhappily. "I don't remember, but I know it's *important*," he meowed. "There's something I have to do."

"You have to take care of yourself before you can help any other cat," Tigerstar said firmly, but Shadowkit's tail slashed restlessly from side to side, his paws twitching with frustration.

"I'll give him something to calm him," Puddleshine suggested quietly, and hurried off to his herb stores, returning with a few tiny green leaves and setting them down in front of the kit. "This is thyme, Shadowkit. It'll help you relax."

As Shadowkit licked up the thyme, Tawnypelt asked quietly, "Puddleshine, what do you think this is? This fit he had. Have you ever seen anything like this before?"

The brown-and-white tom shook his head helplessly. "No," he answered. "Have you? Ever?"

Tawnypelt sighed. *Puddleshine's a good medicine cat, but he's so young.* Suddenly she missed Littlecloud, the elderly medicine cat who had preceded Puddleshine, with a sharp pang. Maybe if Littlecloud were still alive, he might know of something that could help Shadowkit.

Or if Flametail were alive . . . She shut her eyes for a moment, pain washing over her. Tigerstar's and Dawnpelt's littermate, Flametail, had been a fine medicine cat, but he'd drowned, a horrible death, before Puddleshine had even been born. Littlecloud had never taken another apprentice before he died; Puddleshine had had to learn on his own, with help from other Clans' medicine cats.

"No," she mewed sadly. "I've never seen anything like this."

Puddleshine gulped, looking between Dovewing, Tigerstar, and Tawnypelt, then led them to the far end of the den. "I know that you believe Shadowkit is meant to be a medicine cat," he began, quietly enough that the kit wouldn't be able to hear him. "But the way he was thrashing around in pain . . . even for a medicine cat, it's not normal."

Fear prickled along Tawnypelt's spine. "You think there's something wrong with Shadowkit."

Tigerstar looked alarmed. "Is he sick?" he asked.

"I don't know," Puddleshine said, his tail drooping. "That's what worries me. I can't treat him if I don't understand what's wrong." He looked so anxious that, amid her own worry over Shadowkit, Tawnypelt felt a flash of pity for him: No one liked to watch another cat, especially a kit, suffer. But it must be worse for a medicine cat, who was *supposed* to be able to help.

"If you don't know what's wrong, you'd better get another medicine cat here," Dovewing meowed sharply.

"I—" Puddleshine began, but Dovewing went on.

"Some of the others are older and have seen more than you have. Why don't you ask Leafpool to examine him?"

Tawnypelt felt the fur bristle along her spine. "We don't need a *ThunderClan* cat sticking her nose in our business," she spat before she could stop herself. *Dovewing will always think*

ThunderClan is better than ShadowClan.

"If my kit is in danger, I'm going to go to any cat who can help him, no matter what Clan they're from," Dovewing growled back.

Tigerstar pressed his shoulder reassuringly against Dovewing's. "I think it's a good idea," he mewed. "Puddleshine, take two warriors and have them escort you to ThunderClan's camp. I'm sure Leafpool will be happy to help."

Puddleshine glanced over at Shadowkit, who seemed to be dozing again, then nodded. "I'll be back as fast as I can."

As the medicine cat hurried from the den, Tawnypelt looked at Dovewing. The other she-cat stared back, her green eyes fierce. "I want to help Shadowkit, too," Tawnypelt mewed apologetically. "But I worry about showing weakness to other Clans. Not now, while ShadowClan is trying to heal."

Dovewing dipped her head in understanding. "I know. But Shadowkit is special. If there's even a chance Leafpool can help him . . ."

Tigerstar's gaze held his mother's. "Without Shadowkit, we never would have made it back home. I'm sure he's important for ShadowClan's future. We need him. Even if we have to get the help of another medicine cat."

Dovewing's ears twitched, and she leaned her head against Tigerstar's shoulder. "Spiresight said that Shadowkit would see into the shadows. I just hope his gift isn't too much for him to handle. He's so young."

Tawnypelt had heard them talk about Spiresight before— the cat who'd dreamed strange dreams and seen visions, who had helped them on their way back to the lake and sacrificed himself to save their kits—but she had never met him. *How can I judge if what he said is true?* She shook her head to clear it. Maybe Shadowkit saw true visions, but maybe he was just a sick kit. Tawnypelt simply wanted him to be okay.

"I remembered!" Shadowkit called across the den, his voice hoarse with sleep but his small face alert.

His parents hurried over, Tawnypelt just behind them.

"You woke up so quickly," Dovewing purred, nuzzling him. "I'm surprised the thyme didn't help you sleep longer."

"I know what I saw," Shadowkit announced, looking up at them solemnly.

"What was it?" Tigerstar asked, his voice gentle.

"There was a big tree," Shadowkit said, his eyes wide. "*Really* big. It had fallen into the river and was floating along. And then the ground ended and the river went right over the side of the world, and the tree fell. But there were cats behind the water. The tree fell onto them." He looked up at Tigerstar, and his voice shook. "I could hear them yowling in pain. I don't think it's happened yet. We have to warn them."

The river went right over the side of the world. "That sounds like a waterfall," Tawnypelt realized.

"There's no waterfall on ShadowClan's territory," Tigerstar pointed out. "Or on any Clan's territory, as far as I know." He turned his gaze back to Shadowkit's solemn face. "Did you recognize any of the cats' voices?"

Shadowkit shook his head.

"Did you see a waterfall on your journey here from the

Twolegplace?" Tawnypelt asked.

"No, nothing like that," Dovewing mewed, and Tigerstar nodded in agreement.

"It wasn't a place I'd been before," Shadowkit explained. "There were a lot of rocks there, and I think the cats were behind the waterfall, somehow. But it felt like a really important place. And there were cats there, cats like us, and they were in *danger*."

Behind the waterfall, in a rocky place. It all suddenly made sense. "I know what he's seeing," Tawnypelt cried, remembering cool, clear air and a cave full of cats behind a tumbling waterfall. "The Tribe of Rushing Water!"

CHAPTER THREE

"I don't believe it," Tigerstar hissed, keeping his voice low. He had hurried Dovewing and Tawnypelt out of the medicine cat's den. Glancing back over her shoulder, Tawnypelt could see Shadowkit craning his neck to watch them, his expression anxious.

"Who else could it be?" Tawnypelt argued. "Important cats living near a waterfall? Shadowkit's having visions about the Tribe!"

"But why would he be seeing them?" Tigerstar demanded. "He's a ShadowClan cat! After all we did to make it back here, Shadowkit belongs in ShadowClan! His future is here."

Tawnypelt turned to Dovewing. "*You've* been to the Tribe. Surely you recognize Shadowkit's description." She thought of the mountain cats who had helped her on the quest to find a new home so long ago. Her chest ached at the thought of them being in danger. Dovewing had traveled to their cave, too, more recently. She had to see how important this was.

Dovewing shifted uneasily from one paw to another. "It *could* be them," she agreed hesitantly. "But I'm not sure. There are other waterfalls."

"With cats living behind them? Who Shadowkit might see visions of?" Tawnypelt's meow rose incredulously, and, all around the clearing, other cats' ears went up in curiosity.

"What's going on?" Grassheart asked, looking up from the frog she and Cloverfoot were sharing. "Is Shadowkit okay?"

"Puddleshine hurried out of here like his fur was on fire," Cloverfoot added.

All around the clearing, cats were listening closely. Tigerstar took a deep breath, looking around at his Clanmates. "We haven't told every cat in the Clan yet," he said, glancing at Dovewing, "but we think Shadowkit has a special connection with StarClan, like medicine cats do. He had a fit—or a dream, whatever it was—in the nursery, because he was having a vision. He saw cats in danger and a waterfall. Based on his description, Tawnypelt thinks he's seeing a vision of the Tribe of Rushing Water."

"In the mountains?" Grassheart asked, surprised. "Why would he see visions about *them*?"

"Are you sure it was a vision?" Whorlpelt, one of the youngest warriors, asked. "Sometimes if I eat too much, I have weird dreams. It might not mean anything."

Juniperclaw flicked his tail. "Why would Shadowkit have visions of a place he's never been to or even heard of? I think Whorlpelt's right. You're getting worked up about a normal dream."

"Shadowkit's had visions before," Dovewing explained. "He saw ShadowClan's camp, long before he'd ever been here."

Tigerstar nodded. "He brought us back to the lake. When

we were lost, he knew exactly how to find the way home. . . .
We never would have made it back here without him."

Tawnypelt watched her Clanmates exchange surprised
glances. She understood their shock. Tigerstar had told her
that Shadowkit had visions, but not that they were so specific
or so accurate. Clearly, Spiresight, whatever he had been like,
had been right: Shadowkit was special.

"I still think it would make more sense if Shadowkit were
having a vision about something important to *ShadowClan*,
though," Cloverfoot mewed. "Where is there a waterfall?"

"Where the Tribe of Rushing Water lives!" Tawnypelt
spat, irritated. Why were they all ignoring the clear answer?

"Calm down, all of you," Tigerstar meowed in a level voice.
"We have to think about this carefully, and not make any
decisions in a rush."

Tawnypelt growled softly. There was only one possible
meaning in Shadowkit's vision—why was every cat debating it?

"Was there something you wanted to say, Tawnypelt?"
Tigerstar looked at her, sounding annoyed.

"Yes!" Tawnypelt replied. "It's clear that Shadowkit is
dreaming of the Tribe. Why won't any cat in this Clan listen
to me? I'm the deputy, and I've been part of ShadowClan longer than almost any of you!"

Scorchfur huffed, a small, sarcastic sound.

"What?" Tawnypelt asked, whirling to face him.

"You were more loyal to *Rowanclaw* than to ShadowClan,"
Scorchfur said, just as fiercely. "Always. You stuck by his decisions when the Clan was torn between him and Darktail.

Everything fell apart then, and you didn't raise a paw to stop it. Maybe *that's* why some of the cats here don't want to listen to you. The ShadowClan you tried to hold on to didn't work! We need to *forget it*!"

Tawnypelt gasped, feeling as breathless as if Scorchfur had just kicked her in the stomach. "I—I did everything I could for ShadowClan," she gasped. "And so did Rowanclaw."

All around the clearing, cats leaped to their feet, hissing and growling.

"It was the Clan who turned on Rowanclaw, not the other way around," Oakfur, one of the elders, hissed at Scorchfur.

"We *lost* ShadowClan because Rowanclaw wasn't strong enough to stand up to the rogues," Strikestone snarled. "Things have to be different now if we're going to survive."

Cats were glaring into each other's faces, less than a whisker's length apart, looking as if they were only a heartbeat from attacking one another. The younger apprentices and the outsider cats who Tigerstar had brought with him from his journey were hanging back, wide-eyed, clearly unsure what to do about their suddenly hostile Clanmates.

"Quiet!" Tigerstar yowled, his voice rising above the chaos. Silence fell over the clearing.

Tigerstar looked around. "This is unacceptable," he meowed coldly. "I am the leader of this Clan, and I've chosen Tawnypelt as my deputy. She *will* be respected." His eyes traveled from one cat to another, and many dropped their gazes, their faces sullen.

Tawnypelt felt cold inside. So many of the cats resented

her, resented Rowanclaw. She didn't want to think about what
Scorchfur had said: that the old ShadowClan, *her* Shadow-
Clan, should be forgotten.

Rowanclaw, Dawnpelt, Flametail—all the lost cats of
ShadowClan, forgotten.

Maybe I don't belong in ShadowClan anymore.

"I'll let you talk this over," she murmured to Dovewing.
"Just . . . I'll be in the forest."

The pale leaf-bare sun had begun to drop low in the sky
by the time Puddleshine returned, leading Leafpool into the
clearing. Tawnypelt watched from above, high in the branches
of a pine tree overlooking the camp, as Dovewing, followed by
Tigerstar, hurried forward to greet the ThunderClan medicine cat, relief clear on her face.

She looks happier, just from seeing Leafpool, Tawnypelt thought,
scrambling down the rough-barked trunk as the four cats disappeared into the medicine-cat den. She remembered how
hard it had been at first, leaving ThunderClan—including her
littermate, Brambleclaw, who she'd missed desperately—and
trying to find her place in the Clan she'd chosen. With a flick
of her ears, Tawnypelt shook the thought away as she leaped
lightly to the ground.

She waited patiently until the two medicine cats emerged
from the den, Dovewing and Tigerstar close behind them.

"What do you think?" she asked, stepping forward and
nodding a polite greeting to Leafpool.

The brown tabby medicine cat looked troubled. "I've never

seen anything like this," she said. "I believe you all when you say the kit has a connection to StarClan. But why would it make him shake and flail and lose consciousness?"

Puddleshine nodded in agreement, looking helplessly at Tigerstar and Dovewing. "I can't find anything wrong with him. He doesn't have a fever; he's not sick to his stomach; nothing is swollen or broken."

"So either he's sick with something we've never seen before, or he's being sent a message from StarClan that's so strong it's sending him into fits," Leafpool suggested. "If that's the answer, what does the vision mean?"

"Did Shadowkit describe his vision to you?" Tawnypelt asked. "The tree, and the river, and the waterfall?"

"He did," Leafpool agreed. "But I'm not sure what it means."

"How much do you remember of where the Tribe of Rushing Water lives?" Tawnypelt asked, watching Leafpool carefully. Leafpool had seen the Tribe's home when the Clans had traveled from the forest to the lake, before Tigerstar or Dovewing had been born. She hadn't spent as long there as either Tawnypelt or Dovewing had, but she must remember.

Understanding dawned in Leafpool's eyes. "It could be," she agreed. "There's the cave behind the waterfall there, and plenty of cats with a connection to the Clans. But there's no way to be sure."

A shock of excitement ran through Tawnypelt. "Unless we go there."

"No," Tigerstar meowed immediately, his face stern.

"Dovewing, our kits, and I just got here after a long journey. We're not going anywhere. Especially not Shadowkit."

"But Shadowkit's vision must be telling him to go there," Tawnypelt argued. Dovewing was looking thoughtful, and Tawnypelt turned to her. "The journey would be worth it if it helped him, wouldn't it?"

Tigerstar hissed, his ears flattening. "He's my kit, and he's staying here."

Tawnypelt stared at Dovewing, wondering how she would react. Tigerstar glanced at her, too, seeming a little surprised by the force of his own words. For her own part, Dovewing looked thoughtful, her green eyes dark until she raised her head and spoke. "I think Tawnypelt is right," she said.

Tawnypelt blinked, pleased at the unexpected support.

Tigerstar's eyes widened. "What?" he spluttered. "Shadowkit is too young to travel. He survived a hard trip here, and now you want to drag him away to some strange cats?" His fur seemed to bush out at the thought. "No, we should let Puddleshine take care of him."

"He doesn't know *how!*" Dovewing insisted. "Leafpool doesn't, either! If we follow his vision, maybe it will help."

"Or maybe he'll be sick in the same way, but far from home, in the mountains, in leaf-bare," Tigerstar retorted fiercely. "What do you expect, for this Tribe to look after him?"

"The Tribe is friendly," Dovewing mewed. "I've been there. Tawnypelt and Leafpool have been there. They'd do whatever they could for Shadowkit, and maybe they'll know something that can help him."

"They were friendly *then*," Tigerstar pointed out. "If anyone knows how Clans can change, it's us."

"However they changed, the Tribe would never hurt a kit," Tawnypelt mewed firmly. "If Shadowkit's vision isn't pointing us toward them, and if they can't help him, we will just bring him home."

Tawnypelt looked at Tigerstar pleadingly. Dovewing's fur brushed against hers, and, for the first time, she felt united with her son's mate. She was *sure* that traveling to the Tribe of Rushing Water would be the best thing for Shadowkit, and she knew that Dovewing agreed.

Tigerstar stared back and forth between them, his tail slashing through the air. Finally, he shook his head. "No," he said. "I'm the leader of this Clan, and Shadowkit is my son. StarClan gave him the knowledge to bring him *here*, and they won't abandon him now. He'll stay in ShadowClan, where he belongs."

CHAPTER FOUR

❧

Twigs were poking into Tawnypelt's sides. She'd never noticed before how uncomfortable a nest could be. *I was so used to having Rowanclaw to cushion me.* The moss and pine needles that now did that job were useless tonight. Grunting, she rolled over, trying to find a more restful position. Was Shadowkit sleeping in the medicine cat's den? Surely there would be some sound if he was ill again. She remembered the rigid flailing of his limbs, his rapid panting, and rolled over again, trying to push the image away.

"For StarClan's sake, Tawnypelt!" Juniperclaw yowled from the next nest. "If you can't sleep, maybe try taking a walk? You're keeping every warrior in the den awake!"

"Remember how we all slept away from each other in the Twoleg den, Slatefur?" Cloverfoot meowed pointedly. "I miss that sometimes."

"Fine," Tawnypelt got to her feet, shaking pine needles from her fur. "But if you liked the Twoleg den so much, Cloverfoot, maybe you should go back there. You're supposed to be a ShadowClan cat now."

Before Cloverfoot could spit a reply, Tawnypelt stalked out

of the den. Outside, she shivered in the night air, looking up at the clear light of the almost-full moon. Already, she regretted losing her temper in the warriors' den. Tigerstar was right: She was easily irritated these days.

But I can't stand what ShadowClan has become. A squabbling group of cats who she didn't know, or who had fought against her and Rowanclaw, when they had just wanted to keep their Clan together.

A sharp pang of loss shot through her, and she suddenly missed Rowanclaw more than ever. Rowanclaw—when he was Rowan*star*—would have listened to her about Shadowkit and the Tribe of Rushing Water. He had always taken Tawnypelt seriously, listened to her opinions about problems in the Clan. But no cat in ShadowClan cared what she thought now.

She *knew* that Shadowkit had to get to the Tribe. StarClan was sending him these visions for a reason, and they wouldn't stop until he did what they wanted. Shadowkit could help the Tribe, and maybe they could help him. But Tigerstar wouldn't listen to her.

Some cat needs to do what needs to be done. Tawnypelt licked her paw thoughtfully, shocked at her own idea. She could take Shadowkit, right now, and sneak out of ShadowClan camp in the night. No cat would be able to stop her.

Tigerstar would be furious. But when she brought Shadowkit back to him, cured, he would forgive her. He would be grateful, even, because she would have saved his kit.

Could she do it, though?

Something brushed against her fur. There was a familiar

musky scent in the air, and a breeze blew through her fur, carrying, almost too soft to be heard, a voice.

You're on the right path.

Tawnypelt jumped, spinning to look around her, but the clearing was deserted. Just for a moment, she had heard Rowanclaw. Her heart ached, a dull pain deep in her chest. Had she really heard him, or had she imagined it?

If I really heard him . . . if he encouraged me from StarClan . . . then I would know that my plan is the right one.

It *was* Rowanstar. Tawnypelt was sure of it.

Slinking from shadow to shadow as quietly as if she were stalking prey, she crossed the camp and crept into the medicine cat's den. Glancing across to Puddleshine's nest, she saw the medicine cat fast asleep, curled up with his tail laid across his nose. Shadowkit was in his own nest, snuggled into a ball of kitten fluff.

Gently, she lifted him by the nape of the neck and carried him outside. As they stepped out into the cold air, he began to stir, and she lowered him to the ground. His eyes were open, and he blinked peacefully up at her. "Hi, Tawnypelt," he mewed softly. "What's going on?"

She looked down at him, affection swelling in her chest. "We're going to have an adventure," she whispered. "Just you and me."

Shadowkit's ears perked with excitement. "Are you taking me to the place from my vision?"

If he's so happy to go, he must know this is what StarClan wants. Tawnypelt touched her muzzle to the top of the kit's head.

"Exactly," she told him. "But we'll have to be very quiet and careful. Strikestone is guarding the entrance to camp, and he'll stop us if he sees us. But we can sneak out the tunnel to the dirtplace and leave without any cat noticing."

"Okay," Shadowkit said. He got up and trotted beside Tawnypelt toward the tunnel, his side pressed trustingly against hers.

They were almost there when a cry came from behind them. *"No!"*

Tawnypelt whipped around. Dovewing was outside the nursery, her face twisted with horror.

"It's all right," Tawnypelt hissed desperately. She didn't want to hurt Dovewing, but this had to happen. "I'm taking him to the Tribe! It's for Shadowkit's own good! I'll take care of him, I promise."

Dovewing took a few steps toward them and then slowed, her tail waving uncertainly.

With a thump of running feet, Tigerstar charged out of his den. "Dovewing?" he asked, breathless. "I heard you. . . . What's going on?"

Tawnypelt watched him take in the sight of her and Shadowkit standing together, close to the tunnel out of camp. She was sure she looked guilty, and Tigerstar's expression changed, his expression moving from confusion to anger.

He charged forward, so fast that Tawnypelt flinched backward and Shadowkit pressed against her legs. Tigerstar's snarl was louder than she'd ever heard it. "Are you . . . you're just *taking* him?"

Holding her ground, Tawnypelt glared back at her son. "I'm doing what StarClan wants. This is the only way to *help* Shadowkit, and you won't be reasonable!"

"*Reasonable?*" Tigerstar's fur bristled. "You're stealing my kit!"

Agitated whispers came from behind her, and Tawnypelt looked around. Slatefur was staring out of the warriors' den, eyes wide, other faces peering past him from inside, trying to get a better look. Berryheart and Yarrowleaf were at the mouth of the nursery, behind Dovewing, their expressions alarmed. The cats of the new ShadowClan, watching her, silent and shocked.

Hot rage rose up inside her. "This is the right thing to do," she hissed. "You wouldn't listen. You *never* listen to me now. You made me your deputy, but you won't let me *be* your deputy."

"That's not true," Tigerstar tried to interrupt, but Tawnypelt went on. It felt good, in a mean, poisonous kind of way, to finally say all the worst things she had been thinking.

"All you care about now is Dovewing and your kits, and these strange cats you've brought back from outside the Clans," she growled accusingly. "And your own power, of course. You *love* being in charge."

Tigerstar's tail was whipping back and forth furiously. "In *charge*? It's impossible to be in charge with you around, Tawnypelt," he growled. "You're stubborn; you argue with everything I ask you to do; you're rude to any cat who wasn't born in ShadowClan. The Clan has changed, but *you* won't change with it." He paused and sighed, his yowl calming a little. "The old ShadowClan didn't work. I loved Rowanclaw, but the Clan *died* when he was leader, and I'm trying to bring it back. It's hard, and you're making it harder by working against me."

Tawnypelt sucked in a breath. *How dare he insult Rowanclaw?* She glanced away to calm herself, but saw Shadowkit staring up at her, his eyes so like her mate's. "I can't believe you'd talk about your own kin—your *father*—like this," she growled bitterly to Tigerstar. "Rowanclaw was dealt some harsh blows. The sickness, Darktail's schemes"—she glanced around at the faces staring at her from out of the dens—"*betrayal* by cats who should have followed him, but he loved his Clan. And he was fair to the cats who followed him. The way you won't listen to me, or Dovewing, or even Leafpool about this—you're acting like a tyrant, not a leader. It reminds me of another Tigerstar I once knew."

Shock passed over Tigerstar's face, and sour guilt curled in Tawnypelt's stomach. That wasn't fair—the first Tigerstar, her father, had nearly torn the Clans apart for the sake of his ambition. Her son would never be so cruel.

Before either of them could speak, Dovewing stepped between them. "Tawnypelt's right."

Tigerstar looked stunned, and she spoke again, quickly. "Not about you, Tigerstar, but about Shadowkit." She gazed up at him confidently. "I've been thinking, and the more I think, the surer I am that Shadowkit's vision *is* of the Tribe of Rushing Water. If StarClan is sending him such strong visions that they're making him sick, then we have to go. It's the only way he can get better."

"What?" Tigerstar looked betrayed. "*No!* I'm the leader of this Clan, and he is *my* kit—"

But Dovewing cut him off. She slipped past him, joining Tawnypelt at Shadowkit's side. "He's my kit, too, Tigerstar," she said angrily, "and I'm going with them. I *know* this is right. I can't stay here and watch Shadowkit suffer." She leaned toward Tigerstar, but he just watched her, his eyes cold. Dovewing pulled away, but she went on, "We will come back and Shadowkit will be better. I'm sure of it."

Tigerstar glared at her. Dovewing turned to Tawnypelt, her gaze uncertain, but Tawnypelt nodded wordlessly. *We both know this is right.* Dovewing nodded back, took in a breath, and seemed to regain her confidence. Together, they turned and walked away, Shadowkit between them. Tawnypelt could feel the eyes of the whole Clan watching her.

We should bring more warriors with us, she thought fleetingly. *It's leaf-bare, and the travel will be treacherous, and Shadowkit is unwell . . . but who would defy Tigerstar to join us now?*

"Don't worry, Tigerstar," Shadowkit called back earnestly, keeping pace with the she-cats. "It'll all be okay. This is what's *supposed* to happen."

Tawnypelt desperately hoped he was right.

CHAPTER FIVE

The chill morning breeze ruffled Tawnypelt's fur, and she shivered, her eyes still closed against the sunlight. She and Dovewing and Shadowkit had fallen asleep curled together, as they'd done the last two nights, but now she could feel that she was alone.

Without opening her eyes, she cocked an ear, listening for them. She heard the soft pad of paws on grass and Shadowkit saying, not far away, "But *why* does it live underground?"

Tawnypelt's whiskers twitched. It was one of the things she had liked best about her own kits at that age: their wide-eyed questioning of the world, always wanting to know *why* things were the way they were.

"Well," Dovewing answered quietly, "I guess voles live underground because they can keep warm there, and be protected from other animals who want to eat them."

"Like us!" Shadowkit cried.

Purring with amusement, Tawnypelt opened her eyes, then climbed to her feet and stretched. Dovewing was now trying to explain to Shadowkit why cats *didn't* live underground, and finding it difficult. *She's a good mother,* Tawnypelt thought.

Patient, and she takes Shadowkit's questions seriously. It surprised her a little; she'd spent a lot of time thinking of Dovewing as the careless cat who'd run away from the Clans and made Tigerheart chase after her. *Maybe she's not so careless after all.*

Dovewing had been very careful of Shadowkit on the two days of their journey so far, watching out for danger, making sure the kit ate and rested as much as he needed to, helping him over difficult terrain. Tawnypelt could see how precious Shadowkit was to Dovewing.

But gazing up at the craggy gray mountain ahead, Tawnypelt saw snow high on its peaks. *It hasn't been an easy journey so far . . . and it will only get worse.* When they left these grassy foothills and moved on to the cold stone of the mountain, the true danger would arise.

It would be easier if we had more warriors with us, Tawnypelt thought with fresh regret. If she hadn't acted so impulsively, perhaps she and Dovewing could have united to argue calmly with Tigerstar, and set out with a proper patrol, instead of storming off with Shadowkit in the middle of the night. *But it's too late now,* she thought, shaking dust from her pelt. *I just have to believe that Shadowkit is right—it was meant to happen this way. And we'll be fine.*

Shadowkit and Dovewing were in a sunny patch of grass, closer to where the mountain slopes rose above them. Tawnypelt padded toward them, and Shadowkit greeted her with a purr.

"We saved you a vole," Dovewing mewed, and Tawnypelt settled beside them and sank her teeth into the prey. She eyed

Dovewing, trying to think of what to say; she still felt a little awkward around the other cat.

"We went hunting before you got up!" Shadowkit announced, breaking the silence. "I helped catch that vole!"

"He certainly did," Dovewing agreed. "He chased it right toward me."

The kit puffed out his chest with pride, and Tawnypelt mewed affectionately, "You'll be a good hunter one day."

Shadowkit's eyes widened earnestly. "I'm going to be a medicine cat, though," he replied.

Tawnypelt's eyes met Dovewing's and they both purred with laughter, the stiffness between them disappearing. "We know, kit," Dovewing chuckled, brushing her tail over his back.

"Even a medicine cat should know how to hunt, though," Tawnypelt added. "You might get hungry while you're looking for herbs."

"I could track prey through the grass like this," Shadowkit said, getting to his paws. He crouched low and waggled his hindquarters, ready to pounce. Both she-cats purred with laughter again, and Dovewing began to move her tail slowly through the grass for him to stalk.

"How much longer do you think it will be until we get to the Tribe?" Tawnypelt asked as they watched Shadowkit wiggling through the grass, his eyes fixed on Dovewing's tail.

"Another day or two?" Dovewing guessed. "We'll have to be careful of Shadowkit on the way. The mountain paths are so narrow."

Tawnypelt shuddered, imagining Shadowkit slipping and falling from a crag, or down into a crevice between mountain boulders. "We'll keep him between us," she suggested. "We'll go slowly over any slippery patches. By being slow and cautious, we can keep ourselves safe." Dovewing nodded, but Tawnypelt could see the doubt in her eyes.

This would be a dangerous journey for a group of warriors—but for two warriors and an unwell kit?

"We should hunt again before we start," Dovewing mewed finally. "The mountain prey—"

She broke off as Shadowkit gave a small, hurt noise and collapsed onto his belly in the grass.

Both she-cats jumped up and rushed to him as the kit began to convulse, his paws drumming against the ground, his body shaking.

"Shadowkit!" Tawnypelt cried. She and Dovewing put their front paws on Shadowkit's side, trying to still his thrashing, but he was jerking violently and they couldn't hold him.

We don't even have any herbs to give him, Tawnypelt thought desperately, suddenly feeling terribly alone and helpless. *Oh, why did I leave so suddenly? Why didn't I ask Puddleshine for something before I brought Shadowkit with me?*

After what felt like moons, the kit's body stilled, and he blinked up at his mother, looking exhausted and panting rapidly.

"Shadowkit, how do you feel?" Dovewing asked gently.

The kit blinked. "All right," he muttered. "But the tree . . ." He broke off, looking puzzled.

"Just rest," Tawnypelt meowed firmly. "You'll be able to think more clearly when you wake up." *Sleep helped him last time,* she thought.

Dovewing gently nosed the top of his head. "Tawnypelt's right. Let yourself sleep." Obediently, Shadowkit closed his eyes.

They watched silently, their sides pressed together for comfort, as the kit's breathing fell into the slow rhythms of sleep.

"I wish I could help him," Dovewing mewed at last. "Each time this happens, it looks like—I don't know how he's surviving this." Tawnypelt knew what she meant: Shadowkit didn't look strong enough to come back from these thrashing, violent fits.

Dovewing shook her head, her face despairing. "If I were a better mother, I'd know what to do," she went on. "Maybe if I had more experience with kits . . ."

"You're a very good mother," Tawnypelt meowed firmly. "Every mother sometimes feels like she doesn't know enough to take care of her kits. Look at me: I raised three kits, but I don't know how to help Shadowkit, either." She nudged Dovewing gently. "You can't blame yourself."

Dovewing sighed, her tail drooping. "He's had such a hard life so far," she said, her voice bleak. "He was born away from the lake, among strangers, all because I dreamed that the ThunderClan nursery wasn't safe. And then we brought him and his littermates on a long, dangerous journey back to the Clans. He saw Spiresight die, and they were so close. And it's been hard for him, learning to live in a Clan. Not every cat has welcomed my kits. Now this. He's sick and I don't know what to do. Are we right to take him so far? On this dangerous journey? What if we don't make it up the mountain? What if we do, and the Tribe still can't help him?"

"I don't know," Tawnypelt admitted. She felt terribly sorry for Dovewing. "Raising kits is hard," she mewed carefully. "You never *do* know if you're doing the right thing, not while you're doing it."

"No," Dovewing agreed, wrapping her tail tightly around herself.

"But those things you talked about—leaving the lake, then coming back home—those were decisions you made because you thought they were right for Shadowkit and the others, weren't they?"

"Of course," Dovewing said, her green gaze shining. "My kits mean *everything* to me."

A pang shot through Tawnypelt. She thought of Flame-tail, her shy, sweet-tempered ginger kit, always eager to help his Clanmates, who'd grown to be a medicine cat and then drowned in icy waters; of Dawnpelt, who'd as a kit been fierce and playful by turns, who'd left ShadowClan for the Kin and been murdered by Darktail. And of stubborn, good-hearted Tigerstar. Her kits meant everything to her, too, and now Tigerstar was the only one left. She closed her eyes and took a deep breath, letting the sorrow rush through her, then opened them and looked at Dovewing again.

"The hardest lesson I've learned as a mother is that you can't control what happens to your kits," she told the younger cat. "All you can do is love them, and guide them, and try to do what you think is right for them when you can. That's what you're doing. You're a good mother."

Dovewing looked back at her, her tail gently twitching as she thought. "Thank you," she mewed at last. "That means a lot. It helps."

They sat in the grass, huddled close together for warmth, and watched over Shadowkit as he slept. The silence between them felt more comfortable now.

After a while, Shadowkit opened his eyes, stretched, and yawned. "I'm feeling better now," he announced. "Are we going onto the mountain?"

Tawnypelt got to her feet, looking up at the narrow ledges they would have to travel to reach the Tribe. She brushed her tail over the kit's back and exchanged a glance with Dovewing. "We'll go as soon as you're both ready."

CHAPTER SIX

Ice crackled beneath Tawnypelt's paws with every step. "I thought you remembered how to get to the cave," she meowed, trying to keep the frustration out of her voice. She raised her paw and shook it to loosen the snow stuck between her paw pads. Her legs were scratched and raw from all the times she'd slipped and lost her footing. It felt as though they'd been climbing up the narrow, icy path forever.

"We must be close. I can hear the waterfall," Dovewing answered. Tawnypelt flicked her ears and then, above the roar of the wind, she could hear the rush of water, too, quite close, but she couldn't see it. The sound echoed off the stones all around them, making it impossible to know which direction it came from.

So close, and yet so far.

She felt exhausted—both physically and mentally. The path was treacherous, but even more exhausting was their worry for Shadowkit, and the constant struggle to keep him safe. Each time he'd slipped, Dovewing or Tawnypelt had lunged forward to grab him by the scruff. Each time he'd groaned or cried out in frustration, Tawnypelt's breath had stopped, and she'd braced herself for another of his fits. Each time a shadow had darkened her vision, she'd cringed and searched the sky for a swooping predator. For a while, it had seemed impossible to her that the three of them would survive this journey with their wits intact. In their frustration, she and Dovewing had started to snap at each other, until they were both so tired that they just fell silent.

Now they were in a narrow, winding cleft between huge boulders. *At least we're safe from eagles,* Tawnypelt thought, looking up to where a black dot circled lazily, high in the sky. "Stay close, Shadowkit," she warned, glancing down at the kit between them. The snow was up to his belly and he looked tired and cold, his tail drooping, but he wasn't complaining.

As they came around a bend, the cleft abruptly ended, sheer gray rock rising ahead of them.

Tawnypelt craned her neck, her heart sinking. She had leaped to the top of boulders like this, the first time she had come to the mountains, but they hadn't been covered with slippery ice. And there was no way Shadowkit could climb up there, even with help. "We'll have to turn back and find another way," she realized, her heart sinking.

Before Dovewing could reply, a growl came from above.

"Who are you?" A lithe young she-cat leaped from the rock overhead and landed in front of them, her teeth bared and ears flat. "You're on our territory." Her pale brown fur was bristling as much as it could beneath smeared patches of mud.

The mud is to hide her from the eagles, Tawnypelt remembered, relief surging through her body. *We've reached the Tribe!*

Shadowkit was pressing close against his mother, frightened of the hostile young cat. Tensing, Tawnypelt prepared to argue. *We've made it this far—now we have to get to Stoneteller.*

"Hold on, Breeze," another voice called. Looking up, Tawnypelt saw several faces peering down at them. "Dovewing, is that you?"

"Snow?" Dovewing called back. With a thump, a white she-cat, her fur barely visible beneath a coat of mud, landed in front of them.

"This is Dovewing," she said to the younger she-cat. "She comes from the Clans, far away in the flatlands. She's a friend to the Tribe." Turning to Tawnypelt, she dipped her head and held out a paw in a gesture Tawnypelt remembered from her last visit to the Tribe. "I am Snow Falling on Stones, and this is Breeze That Rustles the Leaves, a cave-guard to-be."

Tawnypelt dipped her head to them in response and introduced herself and Shadowkit. "I came here with Stormfur, a long time ago, and then with the Clans when we journeyed to our new home," she added.

"You know Stormfur?" Breeze's ears perked up. "He and Brook are my parents!"

"We both know your parents well," Tawnypelt mewed. Stormfur, born a RiverClan cat, and Brook, born in the Tribe, had lived with ThunderClan by the lake for a while before going back to the Tribe at last.

"You must be a younger sister of Lark and Pine," Dovewing commented. "They were kits the last time I saw them. And Snow, you were a to-be when I was here before, but I guess now you're a cave-guard?"

"Yes, I am. We were patrolling the border," Snow said, with a concerned glance at Shadowkit. "But I think getting you back to the cave is more important." She looked up at two cat faces still peering down at them from above. "Moss! Night! Meet us by the thornbush."

As they followed Snow back through the icy crevice between the boulders, Breeze looked down at Shadowkit. "Are you all right to walk a little farther?" she asked.

Shadowkit waded through the snow with his head held high. "I'm very strong and brave," he told her. "I'm a *Shadow-Clan* cat." Despite the icy wind, Tawnypelt was warmed by the pride in his mew.

Snow glanced at Dovewing. "Our kits stay in the cave until they become to-bes," she said with a trace of accusation. "It's dangerous out on the mountain, especially during frozen-water."

"I know," Dovewing replied solemnly. "Our kits usually stay in camp until they're old enough to be apprenticed, too, but this is important. We have to talk to Stoneteller."

The sun was low in the sky by the time they reached the pool at the bottom of the waterfall at last. A steady wall of water crashed down the mountainside, its thunder so loud that Tawnypelt's ears rang.

"It's beautiful," Shadowkit murmured, staring up at it. Sunshine reflected off the falling water, making it shimmer. Where the waterfall pounded into the pool below, a cloud of white mist rose all around, dampening the cats' fur. Shadow-kit turned to peer up into Tawnypelt's face with anxious amber eyes. "But so dangerous."

"Do you recognize it?" Tawnypelt asked, hoping that the kit would say yes. *I need to know this is right.* "Is it the place from your vision?"

The kit squinted at the waterfall and then sighed. "I'm not sure. I only saw part of it. . . ."

Tawnypelt remembered how Shadowkit had trembled and called out, "It's falling!" He'd been seeing a tree going over this waterfall, hurting the Tribe. As they helped Shadowkit up the rocks that led behind the waterfall to the cave's entrance, she and Dovewing exchanged a worried look.

The Tribe of Rushing Water's cave was just as she remembered it. It rose high, as high as the top of the waterfall, and long fangs of rock grew down from the ceiling, high above them. Sunlight shone through the waterfall, giving everything a flickering, dreamlike quality.

I was so young the last time I was here, Tawnypelt thought. She and Rowanclaw hadn't become mates yet; she had barely become a warrior. She and her companions had shared a single focus: finding the Clans a new home. *It was frightening then, but it's good to look back on. Our whole lives were ahead of us.*

Around the edges of the cave, small groups of cats chatted or shared tongues. They quieted as the Clan cats followed the cave-guards into the cave, some standing to get a better look at them. Shadowkit looked around curiously, his eyes bright.

"Dovewing? *Tawnypelt?*" A long-legged gray tom hurried toward them, his tail twitching excitedly. "It's been a long time."

"Crag!" Tawnypelt cried. "I mean, Stoneteller." She had heard that Crag Where Eagles Nest was now the Teller of the Pointed Stones. But it was hard to believe that the earnest young cave-guard she had met on her first visit was now the Tribe's leader and healer, their link to the ancestors who guided them, the Tribe of Endless Hunting.

"It is good to see you both, and to meet this fine kit," Stoneteller mewed warmly after Dovewing had introduced Shadowkit. "But what brings you here?"

Dovewing's gaze was earnest. "Stoneteller, my son had a vision that we think concerns your Tribe. You need to know what he saw, and we hope that you can help him, too."

Glancing over her shoulder, Tawnypelt saw that the eyes of the Tribe were fixed on them. "Can we talk in private?" she asked, dropping her voice.

"Of course. Follow me." Stoneteller turned, heading for a narrow tunnel entrance in the side of the cave.

Inside the next cave, Shadowkit gazed around in wonder, staring at the pale pointed stones that grew up from the floor or down from the ceiling, some meeting in the middle to form what looked like thin, twisted trees. Sunlight fell from a crack high in the cave's roof, throwing long shadows across the floor and glinting off the small pools of water that lay here and there between the stones.

"What is this place?" Shadowkit asked, his eyes wide. He

stepped out from between Tawnypelt and Dovewing for the first time, wandering forward to look up at the rocky ceiling and tentatively dabble a paw in a cool puddle of water.

"This is the Cave of Pointed Stones," Stoneteller explained calmly. "I read the signs of nature here. The fall of a cobweb, the sound of a bird's cry, and the glimmer of moonlight on water all have meaning. In this way, I can understand the guidance of our ancestors, the Tribe of Endless Hunting."

Shadowkit's ears perked. "So you're like a medicine cat?"

"Sort of," Dovewing told him. "Stoneteller is the healer for the Tribe and he speaks to their ancestors, but he's also the leader who tells everyone what to do, like Tigerstar does."

"Wow!" The kit looked at Stoneteller with respect. "That's a big job!"

Tawnypelt and Dovewing both purred with amusement. Stoneteller brushed his tail across the kit's back. "I can tell you're a smart kit," he said. He looked at Dovewing. "He's got a strong spirit, despite his small size."

"I'm going to be a medicine cat," Shadowkit said calmly. "StarClan lets me see things that other cats can't."

Stoneteller sat down near the largest puddle, his eyes thoughtful. "Is this why you've come?" he asked.

Dovewing and Tawnypelt looked at each other. "Like Dovewing said, Shadowkit has been having visions we think are about your Tribe," Tawnypelt began.

"They are, I'm sure of it," Shadowkit broke in. "The waterfall looks just like in my vision." He looked up at Stoneteller appealingly. "There was a huge, huge tree. And it came right over the waterfall and part of it went into the cave and *hurt cats*. You have to protect them."

Stoneteller looked worried. "Did your vision give you any clues about when this will happen?" Shadowkit shook his head, and Stoneteller went on. "I believe that you saw this, but there are no big trees near the waterfall that could fall like that. It's mostly scraggly thorn trees and bushes so high on the mountain. And I can't tell the Tribe to leave the cave during frozen-water, not without knowing for how long. It's too dangerous and cold without our cave's protection."

Shadowkit nodded. "When I have the vision again, I will try to find out," he mewed earnestly.

Tawnypelt's stomach lurched. She didn't want to think about Shadowkit having that vision again. She remembered how he had thrashed and wailed, clearly in pain. "Since Shadowkit's vision is of the Tribe," she added, "we hoped that meant you would be able to help him, too."

"He . . ." Dovewing hesitated, and Tawnypelt could tell she was trying to think of a way of describing Shadowkit's fits without letting the kit know how worried they were about him. "Shadowkit says the visions make his head hurt—don't they, Shadowkit? And then his body shakes and he falls down."

"It makes him very tired," Tawnypelt went on, keeping her voice as calm as Dovewing's. *We shouldn't scare Shadowkit.* She could tell from the glint of concern in Stoneteller's eyes, though, that he realized how frightening Shadowkit's reaction to the visions must be.

Stoneteller crouched down, his gaze level with Shadowkit's.

"I'll have to see if I can help you with that—all right, Shadow-kit?" Looking up at Dovewing and Tawnypelt, he added, "I think it's best if I speak to Shadowkit alone for a little while."

Dovewing hesitated, but Tawnypelt could see the trust in Shadowkit's eyes as he gazed at Stoneteller. "It'll be all right, Dovewing," she murmured softly. "Come with me."

She walked back toward the tunnel to the larger cave, and, after a moment, Dovewing followed.

There were more cats in the cave now that the sun was sinking toward the horizon. The prey-hunters and cave-guards who had been out on the mountain had returned for the night. Kits were chasing one another through the wide-open spaces of the cave, while the older cats shared tongues or chatted quietly.

Unfamiliar cats' faces turned to watch Tawnypelt and Dovewing with interest, and the two Clan cats hesitated.

"Dovewing!" a friendly voice called, and then another.

"Is Jayfeather with you?"

"How is Lionblaze?"

Dovewing brightened. "Moss!" she called in greeting. "Sheer!"

Tawnypelt peered at the cats half-hidden by the cave's shadows. Had it really been so long since she was here that she wouldn't recognize any cat? She stepped closer. Among the elders, wasn't that Bird That Rides the Wind?

"Tawnypelt!" a warm voice meowed, and a brown tabby she-cat rose gracefully to greet her.

"Brook!" Tawnypelt cried. "I'm so pleased to see you."

Beside Brook, she saw a familiar dark gray tom. "Stormfur, how are you?"

The two once-Clan cats made room for her to sit beside them. "We heard from Breeze that you two had arrived," Stormfur explained. "I hope there's nothing wrong back at the lake?"

"No, we had some difficulties, but things are all right now," Tawnypelt mewed. *Are they?* she wondered. *Yes. There is peace among the Clans, even if I'm not sure where my place is in the new ShadowClan.* "Tigerheart is the leader of ShadowClan now," she added. "He's become Tigerstar. And he and Dovewing are mates."

"The little kit belongs to Tigerstar and Dovewing, then? It must have been hard bringing a kit up through the mountain," Brook commented.

"We wanted Stoneteller to have a look at him," Tawnypelt explained. Changing the subject—their worries over Shadowkit weren't hers to spread around—she added, "And you've had more than one litter of kits since I last saw you, haven't you?"

"Yes," said Stormfur proudly. "You met Breeze, and that's her littermate, Feather of Flying Hawk, over there." He gestured with his tail at a stone-gray cat practicing fighting moves with some other to-bes on the other side of the cave.

"And these are our first litter, Lark That Sings at Dawn and Pine That Clings to Rock," Brook said.

Two cats sitting nearby broke off their conversation and dipped their heads politely to Tawnypelt.

"They were only kits the last time any cat from the Clans

was here, but they've grown to be fine cave-guards." Stormfur meowed.

"Like their father," Brook added, and Stormfur purred and gave his chest fur a bashful lick.

"You seem very happy," Tawnypelt told them both. It was true. Like the rest of the Tribe, they were a bit thinner than Clan cats, but their coats were sleek and their expressions full of warm contentment.

"We are," Brook agreed. "Things have been good in the mountains."

"You don't miss the Clans?" Tawnypelt asked. Despite having lived in ThunderClan, Brook had been born in the Tribe and could be expected to be happy here. But Stormfur was a Clan cat, who had only stayed with the Tribe because of his love for Brook.

"Not really." Stormfur wrapped his tail more comfortably around his hind paws. "It was an accident that I ever came here, but it was a lucky one. This is where I belong."

"But they made you leave," Tawnypelt pointed out, puzzled. The old Stoneteller had exiled Stormfur after he had led them in a disastrous battle. He and Brook had lived with Thunder-Clan for moons before they were finally able to return.

Stormfur shrugged. "I forgave Stoneteller for that long ago, and we were friends before he died. This place has been home in a way the Clans never were for me."

"Why?" Tawnypelt was puzzled. "You were born in Riv-erClan." As troubled as she'd felt in ShadowClan lately, she couldn't imagine living anywhere else. Was it possible for a cat to just . . . *leave* the place she'd always called home? And be happy somewhere else?

"I was a half-Clan cat," Stormfur told her. "A paw in RiverClan, a paw in ThunderClan, and never quite accepted in either. Life is simpler here, without all the Clan rivalries and distrust. I mean, you're a half-Clan cat, too. Didn't you ever feel that way?"

"No," Tawnypelt replied automatically. "I chose ShadowClan. I knew it was my home." *But is that true?* She'd been born in ThunderClan and had left because she hadn't felt they'd ever accept her. And she'd fought hard, determined to be a loyal ShadowClan warrior. But now ShadowClan was changing. *Is it still my home?*

"Tawnypelt's deputy of ShadowClan now," Dovewing put in, breaking off from her conversation with Snow.

"That's great, Tawnypelt," Brook purred warmly. "And Dovewing, now that you and Tigerstar are mates, you must be in ShadowClan, too."

"Yes." Dovewing looked down at her paws. "It was . . . hard leaving ThunderClan. We didn't see for a long time how we could be together, not if we wanted to be accepted by either of our Clans."

And so you left, Tawnypelt thought, with a pang of sympathy. *And it took StarClan to bring you back.*

"Clans," Bird, the gray-brown elder, scoffed. "You cats at the lake only make trouble for yourselves by dividing into Clans. You should go where your heart lies."

Once, Tawnypelt would have flicked her ears dismissively:

What did a Tribe cat know about Clans? But now she stilled, doubts filling her. *Where does my heart lie?* she wondered. *Is it still with ShadowClan . . . now that Rowanclaw is dead? And Dawnpelt and Flametail, too?*

"Dovewing! Tawnypelt!" There was a patter of small paws, and Shadowkit flung himself between them. "The Cave of Pointed Stones is full of moonlight, and it's so amazing!"

Tawnypelt felt her heart warm at the sight of the kit. *He does hold a piece of my heart. . . .*

Stoneteller followed Shadowkit across the cave. "I've been trying to read the signs the Tribe of Endless Hunting has for us," he explained. "I still don't know exactly what Shadowkit's vision means, but I *am* sure that he's seeing the Tribe and is here for a reason. We'll keep working together to figure it out. And I hope we can also help him control the symptoms he's been having with his visions." Noticing that the cats around them were listening, he raised his voice a little. "In the meantime, Dovewing, Tawnypelt, and Shadowkit are our honored guests. And now it is time to eat."

Around the cave, cats jumped up and hurried toward the fresh-kill pile. Unlike Clan cats, who ate whenever they liked, Tribe cats ate only one meal a day, together. When Tawnypelt had been here as a young warrior, she had been glad the Clans didn't wait to eat together: When she wanted a mouse, she wanted a mouse. But now, as she looked around at the cats settling down to share a meal, it seemed . . . nice.

Breeze hurried up to Tawnypelt and placed a vole in front of her. Glancing beside her, she saw that other to-bes were bringing Dovewing and Shadowkit prey as well.

"Would you like to share prey with me, Dovewing?" Stone-teller asked. She purred in agreement, and they each took a bite of the prey before them, then exchanged, Stoneteller's mouse going to Dovewing, her sparrow to him.

"I like the way they do that here," Shadowkit said. "Will you share with me, Tawnypelt?"

"Of course," she said affectionately, and they each took a bite and then exchanged their prey. *I like it, too,* Tawnypelt decided, looking around at the cats peacefully eating and sharing their meal.

What must it be like, all being from the same Tribe? There were a few rogues in the mountains, Tawnypelt knew, and that was why the Tribe patrolled their borders, but there were no divided Clans continually arguing over territory, distrusting kits who were neither one Clan nor the other.

No deaths in battle here, Tawnypelt thought. It was a hard life in the mountains, she was sure: vicious eagles swooping from above, unforgiving peaks and sheer cliff faces. But cats did not kill cats.

Darktail would never have come here. This territory is too harsh for him—he wanted the rich prey of the lake.

If Darktail had never come, ShadowClan would never have been torn apart. Dawnpelt and so many others would not have died. Without Darktail's death, no cat would have sought to avenge him.

If we were cats of the Tribe, Rowanstar would still be alive.

The tender sparrow suddenly felt dry in Tawnypelt's mouth.

A gust of cold air blew through the waterfall, a fine mist of cold water falling over the cats. Shadowkit squeaked in surprise.

"A storm's coming," Stoneteller said, "and it is just warm enough to bring rain, not snow. Stay away from the cave entrance until it passes."

The cats were finishing their meal and breaking into smaller groups, the kit-mothers gathering their kits and heading for the nurseries. Other cats were settling down in the nests dug in the dirt floor at the edges of the cave.

"We should sleep, too." Dovewing yawned. Tawnypelt's paws ached with tiredness; it had been a long day.

"I think that Shadowkit should sleep in the Cave of Pointed Stones so that I can watch over him," Stoneteller said.

Dovewing looked at her kit, her gaze uneasy. "He's used to sleeping with me in the nursery," she said slowly.

"Perhaps we could all sleep in the Cave of Pointed Stones?" Tawnypelt suggested, and Dovewing let out a sigh of relief.

"Of course," Stoneteller agreed, then added, "but a kit with such strong visions will travel far from his mother one day."

Dovewing's eyes widened with alarm. Tawnypelt brushed her tail across Dovewing's back. "But not yet," she whispered, and Dovewing twitched her ears gratefully.

We lose our kits soon enough, Tawnypelt thought, thinking of Dawnpelt and Flametail, gone to StarClan. And Tigerstar, who had been a full-grown cat for a long time now. *Let Dove-wing keep hers just a little longer.*

They settled on nests of eagle feathers and moss in the Cave of Pointed Stones, steering clear of the crack in the ceiling through which rainwater streamed. Tawnypelt shut her eyes. Outside, thunder rumbled, and inside, the water dripped steadily. She could hear the waterfall pounding outside, more powerful than ever. The steady rushing rhythm lulled her to sleep.

"No! No!" High-pitched screeching—*a kit in trouble*—jolted Tawnypelt out of her sleep.

"Shadowkit?"

"Shadowkit!"

She and Stoneteller jumped from their nests and rushed toward the kit. Moonlight showed Shadowkit, fur on end, standing in his nest, his eyes stretched wide with horror. Beside him, Dovewing seemed frozen in alarm.

"We have to get them out!" he yowled. "Every cat has to get out of the cave! Now!"

Chapter Seven

❧

"Get out! Get up! Now!" Shadowkit's frantic yowls echoed through the main cave as he burst out of the tunnel from the Cave of Pointed Stones.

Tawnypelt pounded after him, Dovewing and Stoneteller close behind.

"You have to get out of the cave!" Shadowkit screeched, running to the closest nest and leaping on the huddled figure inside. The cat in the nest—*Lark*, Tawnypelt thought—gave a startled squeak and pushed him away.

All around the edges of the cave, confused voices rose from different nests.

"What's going on?"

"Who *is* that?"

"Shadowkit? Are you having a bad dream?"

"Go back to sleep!"

Tawnypelt was nearly close enough to grab the kit by the scruff, but suddenly he reversed course, wriggling underneath her and racing from one nest to another, pummeling the cats with his paws. "You have to leave the cave! *Now!* You're in terrible danger!"

They're not going to listen to a kit. Tawnypelt ran forward and shook the cat in one of the nests. "He's not just dreaming," she said. "You have to wake up."

She could hear Dovewing waking another cat. "I'm sorry, but we have to get moving."

Stoneteller's voice rose above the commotion in the cave. "Every cat on your paws. Shadowkit has had a vision that we are in danger."

Obediently, the Tribe cats began to climb out of their nests, blinking and yawning in the near darkness. A to-be ran off down a side tunnel and returned with a few kit-mothers, their kits whining sleepily around their paws.

"A vision?" Bird meowed. "Why would a cat from the Clans have a vision about us? The Tribe of Endless Hunting doesn't have anything to do with the Clans."

"We don't really have to leave the cave, do we?" Pine yowled anxiously, and several cats chimed in.

"It's pouring!"

"Listen to the thunder out there! Can't we wait until the storm lets up?"

A flash of lightning lit up the cave, and every cat flinched. The rain outside intensified.

"Shadowkit was sent here for a reason," Stoneteller meowed solemnly, raising his voice to be heard over the storm. "Even though I don't quite understand either, I think we need to listen to him. We must leave the cave." He led the way toward the cave mouth, his head ducked low against the water blowing in. Behind him, the cats looked at one another in shock, then slowly began to follow.

The Teller of the Pointed Stones never leaves the cave, Tawnypelt remembered, a sense of relief washing over her. *Stoneteller must really believe in Shadowkit's vision. I was right to bring him.*

Something pressed against her side, and she looked down to see Shadowkit gazing up at her.

"Let's keep him between us," Dovewing said from his other side, sounding grim. "I don't like the look of that storm."

As they stepped through the cave mouth, cold water drenched Tawnypelt's fur, making her gasp in shock. With the storm, the waterfall had increased terribly in size: the narrow path of rocks that usually ran behind the water was soaked, heavy water pounding steadily against it. A harsh wind blew through the waterfall, cutting through the cats' wet pelts and chilling them to the bone.

Tawnypelt scrambled to stop herself from falling as her paws slipped. Instinctively, she and Dovewing moved closer together, almost pinning Shadowkit between them to keep him from being blown off the path.

Past the waterfall, things were no better. The combination of the storm and the pounding of the waterfall was deafening, and the cats huddled together miserably, straining to hear Stoneteller's yowl.

Stoneteller looked down at Shadowkit, his gaze trusting. "Now what?" he asked, raising his voice above the howl of the wind and the steady pounding of the water.

Shadowkit shut his eyes for a moment, shivering with cold. *He's too young,* Tawnypelt thought, her heart heavy with doubt and worry. *He doesn't know what these visions mean.*

Then Shadowkit opened his eyes. "We have to get to the riverbank," he announced without a trace of doubt. With his tail, he gestured to a steep, narrow trail that wound up the cliff beside the waterfall.

Up there? Tawnypelt thought with horror. The path, which looked like it would be treacherous and slippery at the best of times, was awash in rushing, muddy water.

"Are you *sure*?" Stormfur turned to Stoneteller, his face full of dismay and his voice almost a howl. "That's a dangerous path!"

"*All* of us?" one of the nursing kit-mothers wailed. "We can't take the kits up there!"

Shadowkit wheeled to face her, his eyes wide and sure. "It'll be more dangerous for any cat who stays down here," he yowled.

"We must do this," Stoneteller said with a calm certainty. "I will go first." He stepped toward the path.

Stormfur stared at him for a moment, and then sighed and shook his pelt. "Right," he yowled. "A couple of strong cave-guards right behind Stoneteller. Kits and kit-mothers and elders—and you, Tawnypelt, you're not used to the mountains—in the middle. Swiftest prey-hunters right behind them: You're fast and sure enough to catch a falling kit. More cave-guards at the back. Nose to tail, and be ready to grab any cat who slips."

Shivering, water dripping from their fur, the cats followed his direction. The kit-mothers crouched, letting their kits climb up onto their backs, and Dovewing lowered her belly to the ground, too. "Shadowkit, hold on to me with all your strength," she warned as he scrambled onto her back.

The path was rough beneath Tawnypelt's paws, small stones and grit slipping under her so that it was impossible to get any kind of grip on the rocks. Dovewing's tail brushed her nose, and Tawnypelt's muscles tensed, ready to leap to the rescue if Dovewing or Shadowkit slipped. She could feel Brook close behind and was grateful for her, and for the Tribe cats following her—without them, it would be a long, painful fall back down if she slipped.

It was a difficult climb, even harder than she would have predicted. Her claws ached from trying to find a hold on the rocks, and ice-cold water streamed over her face, almost blinding her, and dripped from her whiskers.

Once, a cat ahead of her slipped and skidded a few tail-lengths back, knocking the cats behind her one into the other. Dovewing fell back onto Tawnypelt, who felt her own paws skidding backward into Brook.

But no cat fell, and a moment later they were all pressing forward again, straining against the wind and rain.

At last, her paws sore and her soaking fur plastered against her sides, Tawnypelt followed Dovewing as the path led them to a thin strip of level ground above the waterfall.

Almost touching their paws, the stream rushed past, swollen to river size and overflowing its banks, then plummeted over the cliff. Leaves and sticks were swept along by the current, speeding past the cats before disappearing swiftly down the waterfall. Dovewing crouched to let Shadowkit off her back and then herded him away from the water's edge, placing herself between her kit and the tumultuous water.

"Now what?" Stormfur yowled.

Shadowkit stepped forward. "This is the place," he said, looking around. "We have to pile rocks in the stream. If we can build a strong enough barrier, we can stop the tree from falling."

"*What* tree?" Night wailed, and turned to Stoneteller. "This is crazy. The water's too strong; we can't get *into* it."

"The Tribe of Endless Hunting wouldn't have set us an impossible task," Stoneteller meowed. "Shadowkit has seen what we must do."

There was a long moment of hesitation. The Tribe cats stared at Stoneteller, their thin sides rising and falling quickly beneath their soaked and matted fur.

"There's no time to waste!" Shadowkit yowled, but no cat moved.

I believe in Shadowkit, Tawnypelt thought. There was a rock that rose almost to her shoulder by the edge of the stream, and she braced her paws against it and pushed. The stone shifted. Gathering her strength, she pushed again, and the rock slid toward the river.

Another pelt brushed hers. "Together," Dovewing meowed, and put her paws beside Tawnypelt's on the rock. They heaved, and the stone tumbled into the river. Behind her, Tawnypelt sensed the other cats moving. A little farther upstream, Stormfur's stocky shoulders worked as he forced a boulder into the water. Lark and Pine were working together. Every cat was scrabbling at the surface of the banks, working their paws beneath the stones to loosen them, shoving with legs and flanks. They were soaked, exhausted, and plastered with mud, but determined.

"Faster! Please!" Shadowkit yowled, pacing back and forth beside the river.

As more rocks were pushed into the edges of the water, the current changed, flowing faster still as it was forced into a narrower channel. Tawnypelt began to roll another rock farther into the river. As she stepped into the water, the current slammed into her, pushing her hard against the rock. She braced herself and moved on, her side aching from the blow. Stormfur followed her, shoving a rough chunk of stone ahead of him, and a broad-shouldered cave-guard came behind him.

Stoneteller was in the water, too, his eyes slitted against the storm, fiercely determined.

We're doing it. Already, a line of stones ran almost all the way across the river, water splashing against and pouring over them.

"Roll one along here," Breeze yowled. The to-be was right in the middle of the river. A wave of water washed over her back, but she braced herself and waded toward the rock Night was pushing toward her.

Suddenly, a fresh wave of water hit Breeze head-on. The to-be slipped and disappeared under the surface.

"Breeze!" Brook yowled in horror from the riverbank. The young cat's head popped up and she gasped for breath before being pulled under again and swept quickly toward the waterfall.

"Breeze!" Brook and Stormfur and several other cats plunged into the water, but Tawnypelt was closest. Diving forward, she sank her teeth into the scruff of Breeze's neck. The weight of the to-be's struggling body made her stagger a few steps toward the waterfall, her stomach lurching with fear. Bracing her legs against the bottom of the river, she steadied. Dragging Breeze with her, Tawnypelt fought her way to shallower water, where Breeze was able to get her paws under her again.

"Th-th-thanks," Breeze stammered, shivering with cold.

"You saved her!" Brook yowled, wading out to them and looking her daughter over for injuries.

"We can never thank you enough, Tawnypelt," Stormfur said solemnly, brushing his cheek against hers. At the joy in her old friend's eyes, Tawnypelt felt warm inside despite the freezing-cold water soaking her fur.

"There's no time!" Shadowkit was staring upstream, his amber eyes wide and his fur fluffed out into spikes. Instinctively, Tawnypelt and the other cats turned to follow his gaze.

The horizon seemed dark and empty. "What is—" Dovewing began to ask.

CRACK! Thunder boomed at the same time as a flash of bright white light dazzled them, followed by the sound of something heavy hitting the water in the distance. Tawny-pelt's fur stood on end, the fizz of lightning running through her. "That was close," she muttered.

"Look!" Stoneteller's meow was horrified.

Far upstream, a huge dark shape was in the water, rapidly being borne toward them.

"It's a tree. A tree from higher up the mountain," Stormfur said, sounding stunned.

"It's huge!" Bird whimpered.

"We have to get more rocks into the stream," Stoneteller ordered. "Quickly. If a tree that big goes over the waterfall, it could destroy the whole cave."

Panicking now, the cats waded into the water, pushing more stones into the heaped-up line in the river. Tawnypelt shoved a stone into place, her muscles straining, and imme-diately turned to help maneuver another, bracing it against one beneath the water. Her heart was pounding. *No time, no time.* What would the Tribe do if they lost their cavern? How would they survive a winter, homeless in the mountains?

The dark shape was closer now, sweeping around a bend in the river.

"Get out of the water!" Stoneteller yowled. The tree was too close; there was nothing more they could do. Either the rocks would hold the tree back, or the Tribe's cave would be lost.

Tawnypelt raced with the others to the riverbank, then wheeled around, staring at the tree as the river flung it toward them. Her heart was pounding and her mouth was dry with panic.

What if we waited too long to listen to Shadowkit? We should have been here sooner. . . .

Have we done enough?

CHAPTER EIGHT
❧

The tree hurtled toward them, its branches spread so wide that they scraped along both sides of the riverbank. Flinching, Tawnypelt crouched low and squeezed her eyes shut.

Please, please, she begged StarClan, *help the Tribe save their cave.*

There was a horrible cracking noise, and Tawnypelt's eyes shot open. The tree was huge, as big as one of the oaks back in the woods by the lake, and it dangled half over the drop to the waterfall. Its branches creaked and the tree shifted from one side to the other as the current pulled it, but it had caught on the rocks.

"It worked . . . ," Bird mewed, sounding stunned.

"Shadowkit's vision has saved us," Stoneteller added solemnly.

As one, the Tribe turned toward Shadowkit, their eyes shining with wonder.

"Thank you so much, Shadowkit," Snow purred, and the other cats began to chime in with their own gratitude. Tawnypelt felt warm with pride.

Shadowkit, suddenly shy, looked around at the cheering cats and opened his mouth as if to speak. Then he wobbled and fell, his small legs folding beneath him.

Oh, no. Tawnypelt hurried toward the unconscious kit, but Dovewing reached him first. She bent to nose at his still form and then looked up at Tawnypelt.

"He's passed out again," she cried, her voice desperate. "Why does this keep happening?"

Tawnypelt looked down at Shadowkit's still form. He was breathing steadily, his eyes closed. "I don't know," she said. "I thought things would be better, once his vision came true."

Stoneteller joined them, brushing his tail comfortingly along Dovewing's back. "He's done what he needed to do," he said. "It only makes sense that his body needs rest. He's been pushing himself hard."

"He's only a kit," Dovewing yowled helplessly.

"It's rare for such a young kit to have such strong powers," Stoneteller agreed. "He will wake before long, I am sure."

Tawnypelt gently nosed Shadowkit's shoulder. Rain was running thorough his fur. *Poor kit,* she thought. What Stoneteller said was true: Shadowkit was so young to have such a powerful connection to StarClan. She had never heard of a cat having visions like this at such a young age. *StarClan's given him a heavy burden.*

"We've done what the Tribe of Endless Hunting wanted of us," Stoneteller said to the gathered cats. "Now let's get out of this storm."

As the kit-mothers of the Tribe helped their kits to scramble back up onto their backs, Dovewing bent and gently picked up Shadowkit by his scruff.

"I'll go in front in case you slip," Tawnypelt said.

The climb down was less strenuous, but they all moved slowly over the slippery rocks, nose to tail as before. Tawnypelt placed her paws carefully. With a sigh of relief, she finally reached the pool outside the cave and turned back in time to watch Dovewing safely arrive in the clearing as well, Shadowkit still unconscious.

A strange cracking noise and the rumble of shifting rocks came from above. Up near the top of the path, Lark turned to look behind her. "The tree is moving!" she howled, her face twisted with horror.

The cats already in the clearing below stared up, terrified.

"If it falls now, it'll kill us all," Night said.

"We haven't stopped it," Moss said. "We need to climb back up and get out of the way!"

The cats already behind the waterfall froze, unsure what to do. Another ominous cracking sound came from above.

"There's no time," Brook said, her voice tight.

"Have faith," Stoneteller said. He was standing still at the edge of the pool, gazing up the waterfall. While every other cat was panicking, his voice was calm. "The Tribe of Endless Hunting chose Shadowkit to save us. If we weren't safe, he would be awake."

Tawnypelt saw the Tribe cats exchanging doubtful glances. She *wanted* to believe that Stoneteller was right, but as she looked at Shadowkit's limp form, she couldn't help worrying.

Did we bring Shadowkit here just to get him, and us, and the Tribe killed? Maybe his visions weren't real. Maybe he was too young to understand what StarClan and the Tribe of Endless Hunting had tried to show him.

She had believed in Shadowkit. But so many things Tawnypelt had believed in—*ShadowClan, Rowanstar, my own kits*—had been doomed to fail.

She could see the tips of the tree's branches hanging over the top of the waterfall. Tawnypelt's heart stuttered as another loud crack came from above, and a few loose branches tumbled down into the pool.

The branches landing in the frothing water seemed to act as a signal, and the Tribe cats bolted back toward the path up the sheer rock. Tawnypelt ran with them, her heart pounding, pushing Dovewing along ahead of her.

The cats at the top of the path were yowling. "It's coming loose!"

"It's going to fall!"

There's no chance we'll all make it out of the way in time, Tawnypelt realized. Below, cats were rushing back and forth across the clearing, unsure whether they would be better off hiding in the back of the cave or trying to make it high enough on the path that the tree wouldn't crush them.

The tree creaked louder than before. Tawnypelt was just high enough to see it slide forward, the water pushing it over the rocks. Branches were hanging over the side of the waterfall, and the enormous trunk began to tilt slowly, water streaming down its sides.

It's too late, Tawnypelt thought, her stomach hollow with fear.

There was a crash of thunder, impossibly loud. Bright white light burst blindingly around them. Tawnypelt's fur stood on end.

She blinked hard, and her vision cleared. Sticks and scraps of bark were raining down into the clearing. The cats by the pool screeched and ran, dashing behind the waterfall or sheltering at the clearing's edge. Tawnypelt saw a couple of large pieces go over the waterfall, but they caused no damage.

The massive tree was gone.

"Lightning must have hit it," Stormfur said, his voice hoarse with shock.

"We stopped the tree for just long enough," Brook said in wonder. "Shadowkit's vision saved us after all."

A squeak made Tawnypelt turn. Still dangling by his scruff from his mother's mouth, Shadowkit was blinking sleepily. "What happened?" he asked.

He's all right. Tawnypelt felt weak with relief. *We did the right thing. The Tribe is safe, and so is Shadowkit.*

CHAPTER NINE

Weak morning sunlight was shining through the crack in the roof of the Cave of Pointed Stones when Tawnypelt opened her eyes. She could hear the rush of the waterfall outside, but no more rain was falling. *The storm must be over.*

She stretched and got to her feet, shaking feathers and moss from her pelt. Dovewing and Shadowkit were awake, too, curled together and talking softly. Stoneteller was sitting in his own nest, looking thoughtfully at the light reflecting off pools of water beneath the tall stones.

"Good morning," he said, dipping his head to them all. After they replied, he went on, "I'd like Shadowkit to stay in here with me for a little while today. I've been trying to read the signs the Tribe of Endless Hunting is sending, and I may be able to help him learn to handle his visions so that they don't cause him so much pain."

"How are you going to do that?" Dovewing asked.

Stoneteller's whiskers twitched. "Let's leave that a secret between those of us who speak to the ancestors," he said, casting a look at Shadowkit. "He will be fine in the end."

Dovewing hesitated, wary, but Shadowkit's chest was

puffed out with pride. "It's a medicine-cat secret," he said. "Don't worry. I'll come find you if I need you."

When Dovewing looked to her for support, Tawnypelt said, "I trust Stoneteller. And Shadowkit must practice standing on his own. Soon enough, he'll be a medicine cat and belong to the whole Clan, not just his parents."

"I suppose so," said Dovewing unenthusiastically, her tail drooping.

Kits grow up, Tawnypelt thought, *even if their mothers aren't always happy about it.*

As they padded into the main cavern—without Shadowkit—Brook came over to meet them. "I thought I'd be exhausted after yesterday," she said, "but I woke up early and couldn't get back to sleep. How is Shadowkit feeling?"

"He slept well," Dovewing told her. "Stoneteller is trying to help him find a way to handle his visions better. Once they're done, we'll begin our journey home."

We will? Tawnypelt thought, surprised. She supposed it made sense: They would have done all they'd come here to do. But part of her ached at the thought of leaving the Tribe. The idea of going back to the resentments and squabbles of ShadowClan made her feel terribly tired.

Maybe Stormfur is right. Maybe life is simpler, and better, here.

"If you're leaving today, we should have a feast first, to celebrate and to thank you," Brook suggested. "I'm sure Stoneteller won't mind if we eat at sunhigh instead of dusk."

"That sounds very nice," Dovewing mewed, looking pleased.

"I'll gather some of the other prey-hunters, and Breeze, Lark, and another cave-guard can come to help protect us," Brook mewed, hurrying across the cave. "Stormfur! Do you want to go hunting?"

"I'd like to come," Tawnypelt said, watching Brook gather cats around her.

Brook cocked her head to one side. "It's very kind of you," she meowed, "but you're our guests of honor! I think you should rest now if you're leaving later today."

"I suppose you're right," Tawnypelt agreed, reluctantly sitting down and licking at her chest fur. She watched as the hunting party slipped out of the cave and disappeared beyond the waterfall. Dovewing was settled on the other side of the cave, chatting with one of the kit-mothers. Tawnypelt knew she'd be welcome to join them, but for now she was happy alone, watching the light flicker through the waterfall.

At last, she got up and left the cave, skirting the waterfall and coming out into the crisp cold sunlit day. She would hunt after all.

Brook and the others were long gone, but Tawnypelt didn't worry. Her paws seemed to know the mountain paths, and her steps were swift and sure. At last she came to the bare top of a mountain and looked out. The air was clear, and she could see so far, past rivers and forests and hills.

The sun glinted off distant water, and Tawnypelt craned her neck. Was that the Clans' lake? She thought so, and she could almost imagine Tigerstar beneath the pines, sending out patrols and organizing the repair of Shadow-Clan's camp. It felt so far away. Is that my home? she wondered, her heart aching.

She hadn't spoken aloud, but a familiar voice behind her answered, "It will be."

"Oh, Rowanclaw." Tawnypelt turned and touched her nose to his. His fur was glimmering with stars, but his amber gaze was as warm as ever. "I miss you so much," she whispered. "All the time."

Rowanclaw pressed his cheek against hers. "You've been such a loyal mate to me," he said. "All our lives together, and even after I left you to join StarClan. I'll always love you."

"I love you, too," Tawnypelt responded. His scent and voice were so familiar, so welcome. She wished it were this easy to conjure him all the time.

"But I'm gone now," Rowanclaw said, his voice turning solemn. "I'm dead, and I'm fine. I'm happy in StarClan. We'll be together there, but not for a long time."

"A very long time?" Tawnypelt asked, her heart aching.

Rowanclaw gave a mrrow of laughter. "Many moons, and you'll be happy again, I promise. But the long life ahead of you means you'll have to adjust. Everything changes—you know that. Even your Clan."

"It's hard to forgive them for turning against you," Tawnypelt said softly.

Rowanclaw sighed. "I have. And they will forgive me, too. I wasn't the one they needed during the dark times. Tigerstar is a good leader."

"I know," Tawnypelt agreed.

"You have to give him a chance," Rowanclaw went on. "Remember what a brave, clever cat he's always been? With you and Dovewing supporting him, he can begin ShadowClan anew."

Tawnypelt shivered, the wind cutting through her fur for the first time since she'd reached the mountaintop. "I'm not sure I can," she said, staring at her paws. "Maybe I should start over somewhere else. Stormfur is right: Things are simpler here. It's a good life, and I think they'd welcome me."

Rowanclaw said nothing. After a moment, Tawnypelt looked up to see him watching her with thoughtful amber eyes. He twitched a whisker, as if in disbelief, and Tawnypelt looked away again. He knew her so well.

"But my home is in ShadowClan," she admitted.

Rowanclaw purred. "Your heart is in ShadowClan, too," he said. "Our Clan is changing, but not all change is bad. Give yourself some time, and give Tigerstar a chance." He stepped forward and nuzzled her cheek, his breath warm on her face. "I love you so much, Tawnypelt," he said. "I always will. But it's time to let me go."

Tawnypelt closed her eyes and leaned into Rowanclaw, feeling his warm, muscular body against hers one more time. He was right, she knew it, but it was hard to step away. "Thank you," she whispered. "Good-bye, Rowanclaw."

"Tawnypelt! Tawnypelt!" Small paws poked at her side, and Tawnypelt jerked awake.

"Great StarClan, Shadowkit," she said, tumbling the kit over with a playful paw. "You're getting so strong, you almost kicked me out of the cave." Blinking away her sleepiness, she saw that the light coming through the waterfall had changed— it was probably midmorning now.

"Sorry, Tawnypelt," Shadowkit meowed. "I was just really excited."

He looked happy, Tawnypelt realized. Not the focused, desperate expression he'd carried since he'd had his vision, but how a kit *should* look: bright eyes, shining pelt. He looked like the kit he'd been before the vision had first come. She looked up at Stoneteller and Dovewing, who were behind Shadowkit at a little distance.

"Shadowkit and I had a long discussion with our ancestors," Stoneteller explained. "I think we've read their signs correctly, and they should help Shadowkit."

"Which ancestors?" Tawnypelt asked. "StarClan or the Tribe of Endless Hunting?" *StarClan* watched over the Clans, and she wasn't sure she liked the idea of Shadowkit getting advice from the Tribe's ancestors instead.

"Both," Stoneteller said, his whiskers twitching as if he could see into Tawnypelt's mind and thought her view was a funny one. "Shadowkit is very unusual. His powers stretch beyond borders, beyond the world that one cat can see."

Tawnypelt felt her ears flattening. "It *hurt* him to see those visions of the Tribe," she pointed out. "And how can he be a medicine cat for *ShadowClan* if he's troubled with visions that aren't about us?"

Shadowkit cuddled against her. "I'm *fine* now," he purred. "I promise."

Stoneteller looked down at the kit, affection clear on his face. "I can't promise visions won't hurt him again," he admitted. "But I think what he and I have discussed will help. He's a good kit. A strong kit. He will do much for ShadowClan."

"Maybe Shadowkit will help to bring all five Clans together," Dovewing suggested quietly. "Isn't that what StarClan wants?"

Tawnypelt twitched her tail. *A cat should be loyal to one Clan.* But she pressed her muzzle to the top of Shadowkit's head. He *was* very special. A warm surge of love filled her. The idea that had come to her in her dream—of staying with the Tribe—was nonsense. She could never leave Shadowkit. Or Tigerstar, or his other kits, or even Dovewing.

"I believe you will show us the way to a new ShadowClan, little one," she purred softly, and Shadowkit nodded proudly.

"I want to be the best medicine cat ever," he declared. "I'll try my hardest."

There was a small commotion at the cave entrance as the hunting party returned, bearing prey. Tawnypelt sniffed the air, the scent of rabbit making her mouth water.

"I'm *starving*," Shadowkit announced, bounding away from her and toward the hunting party.

"Now, Shadowkit, don't be greedy," Dovewing scolded, hurrying after him. "Wait your turn."

"Oh, but he saved us all," Brook mewed, dropping a fat mouse in front of him. "Shadowkit should eat first."

"Thanks," the kit said shyly. "Would you like to share prey with me?"

All the Tribe cats purred with delight at Shadowkit's having learned their custom. "So polite!"

Young Breeze brought Tawnypelt a vole and plopped down next to her. "Shall we share prey?" she asked. Tawnypelt agreed, taking a bite of the vole and then exchanging it for Breeze's rabbit haunch.

"I wanted to thank you again for saving me from the river yesterday," Breeze meowed. "I will always be grateful. The whole Tribe will, for all the help you've given us."

"We had to come," Tawnypelt insisted. "The Tribe has assisted the Clans in the past, and we will help you whenever we can." It was curious, she realized. In some ways, she felt closer to the cats of the mountain than she did to any of the other Clans by the lake.

"The Tribe and the Clans are like two trees that have grown around each other," Stoneteller intoned. "Both are strong, and they are intertwined, but each has its own future. Still, the Clan cats will always be welcomed by the Tribe."

"Thank you," Tawnypelt mewed, feeling deeply touched. Dovewing's and Shadowkit's eyes shone as they also offered their thanks.

It seemed like too soon when it was time to go. The Tribe gathered around them, touching noses and offering affectionate farewells and advice for the return journey.

"Be careful in the mountains, little one," Night advised Shadowkit.

"Watch out for eagles," Moss added anxiously. "Here, let's smear some mud on your fur. Then we'll show you the best way down."

Tawnypelt did her best to stay still as the Tribe cats smeared her pelt with cold mud, then moved to brush her cheek against Stoneteller's. "Thank you so much for helping Shadowkit," she said. "I think he's on the right path now." The kit seemed happier and lighter, bouncing between his new friends.

"And you, too, I think," Stoneteller said, looking into Tawnypelt's eyes. "You've found your path again, haven't you?"

"I suppose I have," Tawnypelt said. She could feel something deep inside, pulling her in the right direction. "The right path leads back to where my heart lies. Back to ShadowClan."

She looked at the waterfall—so beautiful, so dangerous, but not her home. *It was foolish to think it ever could be,* she realized now. She couldn't imagine a home without the feathery shadows of pine trees, their strong resin scenting the air. *ShadowClan is where I belong.*

She glanced at Dovewing, who nodded, looking pleased. Tawnypelt nodded back, and together, she and Dovewing, Shadowkit safely between them, turned toward the waterfall. It was time to go home.

CHAPTER TEN

Compared to the cold, sheer stone of the mountain during frozen-water, leaf-bare by the lake was almost warm. As they walked past the border with ThunderClan, Tawnypelt sniffed the air appreciatively. She could smell the familiar scent of the lake water and the trees, a hint of pine. There was a richness of prey, too, and the well-known scents of individual cats. The Clan territories smelled like home. *Now that I'm here,* she thought, *I can't imagine that I ever really wanted to leave.*

"I think we'll be back to ShadowClan's camp before sunset," she told Dovewing and Shadowkit. Shadowkit gave a hop of excitement and walked faster, but Dovewing's steps slowed.

"Are you all right?" Tawnypelt asked her, concerned.

Dovewing stared down at the ground as she walked, her head hanging low. "Do you think Tigerstar will forgive me?" she asked quietly. "Do you think he'll understand why we had to go?"

Tawnypelt felt an answering tightness in her chest. She had been trying not to think about the possibility that Tigerstar might still be angry with them. "I'm sure he'll understand

once he sees how much better Shadowkit looks," she mewed
hopefully.

"Maybe," Dovewing said, sounding unconvinced.

Tigerstar loves Dovewing, Tawnypelt thought. *And he respects her.
Enough to be willing to leave ShadowClan. He'll forgive her.*

"Tigerstar is our leader," she told Dovewing. "But you're
Shadowkit's mother, and you had to do what was best for your
kit. You made the right choice, and Tigerstar will see that. If
not immediately, then soon."

Dovewing's ears perked up a little. "Thanks, Tawnypelt."

"What are you doing?" Two ThunderClan cats—Fernsong
and Rosepetal—suddenly approached from around a bush,
and Tawnypelt's fur bristled instinctively.

"We're not on your territory," she snapped.

"That's not what I asked," Fernsong retorted, twitching his
tabby tail.

"We're collecting herbs for Puddleshine," Tawnypelt lied.
Why should I tell a ThunderClan cat my business?

Fernsong looked dubious, but Dovewing broke in. "How
are Ivypool and the kits?" she asked eagerly.

Fernsong's voice warmed. "They're doing very well," he
mewed. "They're such clever little kits. She'd like you to come
see them again." *Of course,* Tawnypelt remembered. Dovewing's sister was Fernsong's mate.

"And is this one of *your* kits?" Rosepetal asked, looking
down at Shadowkit. "Surely he's not an apprentice yet?" Her
tone was friendly, but curious.

"Not quite," Shadowkit replied, gazing up at her. "But I want to be a medicine-cat apprentice."

"And so we're finding herbs," Dovewing added cheerfully.

Rosepetal nodded, looking slightly confused. "Well, we'd better keep patrolling," she meowed. "Mind you stay on your side of the border."

"Give Ivypool and everyone my love," Dovewing said, and watched as the two ThunderClan cats disappeared into the underbrush. Her face was a little forlorn.

It's hard to leave your family and your Clan behind, Tawnypelt thought with a pang of sympathy. When she had decided to join ShadowClan, the worst thing had been leaving her brother, Brambleclaw.

She came closer to Dovewing and brushed her cheek gently against hers. "We're both still grieving a little, aren't we?" she mewed quietly. "Me for Rowanclaw and the old ShadowClan, you for ThunderClan."

Dovewing leaned against her for a moment, letting Tawnypelt support her. "Yes," she agreed. "It's good to have some cat who understands that."

They stood together for a little while, and then Dovewing straightened, as if she'd found new strength. "Come on, Shadowkit," she called. He was stalking a leaf across the grass. "It's time to go home."

Side by side, the two cats, with Shadowkit following, headed toward ShadowClan at last.

* * *

They made it across the ShadowClan border without running into any patrols and slipped quietly through the tunnel into camp.

Berryheart was watching all the kits—hers and Dovewing's and Yarrowleaf's—tumble around the clearing, and she was the first to see them. "Dovewing!" she yowled, leaping to her feet. "Tawnypelt! You're back! And Shadowkit, too!"

The clearing became pandemonium, cats dashing out of the warriors' and apprentices' dens.

"Where have you been?"

"Did you really go all the way to the Tribe?"

"Shadowkit looks better—is he okay now?"

"We were so worried about you!"

Their Clanmates were brushing their tails over their backs, touching noses, pressing cheeks together, as if they were assuring themselves that Tawnypelt, Dovewing, and Shadowkit were really back—that this wasn't all some crazy dream.

Then a gradual hush fell over the clearing. Tigerstar had emerged from the leader's den. He took a slow step forward, then another, his amber eyes locked on Dovewing. Returning his gaze, her steps equally hesitant, Dovewing came to meet him in the center of the clearing.

They both looked devastated, Tawnypelt realized, their eyes full of heartache and hope. Once again, she was reminded of Rowanclaw. Of how she'd loved him. The memory still hurt, but maybe someday it wouldn't anymore.

"Tigerstar! Did you miss me?" Shadowkit shot forward, crashing into his father's legs and breaking the tension between his parents. Tigerstar purred.

"Of course I did. But how can this huge cat be my little kit? You've grown so much I hardly recognize you, Shadowkit."

"That's silly," Shadowkit said, his tail standing straight up. "We haven't even been gone for half a moon."

"It seemed much longer," Tigerstar mewed, glancing at Dovewing again, his eyes soft.

"A *lot* happened to us," Shadowkit said. "My vision was right!" He began to tell Tigerstar about the mountains and the Tribe of Rushing Water, and about all the adventures he had had. Tigerstar listened patiently, occasionally bending to touch his muzzle to the top of his son's head.

"So your mother and Tawnypelt took you to the Tribe, and you saved them," he summarized at last, when Shadowkit had reached the end of his story. "And Stoneteller was able to help you."

"That's right!" Shadowkit agreed proudly. "Stoneteller said I was *special*, because I can see things that happen to other cats, not only ShadowClan."

"I think you're going to have a very interesting future, my kit," Tigerstar mewed. He glanced up at Tawnypelt and Dovewing, and Tawnypelt could see concern in his eyes. *It isn't comfortable to hear that your kit is different,* Tawnypelt thought. *Even though you're proud of them.* Then he straightened and spoke to Tawnypelt directly. "Part of being a good leader is admitting when you're wrong," he said. "I should have listened, Tawnypelt. And I shouldn't have tried to stop you. I knew you had Shadowkit's best interests in mind, and I wish I had trusted you."

"I wish I had trusted *you*," Tawnypelt replied. "I should have tried to convince you again instead of running off with Shadowkit." She felt a great swell of relief, as if something tight that had been holding her back had finally loosened. "I'm just glad Shadowkit's okay."

"Thanks to you and Dovewing," Tigerstar purred.

"And," Tawnypelt added, "I have an announcement to make." She felt sure at last, as if her path were laid out in front of her. "I've decided to step down as deputy."

"No!" Tigerstar cried. "You're the best cat to help me run ShadowClan. No one knows this Clan better than you do."

But Tawnypelt shook her head. "ShadowClan is changing. It makes sense to choose a new deputy. Someone who will be the future of our Clan instead of the past."

Tigerstar still looked worried. "I'll think about it," he mewed slowly. "Choosing a new deputy isn't something to take lightly."

"I'll help you for as long as you want me to," Tawnypelt offered. "But I'm sure you'll make the right choice."

Tigerstar didn't say anything, his tail drooping. But Tawnypelt wasn't worried. *Soon he'll see that a younger deputy will be better for him than his mother—I can't quite stop seeing him as my kit, no matter how strong a leader he becomes.*

"Want to share some prey, Tawnypelt?" Dovewing offered. "I'm so hungry after our long journey."

Tawnypelt suddenly realized that she wasn't hungry, but she was *exhausted*. "No, thanks," she replied. "What I need is a nap."

She slipped into the warriors' den. Settling into her nest, she looked back out the entrance at the cats gathered in the clearing. Shadowkit was playing with Pouncekit and Lightkit and the other kits of the Clan, squealing with delight as they chased one another around the clearing. Tigerstar and Dovewing were sharing a rabbit, their heads close together as they talked. Scorchfur, Blazepaw, and Juniperclaw were lying in a patch of sun, all three purring with laughter. Berryheart, one eye on the kits, was resting her head on Cloverfoot's flank.

It was a Clan at peace.

Tawnypelt curled up more tightly, closing her eyes. She scented the air, picking out the familiar smells of the cats she knew, the scents of ShadowClan.

I'm home.

WARRIORS

SHADOWSTAR'S
LIFE

ALLEGIANGES

SHADOWCLAN

LEADER **SHADOWSTAR**—black, thick-furred she-cat with green eyes

DEPUTY **SUN SHADOW**—black tom with amber eyes

MEDIGINE GAT **PEBBLE HEART**—gray tabby tom with white mark on his chest and amber eyes

HUNTERS **JUNIPER BRANCH**—long-furred tortoiseshell she-cat with green eyes

RAVEN PELT—black tom with yellow eyes

MOUSE EARS—big tabby tom with unusually small ears

MUD PAWS—pale brown tom with four black paws

BUBBLING STREAM—white she-cat with yellow splotches

DANGLING LEAF—black tom with an orange tail

SHADE PELT—dappled brown tom

DUSK NOSE—tortoiseshell she-cat

THUNDERCLAN

LEADER **THUNDERSTAR**—orange tom with big white paws

DEPUTY **OWL EYES**—gray tom with amber eyes

MEDIGINE GAT **CLOUD SPOTS**—long-furred black tom with white ears, white chest, and two white paws

HUNTERS

VIOLET DAWN—sleek dark gray she-cat with bits of black around her ears and paws

PINK EYES—white tom with pink eyes

LEAF—black-and-white tom with amber eyes

MILKWEED—splotchy ginger-and-black she-cat with scar on muzzle

CLOVER—ginger-and-white she-cat with yellow eyes

THISTLE—ginger tom with green eyes

GOOSEBERRY—pale yellow tabby she-cat

YEW TAIL—cream-and-brown tom

APPLE BLOSSOM—orange-and-white she-cat

SNAIL SHELL—dappled gray tom

BLUE WHISKER—white she-cat with yellow splotches

APPRENTICES

HAZEL BURROW—black-and-white tom

MORNING FIRE—dark brown she-cat with amber eyes

SHIVERING ROSE—black she-cat with white splotch on one ear and amber eyes

KITS

PATCH PELT—ginger-and-black tom kit

BEECH TAIL—pale ginger she-kit

WINDCLAN

LEADER

WINDSTAR—wiry brown she-cat with yellow eyes

DEPUTY

GORSE FUR—thin gray tabby tom

MEDICINE CAT

MOTH FLIGHT—white she-cat with green eyes

DUST MUZZLE—gray tabby tom with amber eyes

SLATE—thick-furred gray she-cat with one ear tip missing

WHITE TAIL—dark gray tom-kit with white patches and amber eyes

SILVER STRIPE—pale gray tabby she-kit with blue eyes

BLACK EAR—black-and-white patched tom-kit with amber eyes

SPOTTED FUR—golden-brown tom with amber eyes and a dappled coat

ROCKY—plump orange-and-white tom with green eyes

SWIFT MINNOW—gray-and-white she-cat

REED TAIL—silver tabby tom with a knowledge of herbs

JAGGED PEAK—a small gray tabby tom with blue eyes

HOLLY—she-cat with prickly, bushy fur

STORM PELT—mottled gray tom with blue eyes and thick bushy tail

DEW NOSE—brown splotchy tabby she-cat with white tips on nose and tail, yellow eyes

EAGLE FEATHER—brown tom with yellow eyes, broad shoulders, and striped tail

WILLOW TAIL—pale tabby she-cat with blue eyes

SKYCLAN

LEADER

SKYSTAR—light gray tom with blue eyes

DEPUTY   **SPARROW FUR**—tortoiseshell she-cat with green eyes

MEDICINE CAT   **ACORN FUR**—chestnut-brown she-cat

HUNTERS   **STAR FLOWER**—she-cat with thick, golden tabby fur

DEW PETAL—silver-and-white she-cat

FLOWER FOOT—she-cat with tan stripes

THORN—splotchy brown tom with bright blue eyes

QUICK WATER—gray-and-white she-cat

NETTLE—gray tom

BIRCH—ginger tom with white circles of fur around his eyes

ALDER—gray, brown, and white she-cat

BLOSSOM—tortoiseshell-and-white she-cat with yellow eyes

RED CLAW—a reddish-brown tom

HONEY PELT—striped yellow tom

RIVERCLAN

LEADER   **RIVERSTAR**—silver long-furred tom with green eyes

DEPUTY   **NIGHT**—black she-cat

MEDICINE CAT   **DAPPLED PELT**—delicate tortoiseshell she-cat with golden eyes

HUNTERS   **SHATTERED ICE**—gray-and-white tom with green eyes

DEW—gray she-cat

DAWN MIST—orange-and-white she-cat with green eyes

MOSS TAIL—dark brown tom with golden eyes

DRIZZLE—gray-and-white she-kit with pale blue eyes

PINE NEEDLE—black tom-kit with yellow eyes

SPIDER PAW—white tom

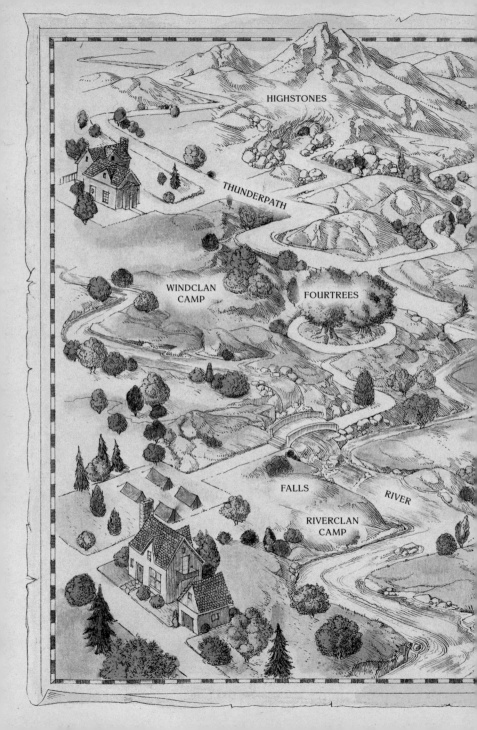

HIGHSTONES

THUNDERPATH

WINDCLAN
CAMP

FOURTREES

FALLS

RIVER

RIVERCLAN
CAMP

CAT VIEW

SHADOWCLAN
CAMP

THUNDERCLAN
CAMP

SKYCLAN
CAMP

NORTH

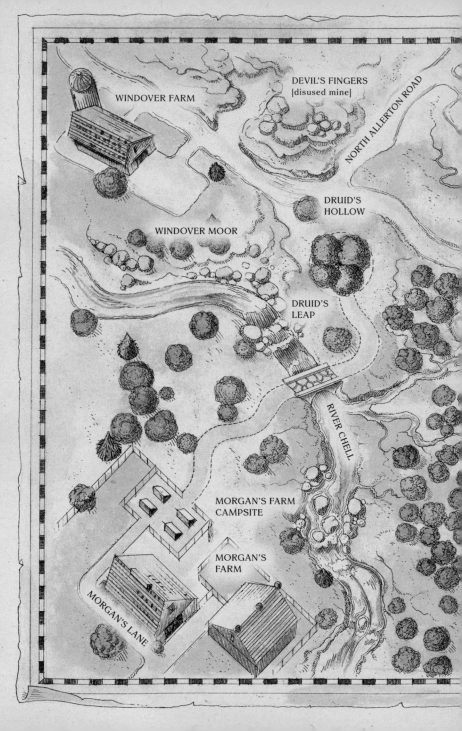

WINDOVER FARM

DEVIL'S FINGERS
[disused mine]

NORTH ALLERTON ROAD

DRUID'S
HOLLOW

WINDOVER MOOR

DRUID'S
LEAP

RIVER CHELL

MORGAN'S FARM
CAMPSITE

MORGAN'S
FARM

MORGAN'S LANE

NORTH ALLERTON
AMENITY TIP

TWOLEG VIEW

WINDOVER ROAD

WHITE HART WOODS

NORTH

CHAPTER ONE

❧

"*I think you should wait and* see what happens," Shadowstar told Skystar. Her old friend, the SkyClan leader, stood next to her, watching the last of the ShadowClan cats begin the walk home from Fourtrees. "It's hard to know what Twolegs will do. . . ."

Distracted, she trailed off as her medicine cat, Pebble Heart, glanced back at her and at ShadowClan's deputy, Sun Shadow. Shadowstar twitched her ears, signaling that he should lead the Clan back to their camp. She and Sun Shadow would stay behind to calm Skystar down.

Skystar bristled, his tail slashing through the air. "It's quite clear to *me* what these Twolegs are doing," he mewed bitterly, "even if the other leaders don't seem convinced. Every day, my patrols report the same Twolegs on our land, looking around as if they're marking territory. I think they're drawing their own borders."

"I know you do," Shadowstar replied patiently. Skystar had spent much of tonight's full-moon Gathering explaining his concerns about the Twolegs. "But why would Twolegs want your territory? They have their own places."

Skystar sighed, his shoulders drooping. "You don't understand. You would feel differently if it were ShadowClan's territory at risk. At least promise me that if the Twolegs keep patrolling on SkyClan's territory, you'll stand with me at the next Gathering. We'll need to convince all five Clans to act together."

"Of course I will," Shadowstar promised, touching her nose to his. *But I'm sure I won't have to. What could Twolegs want in the forest?*

She and Sun Shadow at last said good-bye to Skystar and headed out of Fourtrees toward their own camp. The full moon hung high overhead, lighting their path through the darkness, and Shadowstar matched her pace to her deputy's, both running lightly through the night. In the moonlight, Sun Shadow's slender, dark-furred shape reminded Shadowstar so much of her brother, Moon Shadow.

Shadowstar sighed. Lately she'd been thinking of her littermate, Sun Shadow's father, so often. Moon Shadow had been the cat she'd felt closest to, and he'd died—horribly, in a fire— not long after they had traveled from the mountains to the forest, many seasons ago. *Part of me died with him,* she thought now.

She wished that Moon Shadow had lived to see the life she and the other cats from the mountains had built here: their five thriving Clans, the peace between them, and the fine hunting around their territories, so different from the starvation they'd fled. They'd found the future they'd been hoping for when they left the mountains, but her brother had not been with them to enjoy it.

Sun Shadow, who'd arrived from the mountains long after Moon Shadow's death, had never known his father. But he had Moon Shadow's determination and pride. *He'll be a brave leader one day,* Shadowstar thought. When she lost her final life—far in the future, she hoped—he'd guide ShadowClan well.

They'd crossed the Thunderpath onto ShadowClan land and were surrounded by pine trees when Sun Shadow suddenly stopped, sniffing the breeze.

"What is it?" Shadowstar asked, halting beside him. Before her deputy could answer, she scented it herself. "Dogs!" The thick, meaty scent made her wrinkle her nose in disgust, even as her chest constricted with tension. *What are dogs doing on our territory?*

"Do you think our Clanmates could have run into them heading back to camp?" Sun Shadow asked, his mew sounding much younger and less sure of himself than usual.

Shadowstar tasted the air. She could scent that several dogs had been here very recently, and ShadowClan would have passed this way on their way home. "There's no fear-scent," she said hesitantly, "no blood or anger. I don't think our Clanmates met the dogs."

"Thank StarClan," Sun Shadow said. Then a rough bark sounded in the distance—*not distant enough,* Shadowstar thought—and he stiffened. More barks and howls joined in. Sun Shadow's eyes rounded with fear. "They're coming this way. What should we do?"

Shadowstar thought quickly. *No dogs should be taken lightly, but those barks are deep enough to come from large dogs. We have to lead them away from ShadowClan's camp.* "Let's head back toward the Thunderpath," she decided. "Maybe they won't be able to track our scents over the Thunderpath stink."

Together, they hurried back toward the edge of Shadow-Clan's territory. The full moon was beginning to move down the sky, throwing long shadows across the ground. As she crossed beneath the low-hanging branches of a pine tree, Shadowstar's pelt prickled and the fur on her back rose. It felt like unfriendly eyes were watching her. Hesitating, she looked up into the tree, her steps slowing.

The branches above her were empty. The smell of the dogs was stronger than ever, and a howl sounded close behind them.

"What is it?" Sun Shadow hissed.

"This way," Shadowstar told him, turning to run parallel to the Thunderpath. "Let's put some distance between us and our camp." Flicking her tail, she dismissed the odd feeling of being watched. *Who could it be?* There had been peace between the five Clans for many moons now, and no rogue or loner would dare attack a Clan cat on their own territory.

The snarls and howls were louder now, the dogs eagerly following their scent. *They're going to catch up with us,* she thought. Flattening her ears, she ran faster, Sun Shadow by her side.

Four dogs burst out of the trees behind them, barking. Shadowstar's heart pounded, and her breath was quick and shallow. *We should have climbed up onto a branch,* she thought, but there was no time now, and they were away from the trees, the hard surface of the Thunderpath beneath their paws. She stretched her legs and ran her fastest; they were almost to the

Twoleg bridge. *Maybe they won't chase us far.*

A fifth dog, a shaggy brown one even bigger than the rest, stepped out of the shadows to block their path. It snarled, showing sharp white teeth. Shadowstar and Sun Shadow skidded to a stop, their claws scraping the Thunderpath. Panting, they started to double back—but the dogs who had been chasing them were too close now, their jaws gaping and their tails waving. Their scent was overwhelming. *Where are they coming from?*

The warriors pressed together, craning their necks to watch all five dogs. Crouching low, Sun Shadow hissed, and an answering growl came from the dogs. Two were black, both almost as big as the shaggy brown one. One was medium-sized, close-furred, and brown, and one was smaller and white with curling fur, its pink tongue dangling as it panted eagerly.

She could feel Sun Shadow trembling.

"Let's take on the smallest one together," Shadowstar murmured quickly. "Then we'll head for the trees. Once we're up a tree, they won't be able to reach us." The largest dog was coming closer, growling gutturally.

Sun Shadow nodded and took a deep breath. "I'm ready," he mewed, his voice quiet.

Shadowstar tensed her hindquarters. "Now!" she yowled, and dashed toward the white dog, Sun Shadow a blur of motion beside her.

Shadowstar swiped her claws across the white dog's face, and it flinched backward, blood running from the scratch. Sun Shadow launched himself at the dog's side, clawing at its shoulder, and it turned, yelping, to face the new threat.

"Go!" Shadowstar jumped onto the dog's back and dug in her claws. It howled, twisting and snapping, trying to reach her, and Sun Shadow dived between its legs and came out behind it, dashing toward the trees. The other dogs were barking in confusion and rage.

Balanced on the dog's back, Shadowstar looked toward the trees, gauging how far she'd have to run. For a moment, she thought she saw amber eyes—cat eyes—blinking at her from the shadowed branches. Was help coming? But the eyes didn't move. They just watched. Shadowstar leaped from the dog's back, heading for safety.

In midair, she was suddenly jerked back, a sharp pain shooting through her hindquarters. One of the larger black dogs had caught her in its jaws as she jumped. *Like prey,* she thought, horrified, and twisted to claw at its muzzle. Her vision clouded with agony.

The dog snarled, shaking her as she tried desperately to run, her forepaws churning. Through her shock, Shadowstar could see Sun Shadow near the tree line, looking back in horror.

Run, she thought desperately, *run! ShadowClan needs you.*

Sun Shadow turned and began to run—*back,* toward the dogs, toward Shadowstar.

No! she thought, and then everything went dark.

The sun was warm on Shadowstar's back. The pain was gone. She lay still for a moment, her eyes closed, breathing in the rich scents of prey and growing plants all around her.

She knew where she was.

Those dogs killed *me,* she thought, outraged. *Now I have only one life left.*

When Windstar's daughter Moth Flight had told the Clans' leaders that StarClan had given them each nine lives, guaranteeing they would be able to take the risks a leader must and still have all the moons they'd need to guide their Clans, Shadowstar had been dubious. How could a cat die more than one death? But then she had died—after an attack by a badger—and gone to StarClan and woken again, healed, with a memory of this warm, green place.

She had died eight times: from the badger's attack, a miserable coughing illness, a Twoleg monster on the Thunderpath, and a fight with a rogue before the Clans had fully established their rights to the forest. She'd fallen from a tree while hunting, she'd been swept away by the river—she'd saved a kit from drowning, so it had been worth it—and she'd had an infected wound that even Pebble Heart hadn't been able to treat. And now these mangy dogs.

Only one more life.

It would be fine, Shadowstar reasoned. Most cats—*all* cats who weren't Clan leaders—had only one life. All through the long struggle to find territory and establish her Clan, those terrible moons when all the cats seemed to turn their claws against one another, she'd had only one life.

Still, she now felt vulnerable. As if a great owl were hovering above her, its talons outstretched.

Most cats have only one life, she reminded herself again.

Most cats. Shadowstar's heart gave a sickening thud. *Please, StarClan, please let Sun Shadow have gotten away.*

But when she opened her eyes, her heart sank. Sun Shadow was on his feet beside her, blinking nervously at two cats who stood before him. *The dogs killed him, too.* "Gray Wing?" he asked tentatively. "But you're . . ." He turned to face the other cat, a black tom. "And I don't know *you.*"

Shadowstar climbed to her paws and pressed her shoulder against his. "This is your father," she mewed gently, taking in her beloved brother's outline, now glittering with faint stars. "Hello, Moon Shadow. It's been a while. Hello, Gray Wing."

Both StarClan toms dipped their heads to her, their eyes warm with affection. Shadowstar turned to face Sun Shadow, and now she noticed the stars shining in his fur, too. "I'm so sorry," she told him. Guilt flooded through her. *I should have protected him.*

"It's not your fault. You told me to run. But I couldn't leave you to fight them off alone." Sun Shadow's amber eyes were wide. "But . . . I'm dead? I don't remember exactly. . . ."

Moon Shadow stepped forward and brushed his cheek against his son's. "I've been watching you since you came to the forest," he meowed gently. "I'm so proud of you. This is where you belong now."

"It is?" Sun Shadow looked at Shadowstar anxiously, his ears twitching. "But what about ShadowClan?"

"We will watch over them together," Moon Shadow told him with a purr. "Come with me."

Hesitantly, Sun Shadow stepped toward him. In a moment, they were gone, leaving a trail of starry paw prints in the grass. Shadowstar looked after them, aching inside. Whatever Sun Shadow said, she should have been able to prevent his death. She was his leader. What would she do without her deputy?

In the grass at some distance, she could see a faint black shape. Herself, stars glimmering in her fur. Each time she came here, the shape was a little clearer, a little firmer. Next time, it would *be* her.

She brushed her tail against Gray Wing's. "I only have one more life," she mewed.

"I hope it'll be enough." Gray Wing's expression was grim.

Alarm stirred inside Shadowstar. "What do you mean?" she asked.

Gray Wing shook his head. "I don't know what it will mean for ShadowClan, or for any of the Clans, when you die," he told her, his gaze steady. "None of us do. A leader's never lost all nine lives before. I hope that ShadowClan will be strong enough to survive your loss. If ShadowClan falls apart, it could destroy all the Clans."

Shadowstar shuddered, suddenly chilled. She'd founded ShadowClan. She'd brought all those cats together and built their life in the pine forest. Would they stay together without her? The feeling of vulnerability was back, stronger than before. One life was such a fragile, temporary thing.

And it wasn't just her own life that was at stake. It was also the life of her Clan.

CHAPTER TWO

❧

Vroooom.

At the sound of a Twoleg monster roaring by, Shadowstar opened her eyes. She was lying in the grass near the side of the Thunderpath, not far from the Twoleg bridge. Dawn was breaking, soft pink and golden clouds at the horizon.

For a moment, Shadowstar felt as if she were waking from a long, good sleep. She got to her feet and arched her back, stretching her paws in front of her, enjoying the loosening of her muscles.

Then her eyes fell upon the bridge, and she pictured the fierce dog stepping out from the shadows, its teeth bared.

I died, she remembered with a shudder. Gray Wing's worried face came back to her.

When I'm gone, not even StarClan knows what will happen to the Clans. There *had* to be five Clans. That was one thing they'd learned as they had fought against one another and then come together at last. If ShadowClan fell apart at Shadowstar's death, then all the Clans might be destroyed.

Of course, that was why she, and every leader, had named

a deputy. *But . . .* Her stomach gave a sickening twist, and she looked around.

Sun Shadow lay in the grass a little way off. He looked as though he could have been sleeping, his eyes closed, his face peaceful. But a long gash ran along his belly, and his fur was matted with blood.

"Oh, Sun Shadow," she whispered, pressing her muzzle against his shoulder. "I'm so sorry." He was cold, and the stench of blood and dog overlaid his own familiar scent. Her deputy, her friend, her kin, killed by *dogs*. Rage and sorrow flooded through her, and she dug her claws into the grass.

"Shadowstar!"

Raising her head at the call, she saw a black tom hurrying toward her from the pine trees. For a moment, it looked like Sun Shadow.

"Where have you been?" the tom yowled, and Shadowstar felt her shoulders sag. It wasn't her deputy—of course it wasn't. It was Raven Pelt, a loyal ShadowClan warrior, and his yellow eyes were bright with concern.

"You and Sun Shadow never came home last night," he said. "Half the Clan's out looking for you. I—" He halted, catching sight of the dead body at her paws. "What *happened*?"

In as few words as possible, Shadowstar told him how they had been attacked. Her chest ached with sorrow as she spoke. "I will wait with Sun Shadow," she said at last. "Go find some warriors to help carry him back to camp. We need to say good-bye."

* * *

The sun was setting, and Sun Shadow's body lay in the center of camp. Pebble Heart had cleaned his wounds as well as he could, but the impression Shadowstar had gotten at dawn, that Sun Shadow could be sleeping, was gone now. He didn't look anything but dead.

She dipped her head to touch her nose gently to her deputy's forehead and then spoke. "Sun Shadow first came to the forest as a young cat, searching for his father. Even though Moon Shadow was gone, he found his kin here. More than that, he found his Clan. He proved his loyalty many times: in battle, in the hunt, in the way he always put the good of his Clanmates first." She paused, misery rising inside her, and took a deep breath. "Sun Shadow was the best deputy I could have asked for. He was a brave, compassionate cat who cared about every cat in this Clan, and he deserved a better death. He died trying to save me."

From where he sat by Sun Shadow's side, Dangling Leaf raised his head. "Sun Shadow taught me how to catch frogs," he began.

As her Clanmates shared their memories of Sun Shadow, Shadowstar looked around at them all. Juniper Branch and Raven Pelt were huddled together for comfort, Juniper Branch's head resting on her mate's flank. Bubbling Stream's blue eyes were full of sorrow—the young cat had looked up to Sun Shadow. Mud Paws stared mournfully at the ground as Dusk Nose told a story about Sun Shadow and a rabbit. Pebble Heart's amber gaze—

Amber eyes . . .

Shadowstar gasped as she remembered the eyes she'd seen watching her from the dark woods as she fought the dogs. She knew she had not imagined that cold, unblinking gaze. But would one of her Clanmates have looked on as she and Sun Shadow died? Without trying to help? A cold feeling spread through her belly. *Some* cat had watched them die.

Mouse Ear had amber eyes, too. So did Shade Pelt.

Shadowstar barely heard the rest of the stories her Clanmates told as they spent the night watching over Sun Shadow's body. Once the vigil was over and dawn was breaking, she headed for her den, her shoulders tight. *I'm not thinking straight,* she told herself. *Once I've slept, maybe I'll realize that what I'm afraid of can't be true.*

She had almost reached the oak tree that sheltered her den when Mouse Ear fell into step beside her.

"Shadowstar?" the big tabby tom said eagerly. "You must be really tired. I can organize today's hunting patrols if you want."

Shadowstar blinked in surprise. *That was Sun Shadow's job.* "I guess that's okay," she said slowly. "Thanks." Meeting Mouse Ear's amber gaze made the hairs rise on her shoulders, but she pushed the feeling away. *Lots of cats have amber eyes.*

"We should be careful in case those dogs are still sniffing around," another voice said from behind her. Shadowstar turned to see Juniper Branch, her tail held high. "I'll make sure there are extra cats on every border patrol, in case they need to drive them off."

"Okay," Shadowstar said slowly. The two Clanmates were glaring at each other, the tips of their tails twitching. *What's going on?* "Thank you both."

"I'll do anything I can to help my Clanmates," Juniper Branch said, her green eyes bright.

"Me too," Mouse Ear added.

Shadowstar's jaws clenched as a thought struck her. *Are they competing to take Sun Shadow's place?* She could understand wanting to be ShadowClan's deputy and second-in-command, but Sun Shadow hadn't even been buried yet. She opened her mouth to snarl at them—*you need to have more respect for Sun Shadow's memory*—but then changed her mind. Better to let her Clanmates show their true colors. "I'm going to my den," she told them coolly.

"Okay, Shadowstar, get some sleep," Mouse Ear meowed.

"I'll make sure no one bothers you," Juniper Branch added.

Turning her back on them, Shadowstar slipped beneath the oak tree's roots and curled up in her nest. She was very tired.

I won't be rushed into choosing a new deputy, she thought. *I only have one life left, so this choice might be the most important one that I ever make.*

Shadowstar sat outside her den, a breeze ruffling her fur. Nearby, Raven Pelt was sharing a mouse with Dusk Nose. Mud Paws was grooming Dangling Leaf, while Shade Pelt and Bubbling Stream were sorting through herbs, no doubt at Pebble Heart's request. Every once in a while, one of her Clanmates glanced at her, their expressions troubled. Each time she caught them looking, she felt a claw of dread in her belly, wondering if any of them had worked out that she was on her last life.

No cat knows, she told herself. And she couldn't tell them now. Surely, if her Clanmates knew that her next death would be her last, they would form a protective ring around her at all times.

Well, some *of them would. . . .*

It had been three days since they'd sat vigil for Sun Shadow, and Shadowstar knew her warriors worried about how much time she'd been spending in her den, separated from the rest of the Clan. Maybe they thought she was mourning Sun Shadow.

And I am . . . but that's not why I don't want to be with my Clanmates.

She couldn't stop remembering the amber eyes shining out of the dark woods as she fought for her life. And she kept looking at her amber-eyed Clanmates, wondering if one of them . . .

That's ridiculous. If she didn't trust her Clanmates, what use was a Clan?

Juniper Branch scrambled in through the thorn tunnel at the camp's entrance, closely followed by Mouse Ear. There was a long scratch across Mouse Ear's nose, and Juniper Branch's ear was torn and bleeding.

Shadowstar jumped to her feet, her worries forgotten. "What happened?" she asked, hurrying over to inspect their injuries. "These were made by another cat. Did some cat cross our borders?"

Is another Clan attacking us, after such a long time of peace? A chill ran through her. *Is this how I'll lose my final life?*

Mouse Ear looked embarrassed. "No," he admitted. "We fought each other. Juniper Branch wouldn't listen to me."

"Why should he tell me where to hunt?" Juniper Branch snarled. "I'm a better hunter than he is."

"Because I know our territory better than you do," Mouse Ear growled back. "I've been with ShadowClan ever since we came here."

Juniper Branch began to reply, but Shadowstar had had enough. "Quiet!" she snapped. "What kind of mouse-brains are you two?" Both cats looked indignant, but she went on before either could reply. "Because of your foolishness, you didn't catch any prey. You *failed* your Clan. Now someone else will have to hunt, because you were too busy fighting to do your duty."

"This is your fault," Mouse Ear growled at Juniper Branch. "You're the one who started the fight."

Juniper Branch snarled and swiped at him, reopening the scratch across his nose. Hissing, the big tabby leaped at her, tumbling the smaller tortoiseshell onto the ground.

"Stop it!" Raven Pelt, Juniper Branch's mate, charged toward them, quickly followed by Mud Paws and Dangling Leaf.

They pulled the snarling cats apart. Blood was running down Juniper Branch's cheek, and a patch of fur was missing from Mouse Ear's shoulder. They glared at each other, their tails slashing from side to side.

"You're acting like stupid kits," Mud Paws yowled,

exasperated. "Why would you fight like this?"

Juniper Branch snarled at him. "Stupid kit yourself," she hissed. "You always stick up for Mouse Ear, even when he's wrong."

Mud Paws narrowed his eyes. Before he could retort, Raven Pelt stepped up beside his mate protectively, his ears pressed back in anger.

They're practically at each other's throats, Shadowstar thought, dismayed. *How will this Clan stay together without me?*

She stepped between Juniper Branch and Mouse Ear and glared around at all the warriors. "No more," she said firmly. "You should be ashamed. Is this how a Clan behaves? Or are you rogues with your claws turned against each other?"

The angry cats' tails drooped. "I'm sorry, Shadowstar," Juniper Branch muttered, and Mouse Ear nodded.

"Go to Pebble Heart's den and let him treat your wounds," she ordered. "After that, you can work *together* and change the bedding in all the nests." Juniper Branch looked as if she was about to object, and Shadowstar gazed at her sternly. "If you two are going to act like kits, you can take on some apprentice duties."

She watched as they hurried off toward the medicine cat's den, looking abashed; then she turned to the rest of her Clanmates. "I'm going to lead a hunting patrol," she announced. "Maybe that way, we'll be able to focus on actually catching some prey. Who wants to come with me?"

"I will," Dusk Nose volunteered quickly, and Bubbling Stream stepped forward to join them. With a nod of approval,

Shadowstar turned and headed for the tunnel, the two younger cats following.

Out in the forest, the familiar pine scent made Shadowstar feel a little calmer. The earth was cool and damp underfoot. She sniffed the air, searching for prey.

"There were a lot of mice over by the Thunderpath yesterday," Bubbling Stream suggested.

"We'll head over there, then," Shadowstar mewed briskly. Her muscles tightened at the idea of going back to where Sun Shadow had died—where *she* had died—but she wasn't going to avoid any part of her own territory.

There was long grass just past where the tree line ended, and Dusk Nose stiffened. "There," he meowed. "In that clump of grass." The air was heavy with the scent of mouse, and Shadowstar could hear several quick heartbeats coming from the grass.

"Drive them out and Bubbling Stream and I will catch them," she told him, and she and the white she-cat slipped forward, passing on either side of the clump of grass where the mice were concealed. Once they were a few steps closer to the Thunderpath, Dusk Nose charged into the grass. Four mice, panicked, ran straight toward the she-cats.

Bubbling Stream pounced at once, pinning one mouse beneath her paws. Shadowstar was a heartbeat too slow to catch the other three and whipped around to leap after them.

They were so close to the Twoleg bridge. For a moment, she expected the shaggy brown dog to step out and block her path. Her heart thumped painfully, and she hesitated.

The mice dashed out of sight.

"What *happened*?" Dusk Nose burst out, and then licked at his chest fur, embarrassed.

Shadowstar shifted uneasily from one paw to another. "I'm just tired," she lied. Both her Clanmates were staring at her with concern, and she flicked her ears at them. "Come on," she meowed. "Let's try a little farther into the woods."

I need to get over this, she thought as she led them farther on. *It's because I can't forget that this is my last life. I have to make sure my Clan is ready to go on without me before I die, but I can't be so afraid of death that I don't act.*

Catching a rich prey-scent, she peered around. *There.* A small squirrel was sitting up, its back to them, clutching a nut.

Shadowstar didn't hesitate this time. She took off, running fast. Excitement shot through her as the squirrel, startled by her movement, began to run too. She could leap before it reached its tree.

Then she stumbled, a blinding pain shooting through her foreleg. Looking down, she realized that she had stepped into a hole and twisted her limb.

I would have seen it if I hadn't been so reckless. But she'd had to charge, hadn't she? Otherwise, she would have frozen up again.

As Bubbling Stream and Dusk Nose hurried toward her, Shadowstar wondered bleakly if she'd lost her nerve for good.

CHAPTER THREE
❧

Shadowstar gingerly lowered her paw, shifting her weight onto her foreleg, then relaxed. It barely twinged. It had taken half a moon, but her leg was finally healed. Still, she knew Pebble Heart would insist on examining it one last time.

As she waded through ferns to the cave beneath the Clanrock where the medicine cat made his den, she could hear him treating one of her warriors.

"Hold still and I'll soon have that out," the gray tabby tom was saying gently. Looking through the cave entrance, Shadowstar saw Shade Pelt holding one paw in the air as Pebble Heart worked a thorn out of his paw pad.

"There," he said cheerfully to the younger cat. "I'll put some comfrey on to help you feel better."

Shadowstar watched as Pebble Heart chewed the comfrey leaves into a paste and licked it carefully onto Shade Pelt's paw. *He cares so much,* she thought. *He's always looking out for every member of ShadowClan.*

The medicine cat's amber eyes glinted as he looked up at Shade Pelt. "Keep off it for the rest of today."

Shadowstar caught her breath. *Amber eyes.* Again she

pictured the cold eyes that had watched her from the forest as she struggled and died.

Pebble Heart would never do something like that. She was quite sure that if she could trust any cat, she could trust Pebble Heart. She had known him since he was a kit, and he was a medicine cat—charged by StarClan with the duty of taking care of his Clanmates.

Shade Pelt limped out of the medicine cat's den, dipping his head respectfully to Shadowstar as she ducked through the entrance.

"How's the leg feeling?" Pebble Heart asked.

"Much better," Shadowstar told him, and stood patiently as Pebble Heart felt it over.

"Not hurting at all?" he meowed at last, and she shook her head. "I think you're fine to go back to hunting and patrolling. But let me know if it bothers you."

"Okay," Shadowstar replied, but she lingered, watching as Pebble Heart tidied his herbs. The medicine-cat den was the most peaceful place in camp.

"Are *you* okay?" Pebble Heart asked as he returned the leftover comfrey to the dried herbs at the side of his den. "You've been keeping to yourself lately."

Shadowstar started to say that she was fine; but then she noticed how heavy her fur felt, and how her worries had filled her head like water. "They just keep fighting," she sighed bitterly. "With Sun Shadow gone, some warriors seem so eager to walk in his paw steps that all they do is compete with each other." Despite having been punished more than once, Mouse

Ear and Juniper Branch were still at odds. "And now other warriors are picking sides in their argument." She swallowed hard, her stomach an unhappy ball. "The Clan's being pulled apart."

Pebble Heart looked into her eyes, his own gaze steady. "Take a moment," he told her. "Breathe deeply." He inhaled a long, slow breath, and Shadowstar imitated him. Together they held the breath for a moment, then gradually let it out. "Again."

After a few repetitions, Shadowstar relaxed a little.

"It's true that not knowing who's going to be your deputy is causing some conflict," Pebble Heart said. "It's been more than half a moon since Sun Shadow's death. Maybe it's time to name his successor?"

Shadowstar hesitated. *I can tell Pebble Heart the truth,* she reminded herself. "But it matters so much who I choose as deputy," she told him. "It has to be a cat I can trust."

Pebble Heart cocked his head, looking puzzled. "Is that any different from when you chose Sun Shadow?" he asked. "I don't remember it being such a struggle."

Shadowstar looked down at her paws, wondering if she could tell the medicine cat the truth.

"This is my last life," she finally confessed, keeping her mew as quiet as she could. "My next deputy will have to be ready to lead the Clan *soon*, and be able to keep ShadowClan together."

Pebble Heart looked deeply troubled. "Are you sure?" he asked after a moment. "There was the infection, and the fight with the badger . . . the cough, the time you drowned . . . that fall . . ."

"Er . . . I may have died twice without telling you," Shadow-star confessed. "I was hit by a Twoleg monster and I fought a rogue."

At the stormy look on Pebble Heart's face, she added quickly, "I didn't tell *any* cat. Both times, I died alone and began my new life alone. There was nothing anyone could have done. It seemed safer for the Clan if no cat knew how close I was to my last life."

"Oh, Shadowstar." Pebble Heart's eyes shone with distress. "I'm so sorry. You shouldn't have been alone."

She shrugged. "I wasn't alone. StarClan was with me." She brought the conversation back to what seemed most impor-tant. "Sun Shadow had been helping me lead the Clan for a long time. He was *ready* to lead, if he had to. How can I know if one of the others will be able to guide ShadowClan? How can I know if I can even *trust* . . . ?" She trailed off, thinking of those amber eyes that had watched her die.

"What do you mean?" Pebble Heart asked, staring at her intently.

Shadowstar told him about the eyes she'd seen watching her and Sun Shadow's deaths from the woods. "I thought I might have imagined them, but the more I think about it, the more sure I am that there *was* a cat there. I don't *think* it was a ShadowClan cat, although I can't help wondering . . . but if it wasn't, that's almost as bad. What cat could watch us die with-out wanting to help? It makes me feel like I have an enemy . . .

or ShadowClan does. And Gray Wing said that if Shadow-
Clan falls, all the Clans could fall. . . ."

"I see." Pebble Heart nodded. "You're wondering how you
can leave an untested leader in charge, if the Clans are in such
danger."

"Exactly." Shadowstar felt oddly lighter. She was still worried and frightened, but she was glad that she'd told Pebble
Heart what was bothering her.

"For what it's worth, I have faith in you," Pebble Heart
mewed. "If the Clan *is* in danger, I think you will find that
danger before your final death." He pressed his cheek to hers.
"You've led this Clan so well, I *know* you will leave us safe."

Maybe, Shadowstar thought. *I hope he's right.*

But as she thanked Pebble Heart and left his den, weav-
ing her way past her warriors, she couldn't help thinking of
Sun Shadow's death. She had failed him. *I should have saved him.
I should have made him run to safety. Then he would still be here, ready to
lead the Clan when I die.*

She would need to do a better job protecting ShadowClan.
Slipping into her nest below the oak tree, she shut her eyes.
I have to make sure my Clan is strong enough to survive my final death.

Shadowstar led her Clan into Fourtrees, the full moon
shining above them, bathing the clearing in cold silver. Skystar and Thunderstar were already seated on the Great Rock.
Skystar looked tense, his thick light gray fur bristling and his
large paws shifting restlessly. Shadowstar strode toward them
as her warriors greeted friends and kin from other Clans.

Pebble Heart joined Cloud Spots and Acorn Fur, doubtless to talk medicine-cat business.

Leaping lightly to the top of the Great Rock, Shadowstar nodded to Skystar and Thunderstar. Skystar twitched his whiskers irritably at her. "You're still planning to back me up, right?" he asked urgently.

"I will." *But first I have to hear what's going on.*

Thunderstar, calmer, looked down at where his and Skystar's deputies sat near the base of the rock. "You haven't picked a new deputy yet?"

"No." Shadowstar tried to make it clear from her tone that she didn't want to discuss it, but the big ginger tom only blinked at her earnestly.

"It was hard for me, too, when Lightning Tail was killed," he confided. "But I'm glad that I chose Owl Eyes as my deputy. It's good for the Clan to have another cat they can rely on."

"I will name a new deputy when the time is right," she told him coolly. Her Clan's business was no other cat's concern.

Thunderstar looked as if he wanted to speak again, but seemed to change his mind as Windstar and Riverstar joined them on top of the Great Rock.

"I notice you don't have a new deputy yet," Windstar remarked briskly to Shadowstar. "A leader needs a deputy to bear some of the weight of running a Clan."

Shadowstar's tail twitched with irritation, but Skystar broke in, addressing all the cats in the clearing. "Now that we're all finally here, I need to speak. I don't have time to tell you how our prey is running or to listen to a list of new apprentices in another Clan," he yowled. "We have a serious problem."

"What's the matter?" Riverstar asked.

"I warned you all about the Twolegs," Skystar went on. "I tried to tell you at the last Gathering, but you said not to worry, that there was nothing Twolegs wanted in the forest."

"Oh, *this* again," Windstar broke in with an irritable flick of her tail. "A few Twolegs walk across your territory, and you get all worked up."

"It's not 'a few Twolegs,'" Skystar mewed indignantly. "More and more of them are coming, more often now. Sometimes they come in groups, with big Twoleg monsters. They've been patrolling, looking very carefully at SkyClan's territory. I think they're hoping to take it over as their own. If they do, what will happen to SkyClan?"

"But why would they want your territory?" Riverstar asked reasonably. "Twolegs live in those big dens like mountains. The forest isn't their kind of place at all."

"No, Skystar's right," Thunderstar broke in. "I've seen them, and they're acting like the forest is theirs. Maybe they want to build some of their dens on forest land."

"Even if that's true," Windstar replied, "this sounds like SkyClan's problem, not WindClan's."

There was an outbreak of angry yowling from the cats gathered in the clearing below.

"So WindClan would be happy enough for SkyClan to be destroyed?" Quick Water, one of Skystar's cats, snarled, rearing back onto her hind legs.

"We can't turn our backs on other Clans!" Pink Eyes, a white-furred ThunderClan warrior, looked shocked.

Even Moth Flight, Windstar's own daughter and her Clan's medicine cat, was staring at her mother, hissing: "There *must* be five Clans! We have to protect one another!"

Windstar flicked her tail again, her yellow eyes darkening resentfully.

"If SkyClan lost territory, it would be every Clan's problem," Thunderstar meowed firmly. "We should discuss where SkyClan could go if the worst happened. Maybe we should talk about redrawing our borders."

There was an outcry from the clearing below—cats yowling over one another—and the ginger tom hissed at them for silence.

Riverstar's eyes narrowed, but his voice remained calm. "Are you suggesting sharing some of ThunderClan's territory with SkyClan? It *is* the closest."

Thunderstar drew back. "We're all in this together," he protested. "ThunderClan will change its borders only if *every* Clan does."

From the base of the Great Rock, WindClan's deputy, Gorse Fur, hissed, "WindClan will fight for the moor. We *need* our territory."

"Gorse Fur is right," Windstar agreed. "Changing our borders would mean less prey for every Clan. And prey on the moors is hard to catch—do ThunderClan and SkyClan really think they can survive by hunting rabbits like we do?"

Shadowstar could see cats in the clearing exchanging dubious looks. The warriors who had joined WindClan were the fastest in the forest—long-legged hunters who ran like the wind their leader was named after. ThunderClan and Sky-Clan cats were better suited to climbing trees or pouncing on smaller prey. *And ShadowClan cats are better at stalking through the shadows of the pine forest,* she thought, looking at her stealthy warriors. *As for RiverClan . . .*

"RiverClan cats *swim* for their prey," Riverstar added, echoing Shadowstar's thoughts. "Does any other Clan really plan to share *our* hunting grounds?"

Skystar's fur bristled. "We have always been able to adapt," he said fiercely. "When I came from the mountains, I learned to hunt on the moor and in the forest. SkyClan cats will hunt wherever they need to."

Windstar rounded on him, showing her teeth. "So many cats fought and died to establish our boundaries," she hissed. "Do you think changing them wouldn't lead to new conflict?"

"So would SkyClan being made homeless!" Skystar growled. He turned to Shadowstar. "You said you'd support me with the other Clans if the Twolegs kept patrolling my land," he reminded her. "Will you speak for me now?"

Shadowstar felt as if she'd missed her footing in the dark. Every cat's eye was on her. Did Skystar really expect her to agree to redraw ShadowClan's borders? "I want SkyClan to be safe," she mewed defensively, "but I never agreed to give up territory."

Skystar growled at her, a thick, guttural sound, his eyes

flashing. "I *knew* ShadowClan could not be trusted," he snarled.

The rage in his voice startled Shadowstar. She had thought that time had mellowed the angry, reckless cat Skystar had been when they were young, but maybe he had just learned to hide that fury. She thought again of those eyes watching from the forest as she died. . . .

Skystar had pale blue eyes, but plenty of his warriors—Acorn Fur, Quick Water, and Birch, for instance—had amber ones. *How far would Skystar go?* she wondered.

"I agree with Windstar." Riverstar spoke calmly, interrupting Shadowstar's worried thoughts. "The borders are as they are for a reason. Any cat who wants to can seek shelter with RiverClan, but we will not give up our territory."

Skystar snarled furiously at Riverstar, but the long-furred tom blinked at him, unperturbed.

"Well, RiverClan doesn't have to worry, does it?" Thunderstar said bitterly. "You're across the river from SkyClan. Whatever affects us in the forest won't touch you."

He and Skystar—father and son—had never looked more alike than they did now, their broad shoulders tense and their long tails slashing from side to side. *Thunderstar has amber eyes, too,* Shadowstar noticed, feeling slightly sick.

Was she making too much of this? *No,* she decided. *My task is to protect my Clan and to make sure they will go on without me. If I have an enemy,* ShadowClan *has an enemy.*

Thunderstar sighed. "So even if the Twoleg threat gets worse, WindClan and RiverClan are against redrawing our borders," he meowed. "ThunderClan and SkyClan are for it." He turned to Shadowstar. "You say you never agreed to give up territory, but will you agree now? Your vote can break the tie."

"It's not a *vote*," Windstar muttered, but the others ignored her, their eyes fixed on Shadowstar.

Shadowstar tucked her tail around her legs and thought. The clearing was silent, each cat straining to hear her answer. *Is redrawing the borders the right thing to do?* It was true that changing territories would force the cats of each Clan to learn to hunt in a new way. And there would be less prey if there was less territory.

As well, she still wasn't sure that there really was a Twoleg threat to SkyClan. *Twolegs have wandered through Clan territory before,* she thought. *Maybe Skystar is seeing danger where there isn't any.*

And what if Skystar or one of his Clanmates *had* watched the dogs attack her and Sun Shadow? Could she trust them?

She spoke carefully. "I'm not ready to make this decision. There's a lot I need to consider."

Skystar's tail slashed wildly. "Like *what?*" he yowled. "Do you have to weigh whether SkyClan is worth saving?"

Snarls came from the SkyClan warriors in the crowd below.

"I want to see for myself what the Twolegs are doing on your territory," Shadowstar meowed steadily. "If I agree that there's a threat—"

"There is," Skystar insisted.

"*If* I agree, *then* we'll talk about new territory. Maybe there's somewhere else nearby where SkyClan can carve out a suitable home. We should look around before we discuss shrinking every Clan's hunting grounds."

Skystar glared at her silently for few moments. "Three days," he meowed. There was a yowl of protest from some of his Clanmates.

"We don't *want* a new territory," Dew Petal growled, and some of the other young SkyClan warriors meowed in agreement.

Skystar hissed them into silence. "Three days," he repeated. "You can send a patrol to see what the Twolegs are doing, and I'll listen to any new suggestion you—or any other Clan leader—proposes. But understand I'm not agreeing to anything."

"Of course," Shadowstar replied. Maybe there was livable territory near Highstones, beyond ShadowClan's borders. Anything would be better than trying to get the other Clans to give up their territory—that would only lead to open battle.

She gazed out at the cats massed in the clearing. Every cat, no matter their Clan, looked frightened and hostile.

So many of them had amber eyes.

CHAPTER FOUR

"Ugh." Mud Paws wrinkled his nose in disgust. "I hate the way it smells over here. I wouldn't mind giving this bit of our territory to SkyClan."

"You'll be glad of those rats if we have a hard leaf-bare," Shadowstar reminded him firmly.

Near the edge of ShadowClan's territory was a spot where Twolegs in yellow monsters left crow-food and debris in rotting heaps behind a shining silver fence. It smelled horrible, but it was crawling with rats. Usually, the ShadowClan cats left them alone—rats were fierce fighters, and hunting them was bound to leave a warrior with bites and scratches—but it was good to have the prey to fall back on in the harshest leaf-bare.

Shadowstar led Pebble Heart, Mud Paws, and Raven Pelt past the fence now, resisting the impulse to wrinkle her own nose.

"Anyway," Raven Pelt meowed, "we're not planning to give up *any* territory. That's the whole point, right, Shadowstar?"

"I hope so," Shadowstar murmured. "If there's a likely looking territory, past our borders but not too far away, maybe we can convince Skystar that it's an option."

She had spent the previous day on SkyClan's territory, watching Twolegs tromp, noisy and careless, through the woods. They had seemed more focused and intent than the few Twolegs she'd seen before, examining the land as if they were in fact marking out territory, leaving bright patches of shiny Twoleg stuff on some of the trees.

She still wasn't sure what the Twolegs had been doing. But now she understood Skystar's alarm.

And so she'd brought Pebble Heart and two loyal warriors—ones who *hadn't* been fighting or trying to impress her with what good deputies they would be—to help look for unclaimed land that might make a good SkyClan territory.

It doesn't seem likely that we'll find it here, to be honest.

"I forgot how bleak this place is," she muttered to Pebble Heart, looking up at the Highstones ahead as they crossed out of ShadowClan territory. The medicine cats traveled to the cliffs every half-moon to visit the Moonstone, but Shadowstar hadn't come here since she'd been given her nine lives many moons before. ShadowClan's own territory was fine, if smelly in places, but once you crossed the border, the grass grew thinner and coarser and the land became more and more rocky. There was little shelter—and *very* little prey.

The sky was heavy and gray, ominous clouds hanging overhead. The weather didn't make the territory look any more appealing.

"I don't like leaving ShadowClan territory," Mud Paws muttered, glancing around nervously.

"The Moonstone cannot be on any one Clan's territory," Pebble Heart said, tipping his head back to gaze up toward the entrance to the Moonstone. "To keep that from happening, SkyClan's territory would have to stretch a long way from Fourtrees and the other Clans."

Poor hunting, little shelter, far from Fourtrees. There's no way Skystar is going to accept this as his territory. Shadowstar's tail drooped, but then she lifted it again and spoke briskly.

"Pebble Heart, I want you to scout and see if any useful herbs grow around here." She glanced about, sniffing the air. She didn't smell any dangerous animals or rogues, but you never knew. There were no nearby trees to climb, and only scrubby, thin bushes to shelter beneath. "Mud Paws and Raven Pelt, go with him. I'll look at the land across the Thunderpath." The two warriors should be able to protect the medicine cat if anything happened.

Mud Paws and Pebble Heart nodded, but Raven Pelt paused. "What if you run into something dangerous? Maybe one of us should stick with you."

Shadowstar hesitated a moment. "I'll be fine," she replied eventually. "I'll yowl if anything happens." This was her last life, but she had to keep her nerve. She had never needed other cats to look after her before.

Flicking her tail in farewell, she strode toward the Thunderpath as her warriors followed Pebble Heart toward a scraggly clump of bushes.

Her steps slowed as she got closer, and she sniffed the air again, searching this time for any sign that other cats were in the area. If rogues had claimed the territory, it wouldn't be worth going any farther without reinforcements.

But all she could smell was the stink of the Thunderpath. A huge monster roared by, and she flinched back, flattening her ears and trying not to remember the time she lost a life beneath one of its huge black paws.

This Thunderpath seemed much busier than the one closer to ShadowClan's camp. Another reason for Skystar to reject the territory. Approaching it, Shadowstar's pelt prickled as she felt suddenly vulnerable—as though a predator was watching her.

I'm nervous because I know it's my last life. She reminded herself that she couldn't let that fear control her.

Shaking her pelt as if to throw off her apprehension, Shadowstar craned her neck to watch for monsters. One was racing toward her, but once it passed, she should be able to cross. Its terrible scent was overwhelming.

And then, for just a moment, she caught another scent. *A cat?*

A hard, sudden blow hit her hindquarters. Caught completely by surprise, Shadowstar staggered forward, directly into the path of the Twoleg monster.

There was no time to run. The monster's face with its round blank eyes filled Shadowstar's vision. She squeezed her eyes shut against the oncoming pain and crouched low, her belly pressed against the Thunderpath as she prayed that it would be only her who perished today, and not the five Clans.

A hot wind rushed over her, ruffling her fur; the growl of the monster was deafening.

And then the noise and the wind stopped.

Shadowstar lay still, her eyes tightly shut. *Am I dead?*

She could still smell the foul monster scent, and her belly felt sore and scraped from pressing against the Thunderpath. If this was StarClan, it was very different than it had been before. A raindrop hit the top of her head, and Shadowstar opened her eyes. She was still on the Thunderpath. She was *alive*. Turning, she saw the monster disappearing in the distance. Had it passed right *over* her?

A fine drizzle had begun to fall, and it quickly soaked through her fur. She shook the raindrops out of her eyes, feeling dazed. *I have to get off the Thunderpath.*

She got to her paws with difficulty, her legs weak and shaky, and headed back toward ShadowClan territory.

It wasn't until she reached the grass at the edge of the Thunderpath that she realized: *I was pushed. . . .* It was the only possible explanation.

The cat I scented was trying to kill me!

Before she had quite gotten her bearings, a heavy weight slammed into her side, rolling her onto the ground. Shadowstar's heart was pounding, her blood roaring in her ears, and she kicked out with her hind paws, trying to throw off the attacker above her.

Pain shot through her as a claw sliced at the skin above her eyes. Half-blinded by blood, Shadowstar howled with rage and swiped her front paw across her attacker's side. Shaking the blood from her face, she glimpsed gray-and-white fur.

"Shadowstar!" Her Clanmates had heard her howl.

At the sound of their voices, the cat on top of her leaped away. Gasping for breath, Shadowstar rolled onto her belly and tried to wipe the blood away from her eyes with one paw.

Mud Paws and Pebble Heart were running toward her. Raven Pelt was veering away from them, chasing after the rapidly fleeing cat. It was hard to see through the rain and through the blood running down her face, but Shadowstar recognized her attacker.

Quick Water?

Shadowstar felt a sharp pang of betrayal and disbelief. She and the SkyClan warrior had always gotten along well. . . . Quick Water had been one of the cats who had come down from the mountains with Shadowstar and Skystar, looking for a better life. They'd known each other all their lives.

Had Shadowstar's old friend really become her enemy?

Pebble Heart and Mud Paws reached Shadowstar, and the medicine cat immediately began to pat her over with soft paws—"Does this hurt? Does this?"—and to clean the blood from her fur. It was not until he finally nodded in approval that Shadowstar was able to question them.

"Did you see who I was fighting?" she demanded.

Pebble Heart and Mud Paws exchanged frightened looks.

"It was hard to tell, but it looked like—"

"I wasn't sure, but it looked like—"

"It was Quick Water." Raven Pelt was trotting back toward them, looking tired. "I'm sorry, Shadowstar, I lost her by the carrionplace, but I'm sure it was her."

"I'm glad you made sure," Shadowstar told him. "You've done well." Raven Pelt's yellow eyes brightened at her praise. *He's brave and loyal,* Shadowstar thought, *and he doesn't lose his head in a crisis. Maybe I've finally found my deputy.*

But there was a more pressing matter now. A SkyClan cat— *Quick Water*—had just tried to kill her. Thinking back on the dogs that had tracked her and Sun Shadow through the woods, and the amber eyes that had watched them die, Shadowstar wondered if maybe this hadn't been the first time.

CHAPTER FIVE
❧

They needed to talk to Skystar immediately, Shadowstar decided. The scratch across her forehead still stung, and she ached all over from the fight, but this couldn't wait. She led Raven Pelt, Mud Paws, and Pebble Heart across ShadowClan's territory toward SkyClan.

"What if Skystar knew Quick Water was going to attack you?" Raven Pelt asked. "What if he *told* her to? Should we be going onto SkyClan territory with so few cats?"

Shadowstar twitched her tail, thinking. "Skystar may have had his troubles with the other Clans in the past," she told him, "but I can't believe he'd want to kill me, or hurt Shadow-Clan, no matter how angry he was with me." Raven Pelt began to speak, but Shadowstar went on. "I'm giving him the benefit of the doubt for now. Skystar wants me as his ally; killing me makes no sense. There has to be another explanation for what Quick Water was doing." She wasn't sure if she was trying to convince Raven Pelt or herself. *I don't want to believe it about Sky-star. I won't believe it.*

She had known Skystar since they were kits together, back in the mountains so long ago. He'd made trouble for the other

Clans when he'd felt threatened, but he had grown out of those ways. After the Clans had been formed, he—as much as any leader—had been devoted to the code they'd agreed to follow, in order to avoid any more terrible battles, like the one that had claimed the lives of so many cats of all five Clans. Shadowstar was sure she knew him well enough to trust he was not planning to murder other cats. . . .

I've known Quick Water for a long time, too.

Shadowstar pushed the thought away. "We'll talk to Skystar," she said firmly. "He deserves a chance to make this right."

The moist soil of ShadowClan's territory felt comfortingly soft under her tired paws, but it became firmer and grassier as they approached the Thunderpath dividing their territory from ThunderClan's.

Standing at the edge of the Thunderpath, they watched as one Twoleg monster, then another, sped by. The sound of their round black paws made the fur on Shadowstar's back prickle. For a moment she remembered her belly pressed to that other Thunderpath, the monster rushing toward her, and her mouth went dry. If she had stumbled a few tail-lengths farther, she would have been crushed beneath those round paws.

No. That's not how I'm going to die. Suddenly she was sure of it. The way that StarClan had saved her when she was pushed in front of that monster convinced her: There was too much happening between the Clans right now. She *would not* die, not before ShadowClan was safe.

Recklessly, she charged onto the Thunderpath. Her heart

was thudding, but she kept running, even as a small, two-footed monster with a Twoleg on its back swerved around her, screeching.

It took the others a few heartbeats to catch up with her. "Are you mouse-brained?" Mud Paws gasped, too frightened to show his leader the usual respect.

Shadowstar brushed her tail over his back in a silent apology but said nothing. How could she explain?

On this side of the Thunderpath—ThunderClan territory—the trees were mostly oaks and birches, their branches spreading wider and letting through more sunlight than the pines and occasional oaks of ShadowClan's territory. Shadowstar felt exposed, and she could tell that her Clanmates felt the same. They walked closer together, their pelts brushing.

Shadowstar was glad they didn't run into a ThunderClan patrol. She didn't want to drag any other Clan into this until she had spoken to Skystar. At the edge of SkyClan territory, she hesitated. "Let's wait for a patrol," she said. "If we're going to accuse one of Skystar's warriors of trying to kill me, let's at least go in with his permission."

Mud Paws and Raven Pelt glanced at each other and nodded. Pebble Heart sat down to wait patiently, his gray tabby tail curled around his paws.

It wasn't long before Blossom and Red Claw appeared, Red Claw with a mouse dangling from his mouth.

"Hello," Blossom mewed, looking startled. She dipped her head respectfully to Shadowstar. "Are you—"

"We'd like to see Skystar, please," Shadowstar told her.

"Would you escort us to your camp?"

"Have you had any luck finding us another territory?" Blossom asked. Her tortoiseshell tail curved excitedly over her back.

"We want to see Skystar," Shadowstar repeated. She made sure to sound polite, but there must have been a coldness in her tone, because Blossom's eyes went wide.

"Of course," she meowed. "Follow us." Beside her, Red Claw nodded and gestured with his tail to Shadowstar's Clanmates.

When they reached SkyClan's camp, it seemed both busy and peaceful. Skystar and his mate, Star Flower, were sharing tongues near the entrance to their den. Shadowstar noticed that Star Flower's sides were slightly rounded with a new litter of kits. *No wonder he's so anxious to make sure their home is safe,* she thought. She saw Pebble Heart nod to his sister, SkyClan's deputy, Sparrow Fur, who was sharpening her claws on a birch, and to Acorn Fur, the Clan's medicine cat. Dew Petal and Flower Foot, two of Skystar's grown kits, were changing the bedding in the warriors' den. And Quick Water, looking as calm and relaxed as if she'd spent all day lazing in the sunshine, was sharing a vole with Honey Pelt, another of SkyClan's warriors. She raised her head and gave Shadowstar a long, cool glance. Shadowstar glared back, rage rising in her chest.

"Do you have any news?" Skystar demanded, getting to his paws. "What did you think of the territory near Highstones?"

Shadowstar pulled her attention away from Quick Water

with difficulty. "It might work," she mewed, but she knew she sounded doubtful. "We didn't get much of a chance to look properly."

Skystar's blue eyes widened in outrage. "You didn't *look?*" he yowled. "If you didn't bother, then why are you here?"

The fur rose on Shadowstar's shoulders. "I'm here because one of your warriors tried to *kill* me," she spat. "I'm more worried about that then whether you might need new territory."

Around the clearing, every cat's head shot up. Flower Foot dropped the moss she was carrying.

"Are you a mouse-brain?" Skystar asked. "What are you saying?"

"Something true," Shadowstar told him dryly.

"None of my warriors would do anything like that," Skystar protested, his tail slashing back and forth angrily. "Who are you accusing?"

Shadowstar's eyes locked with Quick Water's amber ones. *"Her."*

Every SkyClan cat—except Quick Water herself—leaped to their paws, hissing angrily.

"Liar!" Sparrow Fur yowled.

"ShadowClan is just trying to make trouble for us," Star Flower growled, showing her teeth. "We should chase them off our territory."

Shadowstar purposefully kept herself from flinching as she wondered if her final death would be at the paws of an angry SkyClan. She continued staring at Quick Water until the gray-and-white cat dropped her gaze.

"Quiet!" Skystar mewed. He stalked closer to Shadow-star, his fur bristling. "If you're coming onto my territory and accusing one of my Clanmates this way, you'd better have some proof."

"I have the proof of my own eyes," Shadowstar told him. "While we were scouting for new territory for your Clan, Quick Water pushed me into the path of a Twoleg monster. After I managed to escape, she attacked me by the side of the Thunderpath. When my Clanmates caught up to us, she ran away."

Raven Pelt stepped up, shoulder to shoulder with her. "I saw Quick Water fighting with Shadowstar and then running away. I chased her. I'm sure it was her."

"I only saw from a distance," Pebble Heart added. "But it looked like Quick Water to me." Beside him, Mud Paws nod-ded.

The SkyClan cats exchanged uncertain glances. Slowly, they turned to look at Quick Water, who was gazing down at her paws.

"And I don't think this was the first time," Shadowstar went on, her heart feeling heavy in her chest. "The dogs that killed Sun Shadow . . . I think maybe Quick Water led them there. I saw eyes like hers watching from the woods." Quick Water raised her head to aim a blazing, amber glare at Shadowstar.

"Nonsense," Star Flower snapped. She was standing beside Skystar, her tail high with indignation. "'Eyes watching from the woods,'" she hissed scathingly, "and you're accusing Quick Water of murder."

"Why would she do something like that?" Skystar asked, sounding bewildered. "I don't believe it. She's been a Clan cat as long as there have been Clans. We all came down from the mountains together. She wouldn't attack you." He looked suddenly older, and tired.

Shadowstar hadn't thought much about *why*: she hadn't been able to wrap her mind around it, and she'd been concentrating on how to tell SkyClan about the attacks. But now she could see Quick Water's reasoning laid out as clearly as a scent trail. "She did it *because* she's a Clan cat," she began slowly. "You've all been so worried about the Twolegs taking your territory. From the lives she knows I've lost, maybe she decided I could be close to my last." She paused, pressing her paws into the earth to keep her forelegs from shaking as she tried to make her tone sound dismissive, like the idea of her being on her final life from StarClan was ridiculous. "Perhaps she thought the opportunity was worth breaking our new code. If Sun Shadow and I had both died, ShadowClan would have been without a leader. It would have been easy to move in and take our territory."

Quick Water dropped her gaze again, working her claws in and out against the ground, and Shadowstar felt a thrill of vindication. *I'm right. She knows I've seen the truth.*

But then the gray-and-white cat looked up, defiant. "I didn't," she meowed. "I don't know who you fought up by Highstones, but it wasn't me."

"Then what were you doing?" Shadowstar asked. "Where were you today?" With her tail, she gestured at Quick Water's side. "That's a nasty scratch you've got there, and I remember scratching the cat I fought." Quick Water hunched, trying to hide the wound.

"She and Honey Pelt were hunting together," Skystar meowed. "Weren't you?"

Everyone looked at Honey Pelt, whose tail drooped. "No," he answered softly. "We ran into each other outside camp, but we weren't together before that."

Every cat looked at Quick Water, and she seemed at a loss, ducking her head silently.

After a moment, Skystar said to Shadowstar, "I never would ask my warriors to attack another Clan's leader. If I were going to steal territory, I wouldn't be working so hard to convince the other Clans to change their borders."

Shadowstar sighed. "I believe you," she told him.

Skystar turned to Quick Water. "If you can't prove where you were . . ." He paused, but Quick Water said nothing, staring back at him, holding very still. "If you can't tell us what happened, then I have to believe you had some part in this," he told her. His blue eyes dropped to the ground, his claws flexing like he was wrestling with his decision.

After a long moment, he lifted his head again. "You leave me no choice, Quick Water. . . . I must exile you."

There were gasps from his Clanmates. Even Shadowstar was stunned. But Skystar drew himself up. "Go," he ordered sharply. "You are no longer a SkyClan cat, and you are not welcome on our territory."

Almost as if she didn't understand, Quick Water stared

at him for a few heartbeats; then she turned and ran out of camp. Even after she disappeared from sight, they could hear the cracks of branches as she forced her way recklessly through the brush.

Skystar looked at Shadowstar again, his gaze bleak. "You made a good case," he meowed sadly. "I had to exile her, since she couldn't explain herself. But I want to be clear that I do not like it."

"I know," Shadowstar told him. She pressed her cheek against his briefly, grateful that her old friend had listened, however unwillingly. "You did the right thing."

As they crossed the border onto their own territory, Shadowstar felt as if a weight had been lifted off her back. *ShadowClan is safer now.*

"It's been a long day," Pebble Heart meowed as they approached their camp. The sun had almost set now, and deep shadows stretched beneath the pines.

Mud Paws and Raven Pelt yowled in agreement. "I can't wait to eat some prey and go to sleep," Mud Paws added.

"There's one more thing before we can rest," Shadowstar told them. Ducking to enter the thorn tunnel, she led them into camp. The rest of ShadowClan had gathered in the clearing and meowed cheerful greetings.

"What did you think of the territory?"

"Pebble Heart, can you look at my paw?"

"Raven Pelt, I saved a vole for you."

The cats quieted as Shadowstar strode across the clearing

and leaped up onto the Clanrock to look down at her Clan. A pale moon was rising over the camp, and it reflected in her Clanmates' eyes as they gazed up at her.

"I've made up my mind," she told them. She was quite sure of her choice. She looked around at them all: Pebble Heart blinking up at her like he already knew what she would say and approved of it, Juniper Branch grooming Dangling Leaf as if he were still a kit and not a full-grown warrior. Bubbling Stream paused mid-step, carrying a mouse over to share with Dusk Nose. And all the others. She looked down at the upturned faces of the cats of her Clan, cats she had promised to lead and protect, and felt a swell of warmth in her chest. When she left them, she would not leave them alone.

"I've chosen a new deputy," she went on. She almost purred in amusement when she saw Juniper Branch and Mouse Ear eagerly pricking up their ears. "This is a brave and loyal cat, one who I know will always try to make the best choices for ShadowClan." She thought of Raven Pelt chasing after Quick Water, of him speaking up to Skystar. He would guide the Clan well. "I say these words before StarClan, so that Sun Shadow and the spirits of our warrior ancestors may hear and approve of my choice. The new deputy of ShadowClan is Raven Pelt."

"Raven Pelt! Raven Pelt!" the Clan cheered, and Shadow-star leaped down to touch her nose to her new deputy's.

"Thank you," he gasped, his yellow eyes wide with surprise. "I'll try to . . . I'll do my best to be a good deputy, I really will."

"I know you will," Shadowstar purred. *And when the time comes, you'll be a good leader.*

The Clan was crowding around, congratulating Raven Pelt.

"If it can't be me, I'm glad it's you," Juniper Branch meowed, brushing her muzzle against his. Mouse Ear seemed less pleased, but even he congratulated Raven Pelt stiffly.

When Shadowstar finally settled in her nest that night, aching with exhaustion, she felt more at peace than she had since Sun Shadow's death. *But is a new deputy enough to keep ShadowClan strong and together?* She hoped so. It was impossible to know for sure.

As she began to drift into sleep, she suddenly shivered. *I've appointed ShadowClan's next leader. Does this mean I've taken a paw step closer to my death?*

Shadowstar was deeply asleep when a screech of terror broke through the night, jerking her awake. *Pebble Heart!* Her heart pounding hard, she scrambled out of her nest. Worried heads were poking out of the warrior den, but she passed them without a word and slipped between the boulders into the medicine cat's den.

Pebble Heart lay in his bed, his eyes wide but unseeing. Every muscle seemed tense, his legs stiff, and he was whimpering, his mouth partly open.

"Pebble Heart!" Shadowstar shook him. "Pebble Heart, wake up!"

He blinked, and gradually his body relaxed and his eyes focused. "Shadowstar," he murmured.

"What's happening? Do you need some herbs?" Shadow-star looked doubtfully at the neatly sorted dried leaves and roots at the side of Pebble Heart's den.

"No, I'm all right." Pebble Heart sat up, still looking groggy. "It was just a dream."

"A regular dream or a medicine-cat dream?" Shadowstar asked apprehensively. Even as a kit, before the Clan had had a medicine cat, Pebble Heart had been sent dreams by StarClan, warning of danger or pointing a path for the Clans to follow.

"I'm not sure," Pebble Heart began slowly. "But it felt *true.*" He looked up at Shadowstar, his amber gaze apprehensive. "I dreamed that the trees around the camp were bending and swaying, like they were being attacked by a fierce wind. But there was no wind. And when the first tree fell, it . . ." He hesitated, his tail swishing across the floor of his den as Shadowstar felt a cold claw scrape at her chest fur. She knew what he was going to say.

"It knocked over the next tree. . . . Soon, every tree was falling down. . . ."

If ShadowClan falls apart, it could destroy all the Clans. That was what Gray Wing had said to her, the last time she was in StarClan. Could Pebble Heart's vision be telling her the same thing?

"But we've just gotten *rid* of the threat," Shadowstar meowed, staring at him. "And now we're in danger again? StarClan, what's going on?"

CHAPTER SIX

❧

Shadowstar and Pebble Heart decided not to tell any other cat, not even Raven Pelt, about Pebble Heart's dream.

"If what you saw is a vision from StarClan, trouble will find us soon enough," Shadowstar had told him grimly, "and if it was just a dream, there's no reason to worry the Clan." Pebble Heart had agreed, but Shadowstar knew that, like her, he was sure the dream had been a warning.

As she and Raven Pelt padded toward ThunderClan's territory, she decided not to think about it. All she could do was try to protect her Clan, and she would do that with or without StarClan's warning.

Instead, Shadowstar would help Raven Pelt learn how to be a Clan leader.

"We'll talk to Thunderstar about the territory up near the Highstones," she told him now. "If he thinks that SkyClan should consider moving there, it'll help all the Clans to come to an agreement."

Raven Pelt's whiskers twitched in confusion. "But it's not a very good territory."

"No," Shadowstar agreed with a sigh. "But it's an option,

and the other Clans will never give up territory. Not without blood being shed. If SkyClan does end up losing its own territory, surely it's better for them to stay close instead of ending up with nowhere to go."

Raven Pelt's tail drooped. "I guess."

"A leader has to think of their own Clan first," Shadowstar told him gently. "But we should try to treat the other Clans as fairly as we can."

As they came out of the pine forest near the Thunderpath, Shadowstar's spine prickled, and she shivered. Something was wrong. She sniffed the air, and then looked around, half expecting to be attacked. Just like yesterday, she'd caught a familiar whiff of cat over the Thunderpath scent. A scent that smelled like . . .

Quick Water?

No, she decided. *I must be imagining it.* After all the danger she'd run into around Thunderpaths, she was seeing trouble where there wasn't any. Quick Water had been exiled; she wouldn't dare intrude on any Clan's territory now.

Side by side, she and Raven Pelt crossed the Thunderpath. The sun was shining brightly, and a warm breeze rustled the leaves of the trees overhead.

The scent seemed stronger here. *I am imagining it,* Shadowstar told herself. *Aren't I?*

Raven Pelt stopped suddenly and opened his mouth to scent the air. "Do you smell that?" he said. "I think it's Quick Water's scent. If she's left Clan lands, shouldn't it have faded by now?"

"It should have," Shadowstar said grimly. So, she hadn't been imagining it. Quick Water must be hanging around ThunderClan territory. Was she trespassing, unwilling to go off alone onto rogue lands? Or was ThunderClan sheltering the cat who had murdered Sun Shadow?

She began to hurry. "We need to talk to Thunderstar."

Just across the ThunderClan border, Shadowstar caught sight of a black-and-white pelt through the underbrush. "Leaf!" she called, and the tom trotted out of the bushes, trailed by a smaller white-and-yellow she-cat.

"Hello, Shadowstar, Raven Pelt," Leaf meowed, dipping his head respectfully. "What brings you onto ThunderClan territory?"

"We need to speak to Thunderstar," Shadowstar told him. "Will you escort us to your camp?"

"Of course," Leaf answered amiably. "Blue Whisker, why don't you go ahead and let Thunderstar know we're coming?" The younger cat flicked her tail in acknowledgment and hurried off. *Well, if Quick Water's in their camp, she'll be long gone by the time we get there,* Shadowstar thought, watching her go.

When they arrived at ThunderClan's camp, the clearing was almost empty, not just of Quick Water, but of most of ThunderClan. No cats were relaxing or sharing prey. Thunderstar sat at one end of the clearing, his deputy, Owl Eyes, and four of his toughest warriors beside him.

Shadowstar eyed them. "What's going on?" she asked. Her pelt was prickling with apprehension, and Raven Pelt pushed closer to her, protecting her side. She had always liked

Thunderstar. But then, she had always liked Quick Water, too. *Is this an attack?* she wondered, and then, sickeningly, *Am I leading another deputy to his death?*

Thunderstar flicked his ears, a friendly gesture. "Nothing's going on," he mewed. "I just wanted these cats to hear what you had to say. You've been up to check out the land by Highstones?"

Shadowstar narrowed her eyes. "We *did* plan to talk to you about that," she meowed. "But right now I'm more worried about something I scented while crossing your borders. Are you . . . Are you sheltering Quick Water?"

The big ginger tom stiffened. "ThunderClan has the right to allow any cat we like onto our lands," he told her. "You and Skystar can't exile cats from our territory."

Dropping into a crouch, Shadowstar felt her ears flatten, as Raven Pelt tensed beside her. "Do you know what Quick Water *did*?" she hissed. "She tried to kill me. She *did* kill Sun Shadow!" This must have been what Pebble Heart's vision was about. The threat to ShadowClan—to all the Clans— wasn't gone.

She wouldn't tell Thunderstar that Quick Water had managed to kill her once. No other Clan needed to know, or guess, how close she was to the end of her nine lives.

At her hostility, the cats beside Thunderstar rose to their paws, but Thunderstar waved his tail at them. "Sit down," he ordered. "Shadowstar, I know what you think happened—"

"What I *think*?" Shadowstar yowled, outraged. "I *know* what happened."

"And I saw it, too," Raven Pelt added. "Quick Water attacked Shadowstar."

Thunderstar shifted his paws uncomfortably. "Quick Water says she didn't do it, and I believe her," he meowed. "You were probably attacked by a rogue who wanted that territory for herself, one who resembled—"

Shadowstar broke in again. "I know Quick Water and I know her scent," she hissed. "Do you really think I would mistake a rogue for her?"

"It was raining, wasn't it?" Thunderstar challenged her. "And with the smells from the Thunderpath, you couldn't have caught her scent well."

Hot rage swept over Shadowstar, and she breathed slowly, willing herself to calm down. She and Raven Pelt couldn't win a fight against these ThunderClan warriors, not alone. "Quick Water is a danger to the Clans," she meowed, glaring into Thunderstar's eyes—*amber*, she noticed. "Even if you don't care about my life, or the threat to ShadowClan, sheltering a cat who tried to kill me could drag all the Clans into battle. Is that what you want?"

Thunderstar flicked his tail. "Your threats won't change my mind," he mewed evenly. "I believe Quick Water, and, if this leads to battle, at least my conscience will be clear." His eyes softened and his voice turned pleading. "You have to understand: I've trusted Quick Water all my life," he added. "She's lived through everything the Clans have had to face. She deserves the benefit of the doubt, doesn't she?"

Shadowstar felt her shoulders slump. "You've known me

just as long," she meowed. "And I thought you trusted me."

Thunderstar looked apologetic, but he didn't drop his gaze. "I believe Quick Water," he mewed again. "And I will protect her."

Shadowstar brushed her tail across Raven Pelt's back. *Time to go.* "This isn't over," she told Thunderstar, who nodded solemnly. She was afraid for a moment that the ThunderClan warriors would spring at her, but she and Raven Pelt left the camp unchallenged.

As they headed back toward their own territory, Raven Pelt asked apprehensively, "What happens now?"

Shadowstar felt a heavy dread settle in her gut. Her mind cast back to one of her earliest memories of Thunderstar—a time when he was known only as Thunder, and she was a cat called Tall Shadow. She'd just killed Fircone, a rogue cat, in front of him, and explained that she'd had no choice. *We must fight or die.*

Was she walking closer to another such day? Was it her final death she could feel right now, circling above her like a hawk?

"We can't let Quick Water stay in the forest," she told him. "She's a threat to ShadowClan. If we can't make Thunderstar see reason . . . we may have to fight."

Fight or die . . .

CHAPTER SEVEN

Shadowstar paced nervously across the Great Rock, waiting for the other Clans. In the clearing below, ShadowClan stood quietly, with none of the usual chatter of a Gathering. It felt strange to be at Fourtrees when the moon was less than half full, but she hadn't been willing to wait for the next full moon to talk to the Clans all together. She had called this Gathering about Quick Water.

Windstar arrived first, leaping up to stand beside her. "I see you've named a new deputy at last," she said, nodding down to where Raven Pelt stood beside her own deputy and mate, Gorse Fur. "Good choice."

RiverClan and SkyClan were streaming into the clearing, and Riverstar and Skystar joined them at the top of the Great Rock. Skystar only nodded solemnly, but Riverstar seemed cheerful.

"I hope you called this Gathering to tell us you've found a great territory for SkyClan," he meowed brightly.

"It's not about that," Shadowstar told him, then raised her head. ThunderClan was entering the clearing. Thunderstar and Sparrow Fur led the way, followed by a group of

ThunderClan's largest warriors, all surrounding a smaller cat. Shadowstar caught her breath. *Quick Water.* Thunderstar had brought her to the meeting, already making a public statement about who he believed. The ShadowClan cats in the clearing muttered to one another, glancing up at Shadowstar in confusion, as did the SkyClan cats. The other Clans looked at one another as if wondering when Quick Water had defected to ThunderClan.

Thunderstar leaped onto the Great Rock without looking at Shadowstar, and sat neatly, his tail wrapped around his paws. Skystar, she saw, was staring at his son, puzzled. *Good,* she thought. *Maybe he didn't know about this. Maybe they're not conspiring together. . . .*

"Since we're all here now, Shadowstar, do you want to report on the territory up by the Highstones?" Windstar asked briskly.

Shadowstar slashed her tail. "The territory's a possibility, but that's not why I called this Gathering." She took a deep breath and quickly told the other cats what had happened, from her suspicions that Quick Water had led the dogs to attack her and Sun Shadow to the *fact* that Quick Water had tried to kill her on the Thunderpath by the Highstones. "Quick Water has broken the code we all promised to live by," she told them. "Skystar did the right thing and exiled her from his territory, only for Thunderstar to welcome her into his Clan. We cannot allow this *murderer* to stay in any Clan's territory. She's no longer a true Clan cat." She looked around. Windstar and Riverstar seemed bewildered, and

Skystar was glaring at his son.

Thunderstar stood up in a smooth, fluid motion. He was the largest and youngest of the leaders, a powerful opponent. Shadowstar didn't want to have to fight him.

"I understand why Shadowstar and Skystar want to exile Quick Water, but I don't think she's to blame for what happened to Shadowstar," he announced. "And I'm not going to drive a cat I trust off my own territory because another Clan tells me to."

Skystar growled at Thunderstar. "If I choose to exile one of my cats, it's my business. It's not your place to interfere."

"You exiled one of your Clanmates without even listening to her side of the story!" Thunderstar growled back. Father and son were facing off now, nose to nose, their teeth bared. "You *abandoned* her!"

Unease rippled through the gathered cats. Every warrior had heard some of the stories about how Clear Sky, as he was then known, had rejected his son for moons, leaving him to be brought up by Gray Wing. Now that they were both Clan leaders, they had long had a more friendly relationship—but right at that moment, Shadowstar worried that old wounds had been reopened.

"I can't believe that Quick Water would do anything like this," Riverstar broke in. "There must be some kind of misunderstanding." The usually serene silvery-gray tom's green gaze was distraught.

Windstar looked out at the cats gathered below the Great Rock. "Let's not fight among ourselves. The best way to resolve this is to hear what Quick Water has to say," she meowed calmly.

Surrounded by her guard of ThunderClan warriors, Quick Water got to her paws, seeming calm and poised despite a quick, nervous flick of her tail. "I've done nothing wrong," she began, and a chorus of hisses and growls from the Shadow-Clan cats drowned out her voice.

"Liar!"

"*Killer!*"

Windstar yowled above the commotion, "*Silence!* We will listen before we decide."

The gathered cats quieted, and Quick Water continued. "I'm sure that Shadowstar and her cats did scent me over near the Highstones." She looked up at Skystar. "I was so worried about maybe having to leave our territory that I traveled up there to scout around. I'm sorry I didn't ask for permission first. But I didn't go there to hurt any cat."

At least she's now admitting she was there, Shadowstar thought. Maybe it had been a spur-of-the-moment attack rather than a planned one. She had seen a vulnerable leader, alone, one whose deputy she knew to be dead . . . it was possible that Quick Water *hadn't* set the dogs on her and Sun Shadow, and that the idea of killing Shadowstar had first occurred to her when she saw her by the Thunderpath. Was Quick Water going to confess?

"And I never even *saw* Shadowstar," Quick Water added pleadingly. "I believe that she was attacked, but I wasn't the one who tried to kill her."

Raven Pelt spoke up angrily from where he stood with the other deputies. "We saw you, Quick Water. I chased you a long way. It *was* you. Explain that."

The she-cat shrugged. "Maybe there was a rogue who looked a little like me. I don't know." Her amber eyes were huge and innocent. She was lying very well, Shadowstar thought grudgingly.

But at least the other Clan leaders know me, Shadowstar thought, *and know I'm not dishonest, or easily fooled.*

"Quick Water is lying," Shadowstar told them flatly. But all four of them looked doubtful.

Should she tell them what Gray Wing had said when she lost her eighth life? If Quick Water had succeeded in killing her, if ShadowClan had fallen apart at the loss of both their leader and deputy, it could have destroyed all five Clans. Would they even believe her? *I don't want them to know I'm on my last life,* Shadowstar decided, and held her tongue.

"Perhaps we should decide together if we believe Quick Water's story," Windstar mewed thoughtfully.

"What?" Raven Pelt yowled from below. "What is there to *decide?* ShadowClan knows the truth!"

Shadowstar stayed silent, a feeling of dread creeping over her. Was there any cat she could trust in the other Clans?

Skystar spoke first. "Maybe Thunderstar is right," he meowed, dipping his head humbly to his son. "I did exile Quick Water without giving her a chance to tell her side of the story." He looked out into the crowd of cats below him, leaning down to look into Quick Water's eyes. "I believe you,

Quick Water. You are welcome to return to SkyClan."

Quick Water held her head high, her eyes shining.

Shadowstar hissed quietly. *That was . . . quick.* Had Skystar, always so proud and stubborn, admitted that he was wrong *too* easily? It would be more like him to cling to his opinion as long as he possibly could. And the way he'd announced his decision, waiting until every cat had fallen silent and was watching carefully . . . *It's like he was speaking to the other warriors, and not to Quick Water. . . . Because Quick Water knew what he was going to say, all along?*

She shuddered. *Maybe they were working together this whole time.*

"I believe Quick Water, too," Thunderstar meowed. "I never stopped." He glanced at Shadowstar apologetically. "I don't want any cat to think that Shadowstar is lying. I'm sure she thought that it was Quick Water who attacked her. But it makes much more sense that it was a rogue."

And Thunderstar is Skystar's son, and Quick Water went to him for shelter. Maybe they were all working together. Shadowstar's stomach was a hard knot. She didn't *want* to be suspicious of the cats in the other Clans—but how could she trust them when so many seemed so deceitful?

"I believe Shadowstar," Windstar said, her thin, brown-striped face thoughtful. "I don't believe she has any reason to lie about this, and I also can't believe she would mistake a rogue for a Clan cat. Shadowstar isn't stupid, and she knows Quick Water well." Ignoring Skystar's grumble, she turned to Riverstar. "We know what Shadowstar thinks. . . . What about you?"

The long-furred tom shook his head slowly. "I *can't* believe that Quick Water would do such a thing. Shadowstar *must* be mistaken."

Shadowstar's heart sank. So, that was it. Quick Water would stay in the forest, and remain a danger to Shadowstar and her Clan. How could she trust the other Clans now?

"So that ends that discussion," Skystar said sternly. "Next time we gather, we will talk *real* Clan business. SkyClan, follow me." In one smooth motion, he leaped from the Great Rock.

Shadowstar watched as the SkyClan cats—including Quick Water—streamed out of Fourtrees.

Windstar gave Shadowstar a lingering look, her eyes full of worry, and then leaped down to lead her own Clan out of the clearing.

At least WindClan is on our side, Shadowstar thought, feeling heavy and numb as Thunderstar dipped his head to her and Riverstar blinked apologetically before they both jumped down from the Great Rock and led their Clans away.

Shadowstar's heart thumped. Quick Water was a Clan cat again. But she was *dangerous.*

She had already sent Sun Shadow to StarClan, Shadowstar was sure of it.

Would she kill again? And if she did, would that be the act that brought down one Clan, and then another, and then another . . . until the Clans were no more?

CHAPTER EIGHT

❧

As they left Fourtrees, the ShadowClan cats bunched together, glancing nervously into the darkness that surrounded them. Shadowstar felt a pang of sadness at the looks on their faces. They'd lost confidence in the safety of the forest. *Is Shadow-Clan already starting to fall apart?*

Turning to lead her Clan toward their own territory, she caught sight of a cat waiting beneath an oak. *Quick Water?* she thought, alarmed, but then she caught Windstar's scent. The WindClan leader was waiting for her.

"Raven Pelt," Shadowstar meowed. "Lead the Clan home. I'll catch up later."

The black tom stopped and stared at her. "Are you mouse-brained?" he asked. "You're not staying here by yourself."

Shadowstar flicked an ear. "Even a deputy has to follow his leader's instructions," she reminded him. Pebble Heart was listening, too, his amber eyes wide and worried.

Raven Pelt pulled back his ears stubbornly. "The last time you went off by yourself, Quick Water pushed you into the path of a monster," he protested.

Shadowstar felt a pang of grief in her heart as she

remembered the last time a deputy had refused to leave her side. *He ended up dead. . . .*

"Raven Pelt," she repeated gently. "Take the Clan back to our territory. I am trusting *you* with their safety. I will be fine." She stared steadily into his eyes until he dropped his gaze.

"Okay," he mewed. "But be careful."

She nodded, and he called, "ShadowClan, follow me!" and hurried forward. Pebble Heart hesitated beside Shadowstar.

"You too," she told him, brushing her tail across his back. "Some cat might have a cough or a thorn in their paw before I get back."

Pebble Heart snorted, shaking his head. "I hope you know what you're doing," he replied. "Let me know when you're back in camp."

Shadowstar nodded in acknowledgment and watched him follow the rest of their Clanmates out of sight. Then she headed for the shadowy figure beneath the oak. "Windstar."

"Quick Water's lying," the brown tabby meowed immediately. "Maybe the other Clans can't bring themselves to see it, but I can. It's not safe to have her on Clan territory."

Shadowstar gave a long, relieved sigh. "It's so good to be believed by a cat outside my Clan," she murmured.

"They're not stupid cats," Windstar meowed, her tail twitching in irritation. "But they're blinded by their fondness for Quick Water. *All* warriors have to follow the code, no matter how much they're liked. If not, how are we any different from rogues?"

"Exactly," Shadowstar agreed. Windstar understood. It

didn't matter how much Quick Water was liked: By trying to kill another cat, she had put herself outside the warrior code, the rules they had all decided each Clan cat must follow for the good of every Clan. Quick Water wasn't a Clan cat anymore. "We have to defend the code if the Clans are going to be able to live together peacefully."

"I know." Windstar kneaded her paws against the ground, unsure. "But what can we do?" she asked. "If we attack SkyClan, ThunderClan will back them up. Skystar and Thunderstar are united in protecting Quick Water now. We won't be able to drive her out."

Shadowstar hesitated. *There's only one way to be sure.*

Instead of answering Windstar immediately, she looked up into the sky, where countless stars shone above them, tiny lights in the deep blackness. Which ones were warriors, she wondered? Was Sun Shadow watching over her? Were Moon Shadow and Gray Wing?

What would they think of what she was planning?

"Quick Water killed Sun Shadow," she mewed quietly. "She cost me one of my lives. She's put herself outside the code now. StarClan would know that killing her was just."

Windstar drew in a shocked breath. "After the Great Battle, we all swore not to kill one another again, not even in the fiercest fight."

"Yes." Shadowstar looked into the brown tabby cat's eyes, seeing a reflection of the same pain she was feeling. "But Quick Water isn't one of us anymore. We have to make sure our Clans are safe. Even if it costs me everything."

"What do you mean, 'everything'?" Windstar asked uneasily.

Shadowstar hesitated. She had never wanted other cats to know how many lives she had left. It made her vulnerable. But she was choosing to trust Windstar. Maybe the WindClan leader deserved to know. "This is my last life," she mewed finally. "The next time I die, I . . . I won't come back from StarClan."

Windstar blinked. "Maybe we shouldn't start any fights, then," she meowed, sounding doubtful. "We don't know what happens to a Clan when its leader runs out of lives."

Shadowstar shook her head. She felt like Moon Shadow, Sun Shadow, Gray Wing, all the cats she had lost over time *were* watching over her. This was the right thing. "I've named a deputy," she said. "If I die protecting my Clan, Raven Pelt will be able to guide them. Even if this battle isn't my last, I have a feeling this will not be a long life. And if this is the end, it'll be okay."

Windstar flicked her ears. "If you say so. I'd prefer to live."

Despite the serious subject, Shadowstar's whiskers twitched in amusement. "Always so practical." Then she got serious. "However we do this, it should be in the open. We have right on our side; we don't have to be sneaky. Let's make a plan."

The next morning, Shadowstar changed the moss and ferns that lined her nest. She'd told her Clanmates about the battle plan for tomorrow—they would confront Quick Water on SkyClan's land—and now all there was to do was prepare.

She worked methodically, carrying out the flattened, dried plants and replacing them with fresh ones, making sure her nest was as soft and cozy as it could be. This was apprentice work, really, but she wanted to do it herself. If Raven Pelt slept in the leader's den tomorrow, he would be comfortable.

After her den was as pleasant as she could make it, she strolled around camp, speaking to her warriors. Juniper Branch was teaching Bubbling Stream a battle move.

"Throw your weight at their shoulders, right here," she meowed, tapping the top of one of the white she-cat's front legs. "If you can get your opponent off balance, then you can take them down."

Shadowstar brushed her tail over Juniper Branch's back. "You're teaching her well," she added. "Show that move to the other young cats. And Bubbling Stream, keep practicing. You're becoming a fine fighter."

She took Dusk Nose and Mud Paws out hunting, and they chased down a rabbit together. The triumph of working with her Clanmates, of taking deep breaths of the pine-scented air of their territory, of pouncing on prey that would feed their Clan, made her paws move faster and her heart fill with joy.

She went from cat to cat all day, unobtrusively offering advice and praising them. Saying good-bye, giving them a last good memory of their leader. Just in case tomorrow *was* the end for her.

As the sun set, they ate together. She shared a starling with Pebble Heart.

"Remember when we left the moors to start our own Clan?" she asked him softly.

Pebble Heart swallowed a bite and nodded. "I was so *young*," he answered. "I didn't think I'd be able to take care of sick cats without Cloud Spots to teach me. But he wanted to go to the forest, and I knew I didn't belong there."

"You did great," Shadowstar told him. "Even that first day, you were giving Gray Wing herbs to help with his breathing, and you treated the injury on Mud Paws's shoulder. You've always taken such good care of the Clan." She shifted closer to him, his side warm against hers. "I'm glad you chose to join us," she added. "And I'm glad you're here to look after our Clanmates."

Pebble Heart blinked at her affectionately, then rested his head on her shoulder. She was pretty sure he knew what she was trying to tell him.

After the Clan's shared meal, she pulled Raven Pelt aside, sitting with him at the edge of the clearing where they wouldn't be overheard.

"I think we're ready," he announced. "Every cat has been practicing battle moves, and Pebble Heart's been out all day gathering herbs for treating wounds and spiderwebs for binding injuries. Although I hope there won't be many injuries. Fight our fight and get out, right?" His leg was twitching with nervous energy, and Shadowstar laid her paw on it to still it.

"We are prepared," she told him. "But I have to tell you something. This is my last life." Raven Pelt started to speak, his eyes wide and shocked, but she spoke over him. "I want you to know that you are the right cat to lead this Clan. I chose you *because* you are the right cat."

Raven Pelt was shaking his head. "No," he meowed breathlessly. "I'll do everything I can to protect you. You can survive this battle!"

"Whether I survive or not doesn't really matter anymore," Shadowstar answered sternly. "I appreciate your loyalty, but you can't let that affect your ability to lead ShadowClan. You have to be ready to become leader if you must."

Raven Pelt blinked sadly. "I'll try to be ready," he told her, sitting still and serious. "But I don't know that I'm strong enough to take your place."

"You *are* ready," Shadowstar told him. "And you *will* be a strong leader. Just never forget to follow what you know is right. Never put anything—not even your own life—above your Clan. StarClan will guide you."

Raven Pelt's eyes were bright. "I hope that this last life of yours is a long one and I don't have to lead for many moons. But, even if it happens tomorrow, I promise to do my best," he vowed. "I will guide and protect ShadowClan and follow the code."

Shadowstar touched her nose to his. "I know you will."

By the time the moon was high in the sky, she had spoken to every one of her Clanmates. But only Raven Pelt and Pebble Heart knew this was her last life. She trusted them to keep that knowledge secret.

She looked up at the stars again. She was sure now that

Gray Wing, Moon Shadow, and Sun Shadow were all watching over her, waiting to welcome her to StarClan whenever she went there for the last time. Would that be tomorrow? Would the coming dawn be the last time she woke in ShadowClan?

CHAPTER NINE

The grass was still wet with dew when they left ShadowClan territory early the next morning, and mist was rising off the river. They stuck to the riverbank as they headed for SkyClan, skirting the edges of ThunderClan's territory.

"It would be better if ThunderClan stayed out of it," she told Raven Pelt, who was padding along at her side, "but I doubt they'll miss us crossing their land. We should expect to see them soon."

Raven Pelt nodded. He was focused, his gaze constantly scanning the woods around them for danger and the cats with them to make sure they were together and all right. His ears were pricked, listening intently to everything Shadowstar said.

He's aware of his Clanmates. He's not afraid to fight, but he's not excited at the thought of shedding blood. He's eager to learn. Shadowstar shook her fur, willing herself to stop assessing Raven Pelt. She had already chosen him, and every time she thought about it, she confirmed for herself that she had made the right choice. Now she needed to concentrate on the coming battle.

Can I really bring myself to kill Quick Water? she wondered. *Even if she killed me first?* From the Great Battle, she remembered the shock of seeing the life go out of a cat's eyes, of *taking* the life of a cat she knew. It had been horrible and deeply shocking, even though the fight had been so desperate. She had never gone into a battle *intending* to kill another cat.

Quick Water is a danger to ShadowClan, she reminded herself. *To all the Clans.* But her reasoning felt suddenly hollow.

Maybe we can convince her to leave Clan territory. Shadowstar felt sick. *She can't live among the Clans anymore. That's for certain.*

WindClan was waiting for them at SkyClan's border.

"Are you sure you don't want to charge in and attack their camp before they know we're here?" Windstar asked, her tail slashing through the air. "It would improve our chances."

Shadowstar shook her head. "We have to do this openly. We're not attacking SkyClan; we're fighting Quick Water."

Windstar looked at her. "It'll come to the same thing," she mewed frankly.

"I know," Shadowstar told her. "But we won't attack them first."

She opened her mouth, scenting the wind. She could smell ThunderClan more strongly now. A few heartbeats later, she could hear what sounded like most of the Clan coming toward them. And SkyClan was coming, too—she'd seen a border patrol spot them and dash back through the woods toward camp, doubtless to alert the Clan.

Thunderstar got there first.

"What are you both doing here?" he asked angrily. His warriors were ranged beside and behind him, their muscles tensed, their claws out.

"You know why we're here," Shadowstar answered. "And our fight isn't with ThunderClan. You should go back to your camp."

Thunderstar shook his head. "This is our fight, too."

"You've come to attack SkyClan." Skystar's voice broke in coldly. He and his warriors had slipped through the trees, lining up on the other side of the border.

"No, we are not here to attack SkyClan, either," Shadowstar told him. "Our quarrel isn't with either of your Clans." She spotted Quick Water among Skystar's warriors, her gray-and-white face defiant. "We're here to protect the warrior code. Quick Water tried to kill me, and she killed Sun Shadow. She's a murderer, she's broken the code, and we can't let her stay in the Clans."

Thunderstar growled in annoyance. "We *settled* this, Shadowstar. Quick Water explained why her scent was there. Let's not let this come down to teeth and claws. You were mistaken about who attacked you." He hesitated, just for a moment. "You must have been."

Shadowstar met his gaze. "I know you want to believe her, Thunderstar, but I'm not mistaken." She turned to Skystar, her voice pleading. "There's still time to avoid a fight. Exile Quick Water. Drive her out of Clan territory, and we'll walk away. No cat will have to fight. . . ."

As she had known he would, Skystar drew back, angry

and offended. "I'm not going to punish an innocent warrior because *you* tell me to. This is SkyClan territory."

Thunderstar's meow was more diplomatic. "We're keeping Quick Water safe because she's done nothing wrong. Please, Shadowstar, Windstar, trust that we can see that even if you can't."

Windstar hissed. "It's you two who aren't seeing clearly. You're blinded by your affection for Quick Water. See the facts!"

Looking from Skystar to Thunderstar, Shadowstar could see that arguing with them would be useless. Quick Water, huddled in the midst of the cats behind Skystar, had her shoulders hunched, as if there were a cold wind rushing over her. *She'll never leave,* Shadowstar thought. *Not by her own choice, anyway.*

Shadowstar charged toward the gray-and-white cat, knocking past Flower Foot, who fell back with a grunt. But before she could reach Quick Water, something slammed into her side, throwing her to the ground. Gasping for breath, Shadowstar rolled over, kicking her hind legs up to throw off her attacker, and saw Thunderstar's large ginger form above her. "Stop this!" he yowled, and she twisted and pummeled him, throwing him off. Climbing to her paws, she came face-to-face with Birch, a SkyClan warrior.

All around, the forest had erupted into battle. Gorse Fur was tussling with Owl Eyes, his teeth bared in a snarl. Mouse Ear and Honey Pelt were rolling over and over, their claws tearing at each other's fur. Windstar was fighting with

Thunderstar now, and Juniper Branch was holding her own against Skystar, dodging the furious swipes of the gray tom's paws. Every warrior in these four Clans seemed to be locked in combat.

Shadowstar clawed at Birch, leaving a long bloody scratch across his chest. *We've been at peace for so long,* she thought miserably. *Now that's ruined.* Birch fell back a pace, then launched himself at her, snarling, and she rose up on her hind legs to meet him.

As they grappled, teeth bared and claws extended, hissing and yowling, she saw past Birch's shoulder.

Raven Pelt!

He and Quick Water were circling each other, backs arched. Shadowstar saw with a jolt of dismay that her deputy had a long bloody gash across his flank. As she watched, Quick Water charged forward, catching Raven Pelt off balance with a blow to his leg.

Raven Pelt stumbled, and Quick Water leaped upon him, her claws extended for a vicious blow.

No. Not again!

Shadowstar was *not* going to stand by and watch another one of her deputies die. She had failed Sun Shadow—but she was not going to fail Raven Pelt.

He *would* live to be the next leader of ShadowClan.

Shadowstar crashed past Birch and sprang at Quick Water, knocking her backward and away from Raven Pelt.

"Get away," she hissed to her deputy. "This is my fight." He drew back but stayed near, his tail slashing the air agitatedly, guarding her back.

As she and Quick Water eyed each other, it felt to Shadowstar as if the sounds of the battle around them quieted. She could hear nothing but her own and Quick Water's harsh breathing.

"You're a murderer," she meowed softly, and she thought she saw a flash of guilt in those amber eyes. "You don't belong here anymore," she went on.

Quick Water looked at her with an agonized, lost expression, and then she sprang, slashing her claws at Shadowstar.

Shadowstar reared up and away, feeling the claws drag down her chest. A sudden warm wetness spread across her body. For a heartbeat, that was all. Then her vision blurred and she swayed on her paws.

Am I dying? Quick Water was staring at her, and behind the gray-and-white she-cat was a circle of other faces: her own Clanmates, SkyClan cats, WindClan, and ThunderClan. It was as if all the fighting had stopped and they were only watching her, still and shocked.

Not yet. I can't die for the last time and leave a murderer in the Clans. With the last of her strength, Shadowstar struck, slicing her claws across Quick Water's belly. She heard Quick Water yowl in pain. Then her legs gave way, and she fell. There was a thud as Quick Water collapsed heavily beside her, moaning.

They were eye to eye, Quick Water's amber eyes staring into her own green ones. Behind and around them stood the

Clans, silent with horror. Shadowstar opened her mouth to speak, to reassure her Clanmates, but she couldn't make a sound. The forest was growing blurry around her. Skystar was pressing his paws against Quick Water's side, trying to close the wound.

"It was true," Quick Water croaked suddenly. Shadowstar blinked slowly, registering the shock on Skystar's face. "I led the dogs to attack Shadowstar and Sun Shadow. I thought if they were both dead, we could take their territory, and ensure the safety of SkyClan. And then I tried to kill Shadowstar again, up by Highstones. I know it was wrong, but I was so *scared.*"

"Oh, Quick Water," Skystar sighed. He was still trying to hold her side together, but he looked heartbroken. "After everything we've been through to form the Clans . . . SkyClan wouldn't have thanked you for betraying the warrior code like that. For killing another Clan cat."

Raven Pelt was above Shadowstar now, trying to clean some of the blood from her face.

The warrior code is what keeps us from being rogues. It makes us Clan cats. If we don't follow the code, the Clans will be more lost than we would be without our territory. Shadowstar wanted to tell Raven Pelt this—he was going to lead ShadowClan now; it was important that he know—but she couldn't speak, only gasp for air. Meeting his eyes, she was sure he knew what she wanted to say.

"Shadowstar, I'm so sorry," Quick Water moaned, her voice weak. "I thought I was saving my Clan. But I should have been trying to keep *all* the Clans safe. All you cats"—she looked around wildly at the crowd, which Shadowstar could barely see now through the blur of her vision—"please know I know I was wrong. Please, forgive me. . . ."

Darkness was filling the clearing. Shadowstar could make out only the shapes of cats , all around them. But she was sure, somehow, that right now they stood united—not Clans, but one great Clan. They wouldn't forget. Her paw twitched as she tried to reach out, tried to touch Quick Water.

I forgive you.

CHAPTER TEN

A warm breeze ruffled Shadowstar's fur, and she stretched luxuriously, enjoying the pull of her muscles in a sleepy, contented way.

I'm dead. For good this time. She opened her eyes and stared out over the lush grass of the clearing. The warmth of the sun, the scents of prey and growing things were stronger, more *real* than she had ever experienced. *Because all of me is in StarClan now.*

She felt . . . surprisingly content. She had had nine good lives. Her Clan was safe with Raven Pelt. She had the strong feeling that her and Quick Water's deaths had brought all the Clans closer together than they had been before. They would take care of one another.

A soft whimper came from beside her, and she turned to see Quick Water. The gray-and-white she-cat's amber eyes were wide with fear and sorrow, and she was shivering.

"Oh, Shadowstar," she whispered. "We're dead. I don't belong here. How can StarClan forgive me for what I did?"

Shadowstar reached out a paw to touch Quick Water's, the way she had wanted to, and couldn't, while they lay dying.

"The Clans will go on," she told her. "That's the only thing that matters." She tried to give Quick Water a reassuring look. "And if I can forgive you for what you did, I'm sure StarClan will, too. . . ."

Quick Water looked doubtful. "So you think my breaking the code and killing you and Sun Shadow—you *twice*—is somehow okay if it made the Clans stronger in the end? I feel like StarClan might see things differently."

"You confessed to what you did," Shadowstar said, "before the Clan cats could kill one another for no reason. That must count for something. You were so sorry before you died." She paused and thought. "I think you might owe Sun Shadow an apology of his own, though."

Quick Water's shoulders drooped.

"You definitely do," a cheerful voice meowed behind them. "But at least I'm in good shape now."

Both she-cats turned to see Sun Shadow—looking healthy and strong—trotting happily across the grass toward them, Gray Wing by his side. Quick Water jumped to her feet and ran to them, clumsy in her haste.

"I *am* sorry," she said, dipping her head to Sun Shadow. "Sincerely. I made a terrible mistake. It's like I've been crazy for moons—all I could think about was whether SkyClan would have to leave our territory. I stopped caring about anything else, even whether other cats lived or died. I don't deserve to be forgiven." She turned to Gray Wing, her tail drooping. "I'm so ashamed."

Gray Wing bent to touch his muzzle to hers. "Old friend, I

want you to see something." He gestured to Shadowstar with his tail. "You too."

Shadowstar and Quick Water followed the two StarClan cats to a pool at the edge of the clearing. "Look," Gray Wing said, nodding at the pool.

Gazing down, Shadowstar watched soft ripples cross the pool's surface. Gradually, the reflections of the sun on the water began to change. She could see the Clan's territories from above. There was ShadowClan's pine forest, and Four-trees. . . .

Beside her, Quick Water whimpered. "What's *happening*?" In the pool, SkyClan's territory was being torn apart. Twolegs and their yellow monsters were felling trees and digging great gaping holes into the earth. "Our territory is gone. . . ." She sounded dazed.

Their view changed. A group of cats was setting out from the ruined territory, heading not toward Highstones but off into strange lands. *It really isn't a good territory by Highstones,* Shadowstar thought. *I guess they couldn't settle there.* "But where is Skystar?" she asked. The tom leading the cats had Skystar's pale gray fur, but it was splotched with cloud-like white spots. And he was small and lithe, not long-legged and broad like the SkyClan leader. But there was something familiar about his determined stride, and the tilt to his ears. "Is he . . . kin of Skystar?" she wondered.

"I don't recognize any of those cats," Quick Water said. "What's going on? They're not SkyClan."

"They *are* SkyClan," Gray Wing corrected her. "Generations on, but kin to the SkyClan you knew. The Twolegs won't take your territory now, but they will someday, and SkyClan will have to find a new home." His voice was sad. "The rest of the Clans will follow them, in time."

Uncertainty ran through Shadowstar. "So every Clan will leave the forest?" she asked. "I thought I could save Shadow-Clan—but nothing I did mattered at all."

Gray Wing raised his head to look at her, his golden eyes full of affection. "Of course it mattered," he said warmly. "Even so many generations on, they remember you. Shadow-Clan survives. And all the Clans will uphold the warrior code, knowing it's what makes them Clan cats."

Quick Water swished her tail. "So what?" she yowled, sounding heartbroken. "I betrayed all the Clans to save Sky-Clan's home, and they're still going to have to leave! They'll be lost without the other Clans."

Shadowstar stroked her tail across Quick Water's back, trying wordlessly to comfort her.

"No," Gray Wing said. "Look." The scene shifted. It was somewhere else now—a lake with open land around it—but there were cats there, hunting and patrolling their borders, sharing tongues and lazing in the sun together. There were thin black cats slinking through shadows, and broad-shoul-dered ginger cats climbing trees, and rangy thin brown cats chasing rabbits, and sleek gray cats swimming after fish. She didn't know any of these cats, but she recognized them: Clan cats. Warriors.

And, coming toward them, walking wearily, but with the

same proud tilt to their ears as Skystar had, and as the cat who had led SkyClan from the forest had: another Clan.

"They come back," Shadowstar breathed.

Gray Wing nodded. "Even apart, the Clans survive. They remember the code, and they look after their Clanmates. And they'll be united again."

Another black cat was walking toward them. *Moon Shadow.* Shadowstar raised her tail to gesture to her brother, feeling suddenly light and free. All the fear she'd carried, fear of her own final death and of what it meant for ShadowClan, was gone now.

The Clans would survive. Their traditions would be passed down for generations of kin, StarClan watching over them all.

I did everything I could, she thought, *and it meant something: ShadowClan will go on. My lives have been truly worthwhile.*

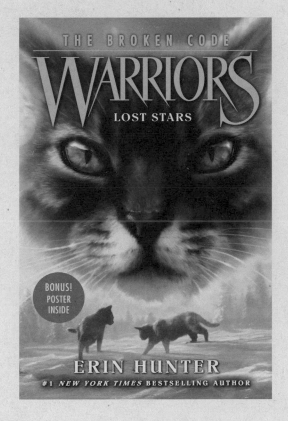

CHAPTER 1

Shadowpaw craned his neck over his back, straining to groom the hard-to-reach spot at the base of his tail. He had just managed to give his fur a few vigorous licks when he heard paw steps approaching. He looked up to see his father, Tigerstar, and his mother, Dovewing, their pelts brushing as they gazed down at him with pride and joy shining in their eyes.

"What is it?" he asked, sitting up and giving his pelt a shake.

"We just came to see you off," Tigerstar responded, while Dovewing gave her son's ears a quick, affectionate lick.

Shadowpaw's fur prickled with embarrassment. *Like I haven't been to the Moonpool before,* he thought. *They're still treating me as if I'm a kit in the nursery!*

He was sure that his parents hadn't made such a fuss when his littermates, Pouncestep and Lightleap, had been warrior apprentices. *I guess it's because I'm going to be a medicine cat. . . .* Or maybe because of the seizures he'd had since he was a kit. He knew his parents still worried about him, even though it had been a while since his last upsetting vision. *They're probably hoping that with some training from the other medicine cats, I'll learn to control my visions once and for all . . . and I can be normal.*

1

Shadowpaw wanted that, too.

"The snow must be really deep up on the moors," Dove-wing mewed. "Make sure you watch where you're putting your paws."

Shadowpaw wriggled his shoulders, praying that none of his Clanmates were listening. "I will," he promised, glancing toward the medicine cats' den in the hope of seeing his mentor, Puddleshine, emerge. But there was no sign of him yet.

To his relief, Tigerstar gave Dovewing a nudge and they both moved off toward the Clan leader's den. Shadowpaw rubbed one paw hastily across his face and bounded across the camp to see what was keeping Puddleshine.

Intent on finding his mentor, Shadowpaw barely noticed the patrol trekking toward the fresh-kill pile, prey dangling from their jaws. He skidded to a halt just in time to avoid colliding with Cloverfoot, the Clan deputy.

"Shadowpaw!" she exclaimed around the shrew she was carrying. "You nearly knocked me off my paws."

"Sorry, Cloverfoot," Shadowpaw meowed, dipping his head respectfully.

Cloverfoot let out a snort, half annoyed, half amused. "Apprentices!"

Shadowpaw tried to hide his irritation. He was an apprentice, yes, but an old one—medicine cat apprentices' training lasted longer than warriors'. His littermates were full warriors already. But he knew his parents would want him to respect the deputy.

Cloverfoot padded on, followed by Strikestone, Yarrowleaf,

and Blazefire. Though they were all carrying prey, they had only one or two pieces each, and what little they had managed to catch was undersized and scrawny.

"I can't remember a leaf-bare as cold as this," Yarrowleaf complained as she dropped a blackbird on the fresh-kill pile.

Strikestone nodded, shivering as he fluffed out his brown tabby pelt. "No wonder there's no prey. They're all hiding down their holes, and I can't blame them."

As Shadowpaw moved on, out of earshot, he couldn't help noticing how pitifully small the fresh-kill pile was, and he tried to ignore his own growling belly. He could hardly remember his first leaf-bare, when he'd been a tiny kit, so he didn't know if the older cats were right and the weather was unusually cold.

I only know I don't like it, he grumbled to himself as he picked his way through the icy slush that covered the ground of the camp. *My paws are so cold I think they'll drop off. I can't wait for newleaf!*

Puddleshine ducked out of the entrance to the medicine cats' den as Shadowpaw approached. "Good, you're ready," he meowed. "We'd better hurry, or we'll be late." As he led the way toward the camp entrance, he added, "I've been checking our herb stores, and they're getting dangerously low."

"We could search for more on the way back," Shadowpaw suggested, his medicine-cat duties driving out his thoughts of cold and hunger. He always enjoyed working with Puddleshine to find, sort, and store the herbs. Treating cats with herbs made him feel calm and in control . . . the opposite of how he felt during his seizures and upsetting visions.

"We can try," Puddleshine sighed. "But what isn't frostbitten will be covered with snow." He glanced over his shoulder at Shadowpaw as the two cats headed out into the forest. "This is turning out to be a really bad leaf-bare. And it isn't over yet, not by a long way."

Excitement tingled through Shadowpaw from ears to tail-tip as he scrambled up the rocky slope toward the line of bushes that surrounded the Moonpool hollow. His worries over his seizures and the bitter leaf-bare faded; every hair on his pelt was bristling with anticipation of his meeting with the other medicine cats, and most of all with StarClan.

He might not be a full medicine cat yet, and he might not be fully in control of his visions . . . but he would still get to meet with his warrior ancestors. And from the rest of the medicine cats he would find out what was going on in the other Clans.

Standing at the top of the slope, waiting for Puddleshine to push his way through the bushes, Shadowpaw reflected on the last few moons. Things had been tense in ShadowClan as every cat settled into their new boundaries and grew used to sharing a border with SkyClan. Not long ago, SkyClan had lived separately from the other Clans, in a far-flung territory in a gorge. But StarClan had called SkyClan back to join the other Clans by the lake, because the Clans were stronger when all five were united. Still, SkyClan had needed its own territory, which had meant new borders for everyone, and it had taken time for the other Clans to accept them. Shadowpaw was relieved that things seemed more peaceful now; the brutally cold leaf-bare had given all the Clans more to worry about than quarreling with one another. They were even beginning to rely on one another, especially in sharing herbs when the cold weather had damaged so many of the plants they needed. Shadowpaw felt proud that they were all getting along, instead of battling one another for every piece of prey.

That wasn't a great start to Tigerstar's leadership. . . . I'm glad it's over now!

"Are you going to stand out there all night?"

At the sound of Puddleshine's voice from the other side of the bushes, Shadowpaw dived in among the branches, wincing as sharp twigs scraped along his pelt, and thrust himself out onto the ledge above the Moonpool. Opposite him, halfway up the rocky wall of the hollow, a trickle of water bubbled out from between two moss-covered boulders. The water fell down into the pool below, with a fitful glimmer as if the stars themselves were trapped inside it. The rippling surface of the pool shone silver with reflected moonlight.

Shadowpaw wanted to leap into the air with excitement at being back at the Moonpool, but he fought to hold on to some self-control, and padded down the spiral path to the water's edge with all the dignity expected of a medicine cat. Awe welled up inside him as he felt his paws slip into the hollows made by cats countless seasons before.

Who were they? Where did they go? he wondered.

The two ThunderClan medicine cats were already sitting beside the pool. Shadowpaw guessed it was too cold to wait outside for everyone to arrive, as the medicine cats usually did. Alderheart was thoughtfully grooming his chest fur, while Jayfeather's tail-tip twitched back and forth in irritation. He turned his blind blue gaze on Puddleshine and Shadowpaw as they reached the bottom of the hollow.

"You took your time," he snapped. "We're wasting moon-light."

Shadowpaw realized that Kestrelflight of WindClan and Mothwing and Willowshine, the two RiverClan medicine cats, were sitting just beyond the two from ThunderClan. The shadow of a rock had hidden them from him until now.

"Nice to see you, too, Jayfeather," Puddleshine responded mildly. "I'm sorry if we're late, but I don't see Frecklewish or Fidgetflake, either."

Jayfeather gave a disdainful sniff. "If they're not here soon, we'll start without them."

Would Jayfeather really do that? Shadowpaw was still staring at the ThunderClan medicine cat, wondering, when a rustling from the top of the slope put him on alert. Looking up, he saw Frecklewish pushing her way through the bushes, followed closely by Fidgetflake.

"At last!" Jayfeather hissed.

He's in a mood, Shadowpaw thought, then added to himself with a flicker of amusement, *Nothing new there, then.*

As the two SkyClan medicine cats padded down the slope, Shadowpaw noticed how thin and weary they both looked. For a heartbeat he wondered if there was anything wrong in SkyClan. Then he realized that he and the rest of the medicine cats looked just as skinny, just as worn out by the trials of leaf-bare.

Frecklewish dipped her head to her fellow medicine cats as she joined them beside the pool. "Greetings," she mewed, her fatigue clear in her voice. "How is the prey running in your Clans?"

For a moment no cat replied, and Shadowpaw could sense their uneasiness. *None of them wants to admit that their Clan is having problems.*

Shadowpaw was surprised when Puddleshine, who was normally so pensive, was the first to speak up. Maybe the cold had banished his mentor's reserve and enabled him to be honest.

"The hunting is very poor in ShadowClan," he replied; Shadowpaw felt a twinge of alarm at how discouraged his mentor sounded. "If this freezing cold goes on much longer, I don't know what we'll do."

The remaining medicine cats exchanged glances of relief, as if they were glad to learn their Clan wasn't the only one suffering.

Willowshine nodded agreement. "Many RiverClan cats are getting sick because it's so cold."

"In ThunderClan too," Alderheart murmured.

"We're running out of herbs," Fidgetflake added with a twitch of his whiskers. "And the few we have left are shriveled and useless."

Frecklewish gave her Clanmate a sympathetic glance. "I've heard some of the younger warriors joking about running off to be kittypets," she meowed.

"No cat had better say that in my hearing." Jayfeather drew his lips back in the beginning of a snarl. "Or they'll wish they hadn't."

"Keep your fur on, Jayfeather," Frecklewish responded. "It was only a joke. All SkyClan cats are loyal to their Clan."

Jayfeather's only reply was an irritated flick of his ears.

"I don't suppose any of you have spare supplies of catmint?" Kestrelflight asked hesitantly. "The clumps that grow in WindClan are all blackened by frost. We won't have any more until newleaf."

Most of the cats shook their heads, except for Willowshine, who rested her tail encouragingly on Kestrelflight's shoulder. "RiverClan can help," she promised. "There's catmint growing in the Twoleg gardens near our border. It's more sheltered there."

"Thanks, Willowshine." Kestrelflight's voice was unsteady. "There's whitecough in the WindClan camp, and without catmint I'm terrified it will turn to greencough."

"Meet me by the border tomorrow at sunhigh," Willowshine mewed. "I'll show you where the catmint grows."

"This is all well and good," Jayfeather snorted, "every cat getting along, but let's not forget why we're here. I'm much more interested in what StarClan has to say. Shall we begin?" He paced to the edge of the Moonpool and stretched out one forepaw to touch the surface, only to draw his paw back with a gasp of surprise.